THE ORPHAN OF SALT WINDS

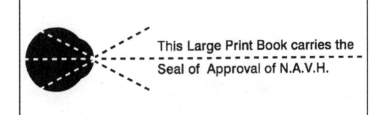

This Large Print Book carries the
Seal of Approval of N.A.V.H.

THE ORPHAN OF SALT WINDS

ELIZABETH BROOKS

THORNDIKE PRESS
A part of Gale, a Cengage Company

A Cengage Company

Farmington Hills, Mich • San Francisco • New York • Waterville, Maine
Meriden, Conn • Mason, Ohio • Chicago

LIBRARY OF CONGRESS CIP DATA ON FILE.
CATALOGUING IN PUBLICATION FOR THIS BOOK
IS AVAILABLE FROM THE LIBRARY OF CONGRESS

ISBN-13: 978-1-4328-6285-5 (hardcover)

Published in 2019 by arrangement with Tin House Books

Printed in the United States of America
1 2 3 4 5 6 7 23 22 21 20 19

For Mum and Dad, with love

The winds and tides remember, as do the birds, and the cockles, and the shrimps, and the sand worms, and the whispering reeds, and the grasses, and the lichens, and every single stone in the old seawall. I know they remember, because they passed the story on to me — a stranger — just as I have passed it on to you.

I can't make any promises. I can only ask you to watch and listen and lift your face to the wind from time to time, in case it's carrying the scent of an ancient magic.

One night you will sense something — glitter on black water, perhaps, or the snapping of a sail in an empty sea, or the call of a curlew — and you will know that the time has come.

— "Call of the Curlew," J. Friedmann

December 30, 2015
Virginia Wrathmell knows she will walk into the marsh one New Year's Eve and meet her end there. She's known it for years. Throughout her adolescence and adulthood she spent the last days of every December on edge, waiting for a sign. So when one finally arrives, in her eighty-sixth year, there's no good reason to feel dismayed.

The sign is lying on her front doorstep, and she very nearly treads on it as she emerges around ten o'clock for a blast of night air. She feels its friable curve under the sole of her slipper and hears a tiny crack, but she pulls back before her foot can come down and grind it to unintelligible dust.

Everything aches when she stoops, but she grunts and clings to her stick and succeeds in scooping it up. Whatever it is, it sits in the hollow of her hand, as light as a ball of tissue, and at first the only thing that frightens her is its fragility. She can't see it, with her back to the hall light, but she holds it tenderly in case it's something wounded and alive. It doesn't move, but when she strokes her thumb across its surface there's a purposeful intricacy to its shape, which makes her think it's a creature of some kind.

The wind makes to snatch it away, and Virginia's fingers form a protective curl. She holds it into the light and sees that it's a bird's skull, unfeathered and unfleshed. Virginia knows the marsh birds well — if she had had her own children she couldn't have known them better — and she recognizes the curlew by its long and gently curving bill. The recognition is paralyzing, and the skull almost falls and breaks on the doorstep. Briefly it occurs to Virginia that a shattered sign would no longer be a sign, but this doesn't ring true. She can't unsee what she's seen.

Virginia touches the papery bone, running a gnarled finger around the empty eye sockets. The skull looks like a tiny rapier; a doll's sword. All these years she's been wondering what the sign will turn out to be, and she's come up with the strangest ideas. Words forming on a misted window. An anonymous note. A ghost. She's never imagined anything as perfect as this curlew's skull.

There's a faint warmth at her back from the electric heater in the sitting room, but Virginia shuffles down the steps, away from it, and away from the wedge of light. There is a semicircle of gravel in front of the house, and the stones hurt her soles; it is easier to walk on the grass that grows thick and long against the flint wall. When she reaches the wall, she leans against it, and the edge digs into her waist. She lays her stick along the top and cups the curlew's skull in both hands.

Ribbons of white hair flutter across Virginia's face, and the lapels on her dressing gown flap. The wind is from the north, gritty with the threat of snow and painful to breathe. She faces the marsh and tries to feel excited; to remember the Decembers past when she's prayed, in vain, for this very thing. There is nothing to see out in the vast blackness, but when she shuts her eyes she imagines she can hear the sucking sands and the boom of distant tides.

It will be cold out there, on Tollbury Marsh. It will be a cold way to go. These bedroom slippers won't last long; they'll be in shreds before she's walked ten yards, and they'll get lost in the reeds, and then she'll be barefoot in the mud. She'll struggle on, ankle-deep, until the mud turns to sand and the sea begins to sound on every side, rushing, creeping in predatory circles. She'll stop and brace herself for the icy slap on her shins and thighs. The tide will rise and race, and by the time it's level with her waist she'll have lost her footing. She wonders if she'll shout their names; she's not sure.

Of course, she's thought about it all before, but the cold has never presented itself so vividly. It's a shame this has to happen on New Year's Eve, instead of a balmy evening in July, but there's no point quibbling.

Virginia runs her hand along the bumpy wall and finds a handful of loose stones, which she pockets. Perhaps she should fetch the flashlight from the kitchen drawer and look for more stones; after all, if the point is to die, then she's better off weighted down. The prospect of returning to the house, even for a minute, is giddying. It's a miniature reprieve. Now that she thinks about it, there are other things she'd like to take. There's Clem and Lorna's wedding photo, though she'll have to remove the frame in order to fit it in her pocket with the stones. There's the book of fairy tales, which will take up all the space in her other pocket.

And, of course, there's the manuscript, but that will fold up very small, so long as she can persuade herself to crease it. She'll carry the curlew's skull in one hand; the other she will need for her stick.

Virginia has everything worked out, and yet she doesn't move from the wall. She's hypnotized by the cold and the fingers of wind that comb her hair. It's silly to feel rushed when she's waited so long, but she can't help thinking that if the sign had come earlier in the day she'd have had time to say goodbye to Salt Winds, room by room. She'd have been able to make arrangements for the cat.

A mile away, at the other end of the lane, the lights of Tollbury Point are pricking like pins through the darkness. When she glances over in the direction of the village, picturing the fireworks that will flare and flower for 2016, Virginia remembers the date. Today is the thirtieth of December. Stupid woman — it's not the thirty-first, after all. New Year's Eve isn't till tomorrow.

She's been granted twenty-four hours grace. Virginia doesn't know what to do with herself. She closes her eyes and presses the curlew's skull to her cheek, taking care not to hurt it.

December 1939

The child held on to Clem's hand through-out the bus ride. There were lots of stops and the brakes were jerky, and after an hour she murmured, "I feel sick." Back at Sinclair House it would have been a risky admission, but Clem didn't seem cross at all. "Nearly there," he said, elbowing her as he rummaged in his coat pocket. "See if you can't hold on another ten minutes." She nodded as Clem blew the fuzz off a mint imperial and pressed it into her mitten.

She was glad to have the new mittens when they got off the bus. Clem didn't wear gloves, but his hands had the impervious look of old leather, so perhaps they repelled the cold by themselves. Apparently, Lorna had knitted the mittens specially for her and they'd bought the coat brand-new, last Saturday, from the big department store in town. It was navy blue with a square collar

14

like a sailor's, and it was a bit tight at her shoulders, but thank goodness she hadn't gotten sick on it. She shivered as the bus pulled away, and Clem said, "Warm enough?" She nodded and he stooped to straighten her scarf, which had gotten tangled with the strap on her gas-mask box.

The child hadn't been outside without her gas mask for months; not since the start of the war. Everyone was supposed to carry one, in case the Nazis dropped poison-gas bombs — the government had said so. At the orphanage you got a proper telling off if you went anywhere without one, so Virginia was troubled — and impressed — to see that Clem had left his at home.

The bus had dropped them by an old church with a tower like a stubby finger pointing at the sky and a sign that said *St. Dunstan's, Tollbury Point.* The little girl turned slowly, taking in the bare trees and the whitewashed cottages, and tried to guess which one was her new home. Most of the cottages already had their blackout curtains drawn; one risked an uncurtained window and an open fire, and looked the nicest in the raw dusk. But Clem adjusted his hold on her slippery mitten, picked up the suitcase, and led her away, down a different road.

Beyond the village, the silence was immense. At Sinclair House there'd been no such thing as silence, even when Matron ordered it; there'd been too many children and too many echoes in the tall, bare rooms.

Clem didn't seem one for talking. When they were trudging down the drive, away from Sinclair House, he'd said, "Best do the buttons up on that coat, Virginia," and she'd obeyed, but perhaps she should have smiled as well, or made some reply, because he'd not said anything after that; not until the mint imperial. When they were on the bus, and now, as they were walking along the road, she kept trying to scrutinize his face without being noticed. It wasn't easy; he kept catching her eye and winking.

Clem nodded at a woman on a bicycle, and they pressed into the hawthorn hedge as a tractor rattled by with an empty trailer. There wasn't much traffic. While they were walking, the afternoon became evening, and when Clem said, "Here we are," she was puzzled. She thought there must be a tiny house hidden in the hedgerow, and she looked for it, warily, all along the verge, but all she saw was a narrow road turning onto a potholed lane. The lane was bounded by a low wall, and she knew then where the great silence was coming from.

Virginia stood on tiptoe to see the silence beyond the wall. What she saw was a silhouette-bird perched a great distance away on a tilting wooden post, amid horizontal strips of earth, air, and water; black and pearl and gray. She saw an emptiness that she could taste on her tongue, although it wasn't the sea. She moistened her chapped lips and gathered herself to ask her first question.

"Clem?"

But a car was coming toward them on the main road, sleek and quiet and all but invisible in the dusk. The blackout laws forbade light, for fear of guiding German bombers, and it was presumably in obedience to this that the car had only one headlight, which was fitted with a slit mask. It drew up beside them, and Virginia forgot what she'd been going to say.

"Wrathmell? That you?" The driver had to lean across the empty passenger seat in order to shout through the window. It would have been easier for him if Clem had gone to the other side of the car, but Clem stayed put at the top of the narrow lane, holding Virginia's hand. He didn't even stoop so as to come level with the window.

"Evening, Deering."

The driver's face was pale, and it seemed

to glow in the twilight.

"Oh! Is this . . . ?" He indicated Virginia with a nod, and although Clem made no perceptible response, the man said, "Goodness! Congratulations!" as if he had.

Clem nodded.

"Marvelous thing for Lorna," the man went on.

"Yes." Clem's quietness was beginning to sound like parsimony, as if talking was charged at tuppence a word.

Virginia looked at the murmuring car, with its great curling wheel arches, and longed to touch it, just to see what it felt like. It was shiny black, like a patent leather shoe.

"Well?" said the man, looking her over once more. "Do I get an introduction to the new Miss Wrathmell, or not?"

Clem lifted his gaze over the roof of the car and squinted at the sky. "Virginia, this is Mr. Deering," he said. "Mr. Deering, Virginia."

Mr. Deering pulled his driving glove off with his teeth and stretched even farther across the passenger seat in order to proffer his hand. Clem nudged her gently in the back, so she approached the car and gripped the outstretched fingertips. Mr. Deering laughed and said, "A breath of fresh air!

18

Just what we need around here!" and Virginia was surprised by a squeamish desire to remove her mitten and touch his handsome moustache, to see what *that* felt like. It was the same shiny black as the car, and it didn't look as if it was made of hair. Perhaps he painted it on every morning, with a thin brush and a little pot of lacquer.

"What age?" said Mr. Deering pleasantly, over her head.

"Vi was ten in August."

"Ah-ha. Same age as Theo. Perhaps a spot of matchmaking is in order? What do you say, Miss Wrathmell? It's his birthday party on New Year's Eve."

Virginia stepped back to the verge and Clem reclaimed her hand.

"Next year, perhaps."

Virginia thought it a rather awkward refusal, but Mr. Deering didn't seem to mind.

"Well," he continued pleasantly. "Hop in, both. Won't take a minute to run you down to Salt Winds."

Clem tightened his hold. "Thanks, Deering, but we'll walk."

"Bit of a stretch for little legs, isn't it?"

Something whistled across the silence — a rising, bubbling echo that repeated again and again — and the men stopped talking

19

in order to listen. Virginia thought of a piccolo.

Clem took a quick breath and looked up, as if he'd heard a cautionary whisper in his ear. There was a new resolution in the way he said, "Listen, Deering, we should catch up properly, and soon. Perhaps you'll bring the children to Salt Winds in the New Year, once Vi's had a chance to find her feet? Afternoon tea, or something?"

Mr. Deering withdrew from the passenger window and sat up properly in his own seat. Virginia studied him in silhouette as he pulled his glove back on, wiggling the fingers until they were straight and tight.

"That would be marvelous," he called. "I'll hold you to it." Virginia could tell he was still smiling, even though his features were invisible. He pushed some pedal, or pulled a lever, and the purring motor roared, drowning out any goodbye. Clem didn't have a free hand, but he raised the little suitcase in salute as the car disappeared around the bend in the road.

Clem squeezed Virginia's hand and led her into the narrow lane. She wished he'd said "Yes" to Mr. Deering's offer of a lift, because her shoes were pinching and the lane seemed to stretch on for miles, straight as an unrolled ribbon, without letup. If you followed it for long enough you came, eventually, upon a gray square, which might be a house — but it was a long way away.

"Here," said Clem, putting the suitcase down and poking about in his coat pocket. "Have another mint to keep you going."

This one was a humbug, and it had stuck, over time, to the bottom corner of a paper bag. Clem peeled most of the paper off in tiny, white shreds, and she popped it into her mouth.

"Do you want to walk on the wall?" he asked. Virginia responded with the beginnings of a smile, and he helped her clamber up on her hands and knees, both of them careful not to scuff the navy coat, or catch it on bird muck. The top of the wall was wide and undulating, like a stone road, and when she stood tall and looked down the lane, the top of Clem's hat was lower than her shoulders.

They started walking, and Virginia glanced at the flatness to her left. It was too dark to see the silhouette-bird now. The deep, arctic blue of the sky was reflected, here and there, in streaks of water, and there was a single star in the sky, but everything else was dark. There was a low, cold wind that Virginia hadn't felt when they were coming from the village, and it numbed the left side of her face as she walked.

The humbug flooded her mouth with minty saliva as she passed it from cheek to cheek, but it hardly shrank at all, so she bit down on it with a loud crack.

"Steady on, old thing," said Clem. "You'll have no teeth left."

She laughed at that: a breathy, stifled sound, which encouraged Clem to go on. "Lorna will be put out if you arrive without teeth. I can hear her now: *I could swear that girl had teeth when I last saw her.*"

"What will you say?"

"I'll say, 'Stop your nagging, woman, she had them all in this morning. I reckon she must have taken them out and left them on the bus.' "

Virginia was outraged; she could barely speak for laughing. "I don't have false teeth! Look!" She stopped and bared her teeth in a fierce grimace.

Clem looked, but before he could say anything the whistle noise sounded its repeated echo across the emptiness, and Virginia forgot about her teeth. She looked left, across the void, and fixed her scarf so that it covered her chin as well as her neck. Her breath dampened the knitted wool, and made it prickle against her lips.

"Clem?" she said. "May I ask you something?"

"Anything. Fire away."

Virginia hesitated, because he'd said "anything," and she took him at his word. She saw half a dozen questions lined up like fancy chocolates in a box, and it was hard to choose a favorite. She was tempted by the chance to find out something about Mr. Deering, but her nerve failed and instead she chose "What is that whistling sound?"

"A curlew. It's a type of wading bird. There are lots of birds on Tollbury Marsh; they like it here. I can tell you all about them, if you're interested. All their names, and so on."

Virginia nodded eagerly, and, as if by agreement, they stopped walking and stared into the wind. She already knew that Clem made his living by writing books about wildlife. It had surprised her, when she first found out, because Clem didn't look like a writer; he looked too sturdy and weathered, as if he spent all his days outside. Of the two Wrathmells, it was Lorna who came across as the rarefied, indoorsy one, and on one occasion Virginia had plucked up the courage to ask whether she was a writer too. The three of them had been sitting in the visitors room at Sinclair House, and Lorna had smiled at the question, but before she could answer, Clem had said, "I think Lorna's got enough on her plate, looking after me. Wouldn't you say so?"

"Is this the marsh?" Virginia asked, indicating the darkening vastness with a nod. "When you say 'Tollbury Marsh,' do you mean all of this?"

"Indeed I do, and Tollbury Marsh is good for birds but bad news for people, so you must promise me that you'll not set foot on it. Never ever. Understand?"

Clem made her look at him. The upper half of his face was hidden by the shadow of his trilby hat, but she could see how his jaw set, and she nodded. The follow-up question of *Why not?* died on her lips.

Clem stuck his free hand in his pocket after that and walked with his head down. Virginia worried she'd done something to make him cross and trotted to keep up with him, her gaze fixed on the trilby hat, and before very long she tripped on a raised stone and banged her knee. Clem noticed straightaway, even though he was well ahead and she hadn't cried out. Her skin was grazed, and, worse, the navy coat had picked up a smear of mud, but she managed not to cry and Clem seemed himself again as he helped her up. He spat on a handkerchief

24

and dabbed at the broken skin.

"Piggyback?" he suggested, and she wrapped her arms around his neck and shuffled onto his back. He hitched her up and they were off, much faster now. She laid her head gingerly against his neck and watched the world through the space between his hat and collar. They were closing on the gray square now, and she could see that it was indeed the front of a house, with long windows and tall chimneys. There wasn't so much as a crack of light, and the only proof that the place wasn't boarded up and abandoned was the smell of woodsmoke that grew stronger the nearer they came. Virginia stared up at the gaunt windows, searching each one for a sign of life, but found only reflections of the evening sky and the backs of curtains.

She closed her eyes and let her head loll on Clem's shoulder. The drone of the wind and the rhythmic swing of his steps made a kind of lullaby. As cold and tired as she was, she didn't want their walk to end.

"Lorna won't be cross, will she?" Virginia was careful to speak softly, so close to his ear.

"What? About the coat?" His words vibrated against her cheek, from deep inside his chest. "She'll have me to deal with if she does. Anyway, I'm sure she won't. It hardly shows at all."

Salt Winds. Virginia raised her head in time to read the name of her new home, carved in a stone gatepost.

Clem flicked the hall light on and eased Virginia off his back. She blinked in the brightness as Clem set her suitcase down and tossed his keys into a bowl. It felt warm inside the house, and there was a strong smell of cabbage and gravy. As soon as she could see well enough, Virginia searched for the mark on her coat and began to scrape at it with her thumbnail.

Someone was tearing about on the floor above them, slamming drawers and making the floorboards squeak underfoot. A terrier came bounding and yapping down the stairs, wagging its stump of a tail, and a woman's voice shouted after it, "Bracken!"

Clem took his hat off and called up the stairs, in much the same tone of voice, "Lorna!" He ignored the dog, though it was racing around his feet and worrying his shoelaces.

"Clem? I'm coming, I'm coming, I'm sorry." There was a final flurry of sound and a pause, as if she'd stopped to gather herself, and then Lorna was coming toward them down the stairs.

"Virginia," she smiled, her hands outstretched in a gesture of welcome. "How wonderful to have you here at last!"

She wore an emerald-green dress with a narrow belt and a necklace of pearls, and she made the stairs and hallway, and even the dog, look drab. Virginia had met Lorna several times at Sinclair House, so she was familiar with that oval face; with her creamy skin and pencil-thin eyebrows and plump mouth. She hadn't seen her yellow hair before, though, or not properly, because Lorna had kept her hat and coat on when they were sitting in the visitors room or walking about the orphanage grounds. It was the sole part of her that didn't seem quite in control. Despite her obvious efforts to keep it combed and lotioned and pinned, curly strands kept flying loose all over, and she kept trying to poke them into submission.

"Welcome, welcome!" Lorna held Virginia at arm's length, her hands trembling. She surveyed the child with a fixed smile and planted a perfumed kiss on her cheek.

Virginia's voice had jammed in her throat, and she didn't dare return the kiss, for fear of marring the powdery perfection of Lorna's face. She cobbled together an awkward, blushing gesture instead, something between a bow and a curtsy, which made Lorna laugh uneasily.

"You must be hungry as a hunter!" she said. "Dinner won't be long."

Clem was on one knee, trying to extract his shoelace from the jaws of the ecstatic terrier. "*How* long?" he demanded, frowning up at his wife. "The poor child has walked her legs off on the strength of a sandwich lunch; she needs a quick supper and straight to bed."

Lorna's hostess smile barely wavered. "It'll be five minutes; ten at most. Mrs. Hill made a splendid rabbit pie this morning while I was doing the beds. It's in the oven now and coming along very nicely." She turned back to Virginia and bent down, so that their faces were level. "We usually eat in the kitchen, but I've set the table in the dining room today, as it's a special occasion. Do you want to come and see? I've put a white tablecloth out, and the silver cutlery, and it couldn't look smarter if we were expecting the king to dinner."

There was nowhere for Virginia to look other than her new mother's expectant face. She felt the tears rising at the back of her eyes and contorted her lips into odd shapes in an effort to stop them falling. It was impossible to explain how much she feared the sumptuous dining room; impossible to confess she wasn't hungry.

"I got a mark on my new coat," she faltered, as the first drops slid down her face. It was the only sensible-sounding apology she could think of. Bracken chose this moment to notice her, and busied over to inspect her ankle socks.

"Let's have a look." Lorna studied the offending patch of coat and brushed it with the back of her hand. "Well, not to worry, it's just a bit of mud. There's surely no call for tears?"

Clem came up behind Virginia and shuffled the coat off her shoulders. "Told you she wouldn't be cross," he murmured in her ear. Virginia slipped her mittens off, and Clem popped them in the coat pockets, one on either side.

"But of course I wouldn't be cross," Lorna exclaimed, her smile hardening. "Goodness, I'm not a dragon, am I?"

Lorna was so patently un-dragonlike that it seemed pointless to say so, but perhaps someone should have bothered to state the obvious because the ensuing silence felt heavy. A tear dropped off Virginia's chin and splashed on the dog's nose. It gave a shrill bark and jumped up at her like a jack-in-the-box.

"Oh Bracken, give it a rest," said Clem, touching the dog's belly with the toe of his shoe. Bracken snarled and pounced, catlike, on his master's foot. Virginia smiled at that, so Clem teased it all the more, moving his foot around the wheeling terrier, with one eye on the child's tear-stained face.

All at once Bracken stopped chasing and began to bark in earnest.

"Stop it!" Lorna swooped on the dog, smacking it hard across the nose. Clem winced. When Lorna hoisted the animal into her arms, its back legs scrabbled and pulled threads from her dress, but she didn't seem to notice.

Virginia shuffled closer to Clem until she was half-hidden by his arm, and Lorna glanced at the pair of them, a blush rising up her neck. "I'll check on the pie," she muttered, stalking off with the wriggling terrier still in her arms. Clem ruffled Virginia's hair. "I'd better go and offer my services to the chef," he whispered.

He showed her into the dining room where a snow-white cloth was laid, as promised, for three. A wood fire crackled in the grate, and the silence was like velvet, except for the occasional clatter from the kitchen. "Have a seat, Vi," he said. "Give those poor old feet a rest." He hovered in the doorway for a moment, as if reluctant to leave, and she managed to smile at him over her shoulder.

After he'd gone she stood by the fire for a moment, with her back to the warmth. The dining chairs were made of dark wood with tapestried seats, and she had to tense both arms in order to pull one out. At first she was content to sit on her hands and watch the firelight dance on the cut-glass water jug, but after a while she picked up her knife to find out if it was as heavy as it looked. It was even heavier, so she tested her fork, and her crystal glass, and after that she slid the silver ring off her linen napkin and rested it on her flat palm.

Salt Winds was a large house; she hadn't expected that. It was large enough to be a small-scale orphanage, if someone wanted it to be, although it would have to be stripped and sterilized first. The ivy-patterned wall-paper would have to be painted over, and the threadbare carpets replaced with lino-leum. The greenish curtains would have to be mothballed and replaced with safety bars. There would be no more leather-bound books on the shelves, no glass-fronted cabinets, no china shepherdesses on the mantelpiece. She twisted in her chair,

31

perversely pleased by her snap calculations. Some of those age-dulled oil portraits might stay on the walls, but the framed photographs — the family weddings, the men with dogs and guns, the sepia babies in sailor suits — would go.

She jumped when the door squeaked, but it was just Bracken nosing his way in. He padded across the carpet, ignoring her proffered hand and friendly cluckings, and slumped down in front of the fire. The voices in the kitchen were a muddle of sound. A tap gushed, and when it stopped she caught the end of Clem's question.

". . . that the two of you enjoyed your little tête-à-tête in my absence?"

Virginia barely recognized his voice, it was so stony and hard.

"I don't know what you mean!" Lorna hissed. "Where did you get that from?"

"Straight from the horse's mouth. He came cruising by when we were walking from the bus, and passed on his 'congratulations.' Well, who told him, if not you? He even gave me a little lecture on 'what a marvelous thing it is for Lorna' — he being the great expert, of course."

"I'm sure he did no such thing," said Lorna tightly. "Mind out of the way, this is hot." Her voice moved to a different part of the kitchen. "If you must know, we met by chance in the line at the post office. He asked after you, and naturally I told him you'd gone to fetch Virginia. What's wrong with that? She's not some unmentionable secret, is she?"

Clem sighed, and there was a long silence between them.

"No, of course not."

An oven door slammed shut. Plates were fetched from a rack and stacked angrily, one by one.

"I'm surprised he didn't offer you a lift," Lorna observed.

"He did."

"But you walked?"

"I wanted to. It was our daughter's first view of Salt Winds, Lorna; I'd pictured it so often in my head."

"You made Virginia walk all the way up the lane, when Max could have driven here in five minutes flat?"

"I'd rather not be beholden."

"*Beholden?* Oh, for God's sake —" Lorna's voice stopped abruptly. There were scuffling noises and fierce whispers, and the sound of someone trying not to cry out. Then there was silence.

Bracken raised his head from his paws and cocked his ears. Virginia held tight to the sides of her chair and fixed her gaze on the water jug. The cut glass made a miniature world, so beautiful and complex that if you stared at it for long enough you could lose your way among its flickering slivers of light.

"Bed?" Lorna suggested, scraping the pie remains from Virginia's plate. It was by no means the first time she'd spoken during dinner — she'd asked Virginia whether she had a favorite book and she'd told her about Mrs. Hill, who bicycled up four days a week to "do" the house — but it was the first thing she'd said with any conviction.

"Good idea," Clem agreed, poking about in the scraps for a morsel of rabbit and then holding it out for Bracken. Virginia had been afraid they'd insist on her leaving a clean plate, but they didn't; they couldn't, in all fairness, when Lorna herself had scarcely managed a mouthful. Clem sighed contentedly, and the chair creaked when he pressed against its back; he was the only one to have done justice to Mrs. Hill's pie. Lorna reached for her husband's plate while Bracken finished licking his hand and watched him wipe his slobbery fingers on a napkin.

Virginia leaned down and patted the terrier's head as Lorna piled the dirty plates and glasses onto a tray. "I think we'll let you off washing-up duties, this once," she smiled, her fist full of greasy knives and forks, and Virginia felt wrong-footed because it hadn't occurred to her to offer.

"Switch the wireless on, would you, Vi?" said Clem, once Lorna had gone. Nobody had ever thought to shorten her name before, and it made her blush with pleasure. It was like being reinvented.

Clem nodded at the box on the sideboard. "Left-hand dial."

Virginia turned the left-hand dial gently, with the very tips of her fingers, anxious not to leave prints on the polished wood. The machine whistled and hummed, and suddenly there was dance-band music all over the dining room. When she turned around, half laughing, Clem was fishing through his pockets, a pipe gripped between his teeth.

"Bet you've never filled a pipe before?" he said, placing a leather pouch and a box of matches on the tablecloth.

"No, and she's not about to." Lorna was watching them from the doorway. "Virginia? Bed."

It was strange, climbing up the carpeted stairs behind Lorna; like a dream that goes on and on. Their shoes made little sound, the music faded, the wind was nothing but a murmur. There was something hushed about the way Lorna walked, with a silky rustle and a languid sway of the hips. She went ahead, carrying the suitcase, and Virginia was surprised by the way its weight seemed to drag on her arm, because there was barely anything in it. A few scraps of clothing. A New Testament. A "Best Wishes" card *from all at Sinclair House.*

Downstairs, the music gave way to the clipped voice of a BBC man.

"Mrs. Wrathmell?" said Virginia, at the top of the stairs. "Clem won't have to go and fight, will he?"

Lorna led the way down the dimly lit landing. "No," she replied, with a faint snort. "Not unless they raise the conscription age."

"What about Mr. Deering?" Virginia wasn't sure what had provoked her to ask, but she wished, straightaway, that she hadn't. She wanted to say and do all the right things.

Lorna turned her head, her expression illegible in the poor light. "Mr. Deering? What makes you ask about him?"

They stopped outside a door halfway along the landing and Virginia shrugged at her shoes. "I don't know."

They stood face-to-face, momentarily stuck, unable to address the awkwardness of Virginia's question and unable to leave it be. Downstairs, the wireless crackle expanded as the dining-room door opened and terrier paws pattered across the hall floor. The front door opened, and they could hear Clem blowing on his hands and shifting from foot to foot while he waited for the dog to wee. A chill draft invaded the house, smelling of tobacco smoke and rain.

Lorna shivered. "Come on. Come and see your room," she said, opening the door and switching on the light. She set the suitcase down at the end of the bed and led the way around, smoothing creases from the baby-pink bedspread and adjusting a stem of yellow jasmine in a jar. "I had so much fun, getting it all ready." She smiled at the memory, as if it were an old one.

It was a big room: newly papered, newly curtained, newly furnished. Virginia followed Lorna from bed to chair to wardrobe, trying to take it all in; trying to find the right thing to say. She stopped at the dressing-table mirror and stared at herself in the unfamiliar light: a whey-faced thing with messy pigtails, eyes hooded with exhaustion.

Lorna picked up a knitted doll from the

pillow and flicked at its woolly plaits. "Oh dear," she said. "You're probably too old for pink, aren't you? And dolls." She tossed the doll back onto the bed and took a cigarette from her pocket.

"No!" Virginia protested inadequately, squeezing her hands together. She couldn't remember what her feelings were for the color pink, if she had any at all.

Lorna put the cigarette back in her pocket and went to the window, where she pulled the curtain aside and stared into the black night. Her face lost all its clarity in reflection; the light and the wavy glass made it seem broken and hollow eyed. It made her look even younger than she was. There had been girls at Sinclair House with the same gawky configuration of bones, the same haunted stare.

"Mrs. Wrathmell," Virginia began, gathering up her shoulders in a deep breath. "Thank you very much for having me. I'm sorry I didn't say it properly when I arrived. I like the room very much. I like pink."

They were like badly delivered lines from a badly written play, expressive of nothing but her own discomfort. Lorna made no response, except to lean her forehead against the glass and feel in her pocket again.

"Why don't you go and have a wash and

get into bed?" she said eventually. "I'll tell Clem to come up and say goodnight. The bathroom's at the end of the landing."

She moved toward the door, a trace of the hostess smile still visible on her features. "You'll find a clean nightie under your pillow."

Virginia nodded dumbly.

Virginia locked herself in the freezing bathroom and took off all her clothes before remembering to run a basin of water. Her teeth chattered as she held her hand under the hot tap, feeling it turn from cold to tepid to cold again. When it turned icy she gave up on the idea of a wash and just dabbed at her face and neck with a smear of coal-tar soap before pulling the new nightie over her head. It was made of white flannel with a pink ribbon at the neck and it was meant for a smaller child, judging by the way it strained across her ribs and dug into her armpits. She wondered what kind of little girl Lorna thought she'd seen in that high-ceilinged room at Sinclair House.

Virginia emerged from the bathroom unable to remember where her bedroom was, and as she stood there, trying to think, she listened to the wind. She bent her head to listen before creeping along the landing to the top of the stairs and peering over the banister.

There was Lorna. She was sitting on the bottom stair with her knees hunched up and her head tucked inside her arms, and Clem was standing over her with one hand over his eyes, pelting her with whispered words.

". . . so you say," he was whispering, "but if that's true, then why are you always hiding from me? I come into the room and you shove a bit of paper on the fire. I ask what you've been doing all day and you say, 'The usual.' I ask you what you're thinking and you say, 'Nothing.'" He threw his hands in the air. "It's enough to make a man commit . . . Lord knows what. And now this."

Lorna held herself tightly, like someone waiting for a storm to pass. She didn't reply.

"I thought all women wanted children? I thought that was the whole problem with — with us? This is the best I can do, Lorna. I'm sorry, but it's the best I can do, and you can't even . . . What kind of human being are you? Do you want me to take her back? Is that it? Is that what you want?"

When Lorna shrugged he grabbed her by the shoulders, but she flung him off and backed up the stairs.

"Get off!" she whispered. "Go away! Why won't you just go away?"

Clem came after her, but halfway up the stairs she sat down abruptly and wept into her hands. He stopped — equally abruptly — and closed his eyes. "Oh God," he muttered, pulling a handkerchief from his sleeve and tossing it into her lap. After a minute Lorna shook it out and blew her nose and Clem said, "Sorry," but he said it in the same bitter tone he'd been using all along.

Virginia leaned over a little farther, anxious to try to understand what she was seeing, and her own shadow loomed on the wall above their heads, sliced through by shadow-banisters. She moved back quickly, before they noticed it too, and though she stayed a little longer she couldn't make out what they were saying any longer and wasn't sure she wanted to. The gist of it was bad enough; any more might stick like splinters in her mind and fester there.

She tiptoed back along the landing and forced herself to imagine another cold walk along the flint wall, back toward the bus stop and Sinclair House. It might not happen — she had a feeling that the orphanage didn't countenance refunds or returns — but it was better to picture it all now, so as to be ready if it did. She found her pink-lit room and stood in the doorway, picturing the scene with all her might. Lorna would ask her to keep the mittens, out of sheer politeness, but she was sure to want the navy coat back. Clem would feel sorry for her and offer up fusty sweets, but he'd be disinclined to hold her hand this time, or call her *old thing.*

The curtains were still half-open, and Virginia went and stood between them, resting her face against the glass like Lorna had done. The wind from the marsh made a constant drone. It never whistled or gusted; it just went on and on, as if the whole house were falling through space.

If Clem did come and say goodnight to her, then she was going to ask him, straight out, whether or not they'd keep her. It had to be better to know one way or another. She stood her ground when she first heard his feet on the stairs, but as he reached the landing her nerve failed. When he was a few paces from her room, she switched the light off and darted between the cold sheets.

"All right, Vi?" he whispered, lowering himself onto the end of the bed. He sat there quietly for a while. Virginia breathed slowly and made no answer, but perhaps he could feel her pulse drumming through the mattress springs, because he knew she was awake.

"Listen, Vi," he said softly. "Don't worry

about Lorna. She's pleased as punch you've come."

Virginia opened her eyes. Clem was sitting hunched over, with his elbows on his knees and his face turned toward her. The landing light was behind him, so she couldn't see his expression, but she could feel his gaze, as if it were a tangible thing with a reach and weight all its own. She gave up pretending to be asleep and sat up.

"Tomorrow's a Wednesday, isn't it?" he said.

Virginia nodded.

"Well, Wednesdays are Mrs. Hill's day off, and my day for going up to town, so you two will have the house to yourselves. You'll be the best of friends before the morning is out, mark my words."

He fell silent after that, and Virginia waited nervously. He had something important to say — she knew it — but he was too kind to get to the point.

"I was thinking . . ." he began, at last, and she leaned forward, readying herself, the tight seams of the nightie boring into her underarms like wires.

"I was wondering," he said, "if you'd mind calling her 'Mother' or 'Mum' or some such? I think she'd like that."

Virginia let out a long breath. She nodded, quite calmly and slowly, and heard herself saying, "Yes. Yes, all right."

The mattress wobbled as Clem sat up straight, placing his hands on his knees. "Good," he said. "That's very good." He paused, as if he were going to say something else, but he thought better of it and stood up to go.

"Clem?" Virginia leaned so far forward that she could have seized his hand if she'd dared, and there was a tearing sound in the vicinity of her left armpit. "Shall I call you 'Dad,' as well?"

"You can if you want to," he replied. "Do you want to?"

Virginia pretended to think. "No, not really."

She sensed his smile in the darkness, just as she'd sensed his gaze before.

"Well, that's all right with me," he said as he stood up. She tensed, expecting the awkwardness of a goodnight kiss, but he mussed her hair instead and she burrowed under the sheets.

She fell asleep thinking about names and colors. *Lorna* was a green and gold name, like sunlit trees in summer, but *Mother* was white, like a blank piece of paper. *Virginia* was as clear as water from a tap, while *Clem* was black, like peat, and smelled of smoke and leather and wet earth.

New Year's Eve 2015

It isn't the dawn that wakes the old woman but the lessening of the darkness that begins an hour or two before, as lengths of gray and silver start to show in the sky. As she opens her eyes she sees the curlew's skull on top of the dressing table. Even in the deepest depths of sleep she hasn't forgotten, but it's still a shock to see it sitting there, so full of its own significance, with its watchful eye sockets turned toward her. She could lie here and contemplate it for hours, but she decides to get up, and the cat yowls and clings to the sheet with his claws as her legs move from underneath him. She continues to stare at the skull while her feet are searching for slippers, and the cat jumps to the floor with a thrash of his tail.

Virginia fumbles for her stick and shuffles to the window: one of the rags must have worked loose overnight, because the frame is trembling inside its casing. She pulls a pile of tights from the back of the armchair and rips off one of the feet with her teeth. The nylon scrap fits nicely between frame and casing, and she jams it down with her fingers until the breath of outdoor air is stifled and the window falls still. She will continue to perform such little routines today. Tomorrow, the house will have to take care of itself.

Virginia returns to the dressing table and picks up the skull, running her gaze over the curves and hollows of its head and down its long, needly bill. She closes her eyes and stands still, her lungs straining, the skull as dainty as a bubble on her hand. Last night, an extra twenty-four hours seemed like an impossible gift; this morning she is less euphoric. A single day is not such a very long time in which to extricate herself, thread by thread, from Salt Winds. There are cupboards full of oddments, which she won't have time to sort through, and drawers of photographs that she'll never see again. She pictures the house, room by room, and plots the route of her farewell tour, mentally circling certain parts and crossing others out. *Clem's desk?* Yes. *The dining room?* Briefly. *Lorna's mothball-smelling wardrobe?* Perhaps not. *The attic?*

The attic. Virginia's eyes snap open. There's a paler sky reflecting off the discolored pink of her bedroom wall, and the outlines of things — the rickety furniture, the stretching cat — have grown bolder.

"The attic." She makes herself say it out loud as she returns the curlew's skull to the dressing table. The phone on the landing begins to ring, and the cat starts and glares at the noise.

Virginia glares at it too. On her last day she's reluctant to commune with anyone except the house and its dead; anything else feels tasteless, if not wrong. She's tempted to let it ring and ring, but Joe will start worrying if there's no answer, and then he'll be driving over to check that she's all right. She steps onto the landing, where the telephone is screwed to the wall, and picks up the receiver. At least it's a chance to make arrangements for the cat.

"Virginia. It's Joe."

The warmth of his voice touches her unexpectedly. Not the emotional warmth — Joe is not emotional — but the sheer blood-warmth of it; the rumbling maleness of the sound.

"Of course it's Joe," she replies. "Who else would it be?"

Virginia has got out of the habit of expressing affection, and Joe misreads her tone.

"Sorry," he says, unapologetically. "I wondered if you wanted any shopping. I'm off to the supermarket shortly."

Something soft brushes against Virginia's leg. It's the velvet curtain that hangs across the attic door. A draft has caught it, and every time it swells outward it taps her on the ankle. Over the years she's stopped seeing that curtain; she's erased it from her field of vision.

"Virginia?"

"Oh. No. No shopping today. Thank you, Joe."

There are woody shadows behind the curtain, and smells of varnish and undisturbed dust. She cranes her neck and glimpses a pale globe floating in the darkness, which puzzles her until she recognizes the porcelain doorknob.

"Could you pop over tomorrow, Joe, and feed Silver? I'll leave some pouches for him by the front door."

"Oh? Well yes, of course . . ."

She can picture him so clearly now, as he frowns and scratches the back of his curly head.

"Why?" he says, inevitably. "Where are you off to?"

"Oh. Not far."

Joe's voice drops.

"This isn't about Monday, is it?"

"Monday?"

"We're popping over to Thorney Grange, remember? Our appointment for Monday morning."

Thorney Grange. Virginia rubs her nose on the back of her hand and tries to pay attention to what Joe is saying. These days it's an old folks' home, and Joe thinks she'd be better off there. Less of a worry.

"Hello?" Joe persists. "Virginia?" He thinks she's going to kick up a fuss, like she did the last time. "We're only looking, and you don't have to. But you did promise . . ."

"Yes, yes, I remember." Virginia's mood lifts for the first time since waking, and she waves her hand imperiously. "Don't worry. I won't make any more difficulties."

"Really? Well, that's good. But —"

"Thank you," she says deafly. "Goodbye, Joe." And she puts the phone down.

"Thorney Grange," she snorts, as the receiver rocks back into place with a ping and the agitated cord swings back and forth. She waits while it slows down and stops, and resists the temptation to set it going again. It feels like her first relinquishment. Her first act of farewell.

■ ■ ■ ■

The biggest of the spare bedrooms has the best view toward Tollbury Point, but it's been a long time since Virginia went in. Her routine has diminished over the years, and nowadays she rarely strays from the well-trodden path that leads from bedroom to bathroom to kitchen and back.

She glances around as she opens the door and advances across the tattered rug with a picture frame in one hand. She doesn't wish to see things too thoroughly. Presumably the other rooms — even Clem and Lorna's — are in much the same state: all dry rot and dust sheets, and curtains hanging in tatters, like bats' wings. It's a bit late now to start wishing she'd taken better care of the place. She sits down in the wicker chair by the window and lays their wedding photo in her lap. It's odd that she should treasure it, she thinks, when neither of them looks the least bit happy. She gazes at them a moment, returning their reluctant smiles in kind, then turns them over and grapples with the pins at the back of the frame. That way, she'll be able to fit it in her dressing-gown pocket.

This room faces west, and dawn hasn't

silvered the western sky yet. Tollbury Point is still a blur on the horizon, but she can see the whole length of the lane, as pale and straight as it was on the day she arrived in her navy-blue coat.

Virginia sits at the window until daylight begins to reach this side of the house and the outline of the village grows clearer. There's a dusting of snow on the marsh and more to come, judging by the bulging clouds. She tries not to shiver and shrink from the cold but to welcome it, the way she's used to welcoming warmth. She tries to yearn for snow-streaked mudflats the way she yearns for bath and bed, but you need years, not hours, to pull off mind tricks like that.

She can at least wear her dressing gown; that's allowed, isn't it? Apart from anything else she'll need the pockets for all her souvenirs and stones. She heaves herself to her feet, but something catches her eye as she's turning away from the window. There's something out there, on the old seawall. An object has appeared a few yards from the house, near the spot where she was standing last night.

Virginia frowns at it and thinks of a cormorant, its bony wings hunched against the weather, its feathers fluttering. She wishes this thing were a bird, but it isn't. It's a person. It's a girl.

The girl is sitting on the wall with her arms wrapped around her knees, staring out at the marsh. The wind is picking at her thin clothes and pulling at her hair. Her hands are bare, and the blue-tinged pallor of her skin is bright in the semidarkness. As Virginia stands and watches, a few flakes of snow drift onto the girl's head and speckle the shoulders of her denim jacket.

Virginia takes a turn around the room, muttering and bringing the stick down hard at every step, but when she gets back to the window the trespasser is still there, quaking now, as if in the throes of fever, her damp hair dusted white. Virginia thinks about rapping on the glass and shooing her away, but that would be communication, of a sort, and she can't bring herself to do it.

She returns to her own room and unhooks her dressing gown from the back of the door. It used to be Clem's, and the unrolled sleeves are long enough to hide her fingers. She knots the belt tight and pulls the collar up as high as it will go, pressing her nose into the brown tartan and catching, or imagining, an ancient whiff of tobacco. She takes another look at the wedding photo and pops it into one of the pockets.

All she has to do is pretend she hasn't seen the girl and proceed as planned. Yet she returns to the spare room and stands at the window, twining her fingers around the handle of her stick. The girl is still sitting on the wall, as before, but she's dropped her chin onto her knees, and there's something about her posture that disturbs Virginia. She feels as though she's seen that tumble of black hair before, and the narrow shoulders, and the tilt of the head — and at the same time she knows she hasn't. Not exactly. But today is bound to be a day for ghosts, and as like as not she'll be seeing them at every turn till nightfall: hanging off coat pegs, glancing from mirrors, flitting past door-ways.

The snow has been falling in dribs and drabs since Virginia woke up, but it's coming more heavily now. It's as though net curtains were being drawn across the view, one by one, veiling the village, and the marsh, and the lane, and billowing around the girl on the wall. Eight o'clock echoes eerily from the church tower, and then quarter past, and Virginia keeps telling herself it's time to get on.

January 1940

"Well, you'll have to take my word for it," said Mrs. Hill, as flour fluttered from her fingertips into the big mixing bowl. "They were as thick as thieves when they were boys." Mrs. Hill would know. She knew such things better than anybody, having served the Salt Winds household for almost fifty years.

All the same, Virginia tilted her head skeptically. "Clem? And Mr. Deering? Were friends?" She pictured the man in the car, whom she'd met on her arrival at Tollbury Point a month ago. She remembered Clem's blank face, and the tight-lipped way in which he had said, "Evening, Deering."

"*Best* friends," Mrs. Hill insisted.

Virginia glanced at her homework and bit her nail. Tollbury School was her first proper school, and she had been there barely a week. She was anxious to keep up.

"I can picture them both now," Mrs. Hill said.

This was hopeless. Virginia closed her exercise book and knelt up on her chair as Mrs. Hill sloshed cold water into the rubbed flour and nodded with tight-jawed conviction. "Young Max was always trudging up here with Clem after school. Coming to play at the big house. It counted as a proper treat for him, in those days." She twisted her wedding ring off and laid it on the table. "His father was a butcher, you know. Deering and Son. Used to have the shop next door to the post office. It's because of Clem, and Clem's father, that Max knows the marsh as well as he does. He wouldn't have a clue otherwise."

Virginia picked up Mrs. Hill's ring and slipped it over her thumb, spinning it in the light so that the gold flashed.

"But they're not friends anymore, are they?"

"What makes you say that?" Mrs. Hill wondered slyly, the fat quivering along her arms as she worked the dough. "He's coming for tea today, isn't he?"

"Yes, but I mean they're not *real* friends, are they? I know Clem doesn't like him." Virginia popped the ring back on the table. "I don't like him either."

"Poor Mr. Deering, I think you're a rotter," said Mrs. Hill, but she smiled at the dough as if it had told her a good joke. "His wife died, you know, and he's had to bring up two children all by himself. He can't be completely bad, can he?"

"Why not? Sad things happen to all sorts of people; it doesn't make them nice."

Mrs. Hill laughed, as if she found it a slightly shocking idea.

"Well," she admitted in an undertone, "some people do say he wasn't a good husband to poor Mrs. Deering while she was alive, and I won't argue against them. I knew that girl since the day she was born, and she wasn't the same after she married him."

"In what way?"

"Oh, I don't know. Just quieter."

Virginia thought for a while. "Is that why Clem doesn't like him? Because he was mean to his wife?"

"Oh, well. No. I don't think it's just that."

"What then? Please tell me." Virginia glanced around, lowering her voice to a whisper. "Is it because of Lorna?"

Mrs. Hill banged the ball of dough onto the floury tabletop and pressed it flat with her palms. She passed Virginia a cutter and took another for herself. They leaned over the dough from opposite sides of the table, their heads almost touching.

"Well," Mrs. Hill murmured, as they pressed their first circles from the dough. "First of all, you tell me. What do you make of your new mother?"

Virginia hesitated. "She's very pretty."

"Oh yes," agreed Mrs. Hill firmly, "she's that all right. And? What else?"

"Well —"

But before Virginia could go on, Lorna burst in from the hall, her heels clicking across the stone floor. "I've just spotted their car," she whispered urgently. "They'll be here any moment."

"Nearly there, Mrs. Wrathmell." Mrs. Hill began cutting the scones and transferring them to the baking tray with mechanical efficiency.

Lorna plucked a few dog hairs from Virginia's sweater and picked up her hands for inspection. Bracken began barking and leaping at the front door, infuriated by the noise of the approaching motor.

"I'll go and clean my nails," said Virginia preemptively, as the car braked at the front of the house and, simultaneously, someone knocked at the back door.

"Oh goodness, who's this?" Lorna cried, dropping Virginia's hands. "We're not expecting anyone else, are we? The grocery boy came yesterday."

Mrs. Hill shook her head and continued cutting scones. Lorna wrung her hands.

"Virginia, go tell Clem the Deerings are here. Quickly. And give your hair a quick brush while you're upstairs."

The unexpected knock came again at the back door. Lorna tutted and crossed the kitchen, through the scullery, to answer it.

Virginia went into the hall, where Bracken was yapping and running in circles. She made ineffective soothing noises as she stepped over him and peered through the window beside the front door. She hadn't seen Mr. Deering since the day she arrived last month, nor had she met his children, though she'd heard about them from Mrs. Hill. The Wrathmells' lives might be circumscribed by Tollbury Point — work and school, church and leisure all took place within a rustic two-mile radius — but the Deerings seemed to venture farther afield. The children went to boarding schools, and Mrs. Hill said they were regulars at the cathedral.

Though she hadn't seen Mr. Deering since December, she had seen his car — just once, last week, when she was sent home from school with stomach cramps. It was a Wednesday lunchtime, and she'd walked halfway down the lane before she spotted it — big and black and unmistakable, and parked right outside Salt Winds. She'd climbed into the field and sat against the hedge for a good hour until she heard it purr away. When Clem came back from town that evening, she'd intended to tell him, but somehow she hadn't.

Mr. Deering was adjusting his hat in the rearview mirror, and the sight of his pale face and skin-tight gloves made Virginia's stomach flutter. She couldn't see much of the son, Theodore: just a mouth, talking away in the back of the car, and a bow tie and a fat neck.

Virginia knew she ought to get a move on — Lorna had finished talking to whomever-it-was at the back door, and was crossing the kitchen with a word for Mrs. Hill — but Mr. Deering's daughter was getting out of the car now and standing upright in the pale sunlight. She wore a blood-red beret and suede shoes, and she was sliding a dog-eared novel into her coat pocket. Mrs. Hill had said, with faint scorn, that her name was Juliet, and Virginia thought the name suited her. She was tall and dark-haired — "the very spit of her poor mother" — and even with her coat on you could tell she had a proper bosom. Virginia looked for as long as she dared, while Bracken ran figure eights around her ankles, but Lorna's high heels were clacking across the kitchen floor, and Mr. Deering was pocketing his car keys, and in the end she had to race upstairs.

She paused on the landing to listen. Downstairs, Lorna had made it to the front door, and voices were raised in greeting. The two grown-ups cried "Hello!" as if they were pleasantly surprised to see one another, though obviously they weren't surprised, since they'd arranged this get-together over the phone a few days ago. Mr. Deering said that something smelled delicious; Lorna apologized for the hysterical dog and admired Juliet's beret. There were sounds of cheeks being kissed and coats being removed. Theodore said, "Daddy, I'm starving," which gave the grown-ups an opportunity to laugh.

"Vi?" Clem's voice was calling down the landing. "That you?"

"They're here," she whispered, before she'd even reached the study doorway.

"Are they? Oh Lord." Clem wrote something with a conclusive flourish and screwed the lid onto his fountain pen. She entered the tobacco smog and leaned against him, and he put an arm around her waist with a sigh. "Bother those Deerings."

"Mother says you're to come down," she said, squinting at his manuscript, though there were more crossings-out than words, and his handwriting was impossible to read. "And Mrs. Hill's made scones."

"Oh well. Every cloud . . ."

Virginia took the top page and read aloud from one of the more legible sections, stumbling over the longer words: ". . . low oxygen levels in the peat, due in part to the frequent tidal submersion of the salt marsh . . ." She shot him a quick sideways glance and stopped. It was silly, because Clem insisted she could say anything to him, but she felt there was a risk attached to the word *marsh.* He'd warned her about its dangers on several occasions since that first walk home along the lane, and had made her promise, solemnly, that she would never, ever set foot beyond the flint wall. As far as she knew, it was the single subject under the sun capable of extinguishing Clem's sense of humor. Even the war gave rise to black jokes.

Virginia thought about Mr. Deering's car parked up outside the house last Wednesday.

Clem sighed and put his pen away in its case, and Virginia shut up. Shutting up was almost always a clever move, she'd discovered, not just with Clem but with everyone. People rarely object to a quiet child.

She leaned her cheek against his head and stared out of the window. Lorna would be calling up the stairs in a moment and they ought to go, but neither made the first move. The marsh looked harmless today — dull, even — like a big, puddly field. Clem's desk was more distracting, littered as it was with curiosities: rolls of typewriter ribbon; tins of tobacco; bottles of colored ink; torn envelopes spilling photographs of birds and eggs; drawings of plants and cross sections of earth. She leafed through the pictures dreamily and pulled one out at random.

"Oh!" she exclaimed, delighted. It was a pencil drawing of a duck in a businessman's suit, with a monocle and a furled umbrella: not at all the sort of scientific illustration she expected to find. It was very well done, and she was tempted to ask if she could keep it, but Clem took it out of her hand, studied it a second, and dropped it into a drawer.

"Don't know what that was doing there," he said, getting to his feet and picking up his jacket from the back of the chair.

"It's really good," Virginia protested. "Did you do it?"

"Me?" He shrugged the jacket over his

shirt and gave a short laugh. "No, I did not; I can't draw for toffee. Come on. We'd better get a move on, or there'll be trouble."

There was a faint noise coming from the back of the house, and it nagged at Virginia's attention all the way downstairs. It was a bit like the monotonous wind she'd grown so used to over the weeks, but it was harsher than the wind, and more localized.

"What's that?" she asked.

"Mmm?" Clem wasn't paying attention.

Whatever it was, it paused before she could ask again, and a sharp laugh rang out from the sitting room.

"Doesn't matter," she said, as Mr. Deering made some inaudible remark and Lorna laughed again. Virginia squeezed Clem's hand, and he squeezed back, crushing her fingers so hard that she almost cried in protest.

"Ah, *there* you are." Lorna's tone of voice was dry, but she stood up hastily when they entered, as if she'd been caught doing something wrong.

"Sorry, darling." Clem placed a hand on the small of his wife's back and kept it there. Lorna stiffened but managed a smile. "How do," he added, nodding at the Deerings.

Lorna looked Virginia up and down, and

64

ran a reproachful hand over her hair before turning her to face the room.

"Juliet? Theodore? This is Virginia. Our new daughter."

Theodore was slouching in the window seat, bouncing his heels against the wall, and Juliet was riffling the corners of the novel she'd brought in with her. Both smiled incuriously and said hello. Lorna put her hands on Virginia's shoulders and propelled her toward Mr. Deering's deep armchair. He leaned forward with his right hand outstretched.

"Ah-ha, Miss Wrathmell," he murmured, as if he and Virginia shared a secret or two. "We meet again."

There was something insistent about the way he held his hand out, and Virginia didn't want to take it, but Lorna shoved her in the back, so she did. She dropped it again, as quickly as she could, and Mr. Deering sank back in the chair with a comfortable sigh, his legs at full stretch and a twitch at the corner of his mouth. Virginia felt, obscurely, that he'd enjoyed touching her hand, and making her touch his, and she wondered if they'd have to go through the same rigmarole every time they met.

"Well!" Clem pronounced, hanging back by the door with his hands in his pockets.

He scratched his head and sniffed. "Well. What's your top sport these days, Theodore? I'll wager you're a cricket man like your father, eh?"

Theodore stuck his lower lip out and continued to swing his legs. "Not really."

Juliet stared out of the window, perhaps wishing to discourage any similar conversational gambits, and Virginia followed her gaze. The sky was a delicate yellow, and she could see a cloud of lapwings billowing over the marsh, miles away. She was pleased with herself for knowing what they were, and would have pointed them out to Clem if the Deerings hadn't been there.

"Juliet's the sporty one, aren't you, Jules?" said Mr. Deering. "She'll be an Oxford Blue in three or four years' time, just like her old dad. You mark my words."

"Dad!" Juliet glared, softening slightly as he mouthed her a private *sorry.* She turned back to the window, and nobody pursued the subject.

"Mrs. Hill will be along in a minute with the tea." Lorna looked for something to do, but there was nothing, so she sat down at one end of the sofa and laid her clasped hands in her lap. Clem sat close beside her and Virginia perched on the piano stool. There was still something humming, intermittently, around the back of the house. It sounded louder in here.

"What is that?" Theodore demanded. His voice was too loud, Virginia thought, as she looked at him properly for the first time. His hair was as black as crude oil, and the skin at the parting was startlingly white. He was a rudimentary version of his father, though not yet so smiling or so handsome.

"What? That whirring noise?" Lorna seemed grateful for the question. "That's just Mr. Rosenthal. The knife grinder. He arrived about the same time as you." She knotted her fingers as if there must be something else she could add. "He's sharpening the kitchen knives. Oh, and Clem? He said he'd take those shears away for mending."

"Right." Clem put his arm around Lorna and rubbed her shoulder gently. She didn't pull away, but she didn't lean in either. Mr. Deering shifted in his chair, making the old springs creak.

"Rosenthal?" he mused. "Not that dirty itinerant with the tricycle? He was loitering near Thorney Grange the other day." He stroked a finger along his thin moustache, as if to check that it was still there. "You know he's a Jerry, Wrathmell?"

Clem took his hand off Lorna's shoulder.

"He also happens to be a Jew," he retorted, and it was obvious that Mr. Deering had said something stupid. The twist in Clem's eyebrows was enough to make Virginia squirm, but Max just lounged back in the creaky chair and stretched his legs out until he was practically horizontal.

"A German *and* a Semite!" he exclaimed in cartoonish horror, making big eyes at Virginia. "Damned on two counts, eh? I'd think twice before letting him anywhere near my knives. What do you think, Miss Wrathmell?"

An expectant stillness fell over the room. Even Theodore stopped swinging his feet. Virginia caught Clem's eye and he forced a smile for her. She opened her mouth and shut it again. Clem was about to say something when Mrs. Hill came rattling across the hall with the tea tray, and Lorna got up to open the door and the moment passed. Juliet offered to help hand out teacups, and Theodore was distracted by the scones. Even Mr. Deering had the good grace to pull his feet in and sit up when Lorna brought him a plate.

For a few minutes, the drone of the knife grinder was masked by the chinking of teaspoons on china, and innocuous chatter about rationing. It was only a few days since the government had begun rationing bacon, butter, and sugar by weight, so it still felt like a novelty. Clem thought it was a jolly good thing; we couldn't be relying on imports now Hitler had got his navy up to strength.

"Which is all very well," Lorna said lightly, setting the teapot down. "Just as long as they don't start rationing tea."

Mr. Deering slipped her a wink. "Rules are made to be broken. I'll make sure you don't go short."

This was the first time Virginia had seen the posh tea set in use. Usually it was on display in a glass-fronted cabinet in the dining room, and Mrs. Hill said that's where it had been kept ever since Clem's grandfather brought it home from a business trip to Meissen, in the 1860s. All the pieces were tiny and translucent and painted with periwinkles, and they made a nervous jiggling sound when they were handed out. The Deerings seemed at home, as if they took tea in porcelain cups every day of the week. Mr. Deering balanced his plate on one knee and ate rapidly but neatly.

"So, Wrathmell," he said, between two gulps of tea. "Been out on the marsh lately?"

"I went shrimping a few times last summer. That's about it. There's not been much call for guided walks; I don't know why. The tourists seem to bypass Tollbury Point these days."

"Mmm." Mr. Deering smiled into his teacup, as if he could think of a few reasons why. Virginia stared at Clem. She didn't want to speak in front of everyone, but she couldn't let this pass.

"How can you have gone out on the marsh?" she whispered, training her eyes on him and blocking out everyone else. "I thought you said the sand swallowed people up? And what about the tides that come in faster than anyone can run —"

Clem reddened, like a liar. "That's all true, Vi," he said. "It really is. But you see —"

"But you see, Vi," Mr. Deering interrupted. "Your daddy has special knowledge." His tone was as jovial as ever, but Juliet shifted in her seat and Lorna started gathering up the half-finished plates and cups. "Hasn't he told you he can bloody well walk on water?"

Clem frowned and scratched the back of his head and barked a kind of laugh, but before he could say anything Lorna banged the stack of plates down on the tray and held them there. It was a punctuation mark; a protest; a hand held up to signal *Stop.*

"Children? There's still a bit of daylight left. Why don't you wrap yourselves up warm and go and get some fresh air?"

The three youngsters hesitated, and Theodore looked as though he was going to complain, but there was something about the way Lorna spoke, and the subdued demeanor of the men, that meant they had no choice. The girls set their empty cups on the table and trooped dutifully into the hall, where their coats and hats were hanging on pegs. Theodore followed, swiping the last scone from the tray and popping it whole into his mouth as he shut the door behind him.

Virginia buttoned her coat slowly and in silence, listening for the buzz that was bound to erupt in the sitting room once they'd gone — otherwise why had they been dismissed? But there was nothing; no sound at all.

Given the vastness of the views from Salt Winds, there was surprisingly little space for playing outdoors. If you went out the front door, as the children did, then you could either hang about in the circular drive, where the Deerings' car was parked, or you could squeeze down the path between the house and the seawall. This would

71

bring you to the back garden, which comprised a few square yards of scraggy grass, an overgrown hedge, a toolshed, and a row of terra-cotta pots, where Lorna and Mrs. Hill struggled to grow herbs.

They circled the big black car for a while, admiring it in silence. Virginia managed to touch it, quickly, while the other two weren't looking, leaving a fingerprint on one of the rear wheel arches. Immediately she wished she hadn't, because Mr. Deering was bound to notice, and even if he wasn't cross he would think about her as he polished it away with a soft cloth and know she'd been curious.

Mr. Rosenthal was still working in the fading light; they could hear the whizz of the grinder at the back of the house. If he really was a German, then Virginia would be interested to see what he looked like; there was no point denying it. His tricycle stood to one side of the house, a large black machine with an integral trunk at the back and a sign that read *Rosenthal Knife-Grinding and Repairs*. Virginia watched as Theodore pinged the bell a couple of times and tried to open the lid of the trunk, but Juliet wasn't interested; she just swung herself up onto the flint wall and sat facing the marsh, her book open on her lap.

Virginia seated herself on the wall beside Juliet — not too close — and tried to imagine what it would be like to be gifted with poise, not to mention a red beret and a proper bust and an age ending in *-teen*. She glanced sidelong, without moving her head, as Juliet searched for her place in the book, but the printed words flicked past, impossible to catch, let alone decipher.

Theodore clambered onto the wall, too, and began pacing up and down, touching the girls' backsides with his foot every time he passed behind them. At first Virginia feared for her navy coat and shuffled closer to the edge, but this just goaded him, and he started prodding the base of her spine each time he went by. Virginia tried to grip the wall, but her mittens were slippery and the stones were smooth, and she couldn't find any purchase. Theodore Deering obviously didn't know — presumably he'd never been told — about the dangers of Tollbury Marsh; about how a body could sink under that earth, slowly and inexorably, like an insect in a pot of glue.

"Don't!" she shouted, the next time he stopped behind her.

"Stop it, Pugface," said Juliet vaguely as she turned another page. Theodore kicked his sister by way of reply, leaving a dusty shoeprint on the back of her coat. Juliet frowned dangerously and closed her book. Undeterred, Theodore plucked the red beret from her head and flung it over the wall. It landed on the marsh, a few yards out, suspended on a tussock of grass.

"All right," said Juliet calmly, setting her book down on the wall and getting to her feet. Her curly hair, unconfined by the hat, flickered across her face. She seized her little brother by the wrist and held on to him with an implacable stillness, while he floundered like a landed fish. Virginia swung her legs over and jumped down on the safe side of the wall before running across the grass and standing to watch with her back against the house. The sister and brother looked like actors on a stage, backlit by the winter twilight.

"You're hurting me!" Theodore squealed.

"Go and get it," said Juliet.

"Oh no!" Virginia cried, pressing her hands to her mouth. "You mustn't make him! It's dangerous! He'll drown!"

Juliet took no notice, but Theodore stared at Virginia and began to cry.

"If you don't go and fetch my hat," said Juliet evenly, "I'll break your arm. No, really, I will." And as if to prove her intent she wrapped the fingers of both hands around her brother's wrist and stuck her elbows out, as if preparing to snap the bone. Theodore's face ran with tears and snot, and his wet mouth gaped as he nodded his acquiescence. Juliet released him and he lowered himself onto the marsh, whimpering like a puppy.

Virginia covered her face with her hands, conscious that she must do something, but unable to move or speak. She waited for the shouts of terror and the hungry sucking sounds, and as she waited she framed the questions that Clem would be asking later on, and tomorrow, and for years to come: *Why didn't you tell them? Why didn't you call us? Why didn't you stop him?* These questions would become her lifelong companions, pacing around in her brain hour after hour, like prisoners in an exercise yard, and for a split second she had a presentiment of the dreariness, the sheer tedium, with which they would go on tormenting her, even when she was grown-up; even when she was an old, old woman with white hair. The prospect of such a life sentence was overwhelming, and she bent double, crushing her face against her fists.

"Thank you, Pugface." Juliet's voice floated over Virginia's anguish, like a bird over the marsh, so light and faraway that it hardly registered at first. "That wasn't too difficult, was it? Let's hope there's no damage; it'd be a pity to have to spend your birthday money on a new one."

Virginia straightened up and tried to breathe normally. Juliet was sitting on the wall, turning the hat in her hands and squinting at it to check for marks. Satisfied, she put it back on her head and stuffed stray locks of hair under the rim. Theodore was standing beside her with his hands in his pockets, scuffing the ground with his heel and scrutinizing Virginia through narrowed eyes. His shoes weren't even muddied.

"Thank you for coming," Lorna said, again, as they gathered in the hall. She'd already said it twice. "Lovely to see you all." She had a kiss for Juliet, a kiss for Theodore, and a hesitant glance for Max, which didn't discourage him from grabbing her hand.

"Lovely," he echoed. "Let's meet again soon."

Clem leaned against the kitchen doorway, chewing his lower lip and keeping his distance from the farewells. Virginia could see Mrs. Hill behind him in the darkened kitchen, getting ready to leave for the night. Even though her hands were busy hanging up damp tea towels and unknotting the strings on her apron, she never took her eyes off the group in the hall. When Max Deering touched cheeks with Lorna, Mrs. Hill pressed her lips together so tightly that her mouth became a fine line, the cutting edge of a knife.

Perhaps it was just as well Mrs. Hill wasn't watching from the same angle as Virginia, and couldn't observe the light wink off Mr. Deering's signet ring as he squashed a paper into his hostess's hand. No doubt it was fortunate she didn't see the smoothness with which Lorna received it and slipped it inside her sleeve.

"Hang on, Vi." Clem stopped Virginia on the stairs as she made her way to her bedroom. The noise of the car was fading down the lane and everyone else had melted away; now she wanted to do the same. Salt Winds felt different after the Deerings' visit, as if they'd left something of themselves behind, or taken something away. Virginia thought she'd go upstairs and read, and wait for the feeling to fade.

Clem placed his hand over hers. "I just want to explain something," he began. "Something Deering said."

He was going to tell her about Tollbury Marsh again, and how it would eat her up if she set foot beyond the flint wall. She sat down on the stairs, resigned to it, and Clem looked up at her through the banisters, like a prisoner. She wasn't sure she could trust what he said anymore, and it was a strange sensation — much worse, and more surprising, than not being able to trust Lorna. On top of that, she kept wondering about the paper in Lorna's sleeve and whether she had a duty to mention it.

"I know I go on about it, but I don't want you thinking the marsh is safe. It's true I've been out there myself, but that's because I grew up with it and it's in my blood. I know Tollbury Marsh; I know it like the back of my hand. But even I wouldn't venture far, and nine times out of ten I wouldn't venture at all. It's about understanding the weather, the tides, the mood . . . not just understanding those things, but feeling them . . . Vi? Are you listening?"

Virginia nodded awkwardly, with her chin on one hand. She was listening as she gazed out of the window at the space where the car had been and toyed with her lower lip. Or at least, if she wasn't exactly listening, the sound of Clem's voice was deep inside her mind, tugging away at her thoughts.

"It's just . . . Vi . . . I don't want you thinking I told you lies, or even half-truths."

Mrs. Hill had left the house by the kitchen door, and now she was wheeling her bike down the lane toward Tollbury Point. Mrs. Hill knew what was what, and how the world worked, and where the truth lay. You could tell by the way she faced the night, with a shopping bag on either handlebar and a headscarf tied stoutly beneath her chin.

"Vi?"

"Yes, yes, I know. I'm listening."

Bit by bit the darkness swallowed Mrs. Hill.

New Year's Eve 2015

Virginia slips the chain, wriggles back the bolt, and braces herself for a rush of cold air. She will have to confront the girl, warn her off, threaten her if necessary. The day will not unfold as it should while someone is sitting outside Salt Winds. She's tried banging on the windows, first with her knuckles and then with her stick. She even managed to force a downstairs window open and shout into the wind, but her voice amounted to little — the creaking of a rusty hinge — and the girl didn't notice.

Virginia props the door open with the umbrella stand, and a flurry of snow blows across the hall floor as she sets off. It's worse being outdoors by daylight. Night-time had given the curlew's message an aura of mysticism, draped the house and marsh in glamorous darkness, transformed the streetlights of Tollbury Point into distant planets. There's none of that now, at half past eight in the morning on the last day of December. As Virginia winces her way down the front steps, one by one, she's pained by the withered dandelion leaves poking up from the gravel, and the flattened lager can that's blown in from goodness knows where and landed on the verge. Today shouldn't be like this. Today has nothing to do with weeds, or litter, or moody teenagers.

As she approaches the wall, all she can make out is a bony back and a jumble of dark hair. Earlier on, the girl had been staring out at the marsh, but now she's bowed her head onto her knees, as if she's dozing. How old is she? Fourteen? Fifteen? The girl's youth frightens Virginia. Their worlds are seventy years apart. It's too big a gap. Virginia will say one thing and the girl will say another, and neither will understand a word.

"I need you to go away!" Virginia speaks slowly, batting at the whirling air with her free hand. "Please! Go away!"

The girl swivels her head as Virginia reaches the wall so that her cheek, rather than her forehead, is lying on her knees. Other than that, she makes no response, registering the old woman's voice without appearing to know, or care, what it means.

They stare at one another doubtfully.

The snowfall is petering out again. There's never quite enough snow on Tollbury Marsh; never enough to throw a dazzling tablecloth across the flat vista and effect a transformation. Virginia has seen proper snow in the States, and in Germany, and of course that winter they spent in Switzerland, but it doesn't happen here, at home. Tollbury snow might freeze you to the marrow of your bones, but it's a measly affair to look at: an impure whiteness shadowed by dirty clouds, stippled with grass tips and stones and pools of mud. It's never the kind of snow you regret spoiling with your footprints.

"Go away!" she repeats, helplessly. The child's gaze is pink and she has obviously done a lot of weeping, but she's stopped for the time being. She's worn herself out. Virginia was expecting antagonism, but the girl has barely enough self-will to lift her head. If Virginia could somehow haul her to her feet, turn her in the direction of the lane, and order her to walk, she would probably obey — though her legs would likely crumple within a few yards.

"Who are you?" Virginia demands. A sudden gust flutters their snowy hair and clothes, and they shudder in unison.

"I'm so cold," says the girl. Her voice, like her eyes, is wet and raw with tears, and she sounds like a much younger child. She sounds almost like a toddler, moaning about the nasty wind as if it were someone's fault; as if it were someone's duty to act.

"What are you doing here?" Virginia persists, but the girl has retracted like a snail, her head and knees wrapped inside her dark-blue denim arms.

"I'm so cold," she cries quietly into her knees as she rocks back and forth. "I feel like I'm going to die."

It's enough to try the patience of a saint. Virginia, conscious of being no saint, grinds her stick against the hard earth. "Then you'd better come inside and warm up."

There's nothing gracious about the offer; it's a calculation, pure and simple. Which will be the worse distraction? Watching the child down a mug of tea in the kitchen while she calls her parents and waits to be fetched? Or glimpsing her body from every front-room window, hunched on the flint wall and turning bluer by the second? Virginia can't think of a third option. She feels she's been cornered, and the injustice of it creates a hollow feeling in her chest.

"Come on then, hurry up. You're not the only one."

In fact, the girl is trying to obey, but it takes some effort to uncurl her frozen limbs and slide down from the wall. Her clothes don't amount to much: a gauzy white shirt under a thin jacket, and jeans that leave her ankles bare. For a moment, Virginia fears that the short walk to the front door will prove impossible, and that she's going to have to phone Joe for help, but it's not so. The girl winces and hobbles a few steps, but that's all it takes to get her young blood flowing and her body supple. They walk to the house arm in arm, though it's not quite clear who's supporting whom. The girl isn't carrying anything — no bag, no purse, no coat — but there's a flat rectangle wedged inside the pocket of her jeans. A phone? There's some reassurance in that. It proves she hasn't simply dropped from the sky or crawled out of the marsh.

"Do you have a name?" Virginia asks, because it's instinctive to want to know, but she regrets the question as soon as it's left her mouth. She shouldn't be asking things like that today. Today is for snapping links, not forging new ones.

"Sophie," the girl replies, her voice brimming with tears and shivers. Virginia wonders what she can offer, other than tea. Brandy would be the thing, but there isn't any brandy in the house. There might be some whisky. She remembers drinking whisky a few Christmases back, and not liking it much.

They find the hall floor a mess, flecked with snow and sand and bits of dry grass, and Virginia moves the umbrella stand aside so that the door can swing shut behind them. The gusty, whistling noises fade, but they don't disappear; Salt Winds is not — has never been — one of those cocoon-like houses that shield you from sight or sound of the bleak outdoors. There are too many drafts about the place; too many empty fireplaces; too many rattling windows. It's not a house that welcomes guests, though Virginia hasn't worried about that for a long time. Nobody calls anymore, except Joe.

Not that she's going to start worrying about it now. Why should she? The girl — Sophie — is standing by the hall table looking lost and otherworldly, like an unattended princess. She seems too absorbed by her own troubles to pay attention to Salt Winds or its owner. Virginia is tempted to poke her with the stick; give her bare ankles a thwack; surprise her out of herself. Instead, she straightens out the crumpled rug for fear the child will trip. Those slip-on shoes are thinner than ballet slippers;

they're so thin that you can make out the shape of the girl's feet, the curves of heel and instep, the delicate struts of the toe bones. Their soles are peeling off too, which is hardly surprising when you consider she's walked down the lane all the way from Tollbury Point, if not farther.

"Come and sit." Virginia takes Sophie by the elbow and steers her into the kitchen. In Mrs. Hill's time the range would have been glowing and the black kettle would have been simmering on top, and there'd have been no better place to warm someone up. These days, the kitchen is probably the coldest room in the house. The microwave sees plenty of use, as does the electric kettle, but the range hasn't been lit in years — decades, probably — and in wintertime, the big window is wet with condensation. Mrs. Hill would have hated that.

Virginia's winter coat is hanging over the back of one of the chairs, and she shakes it out and tucks it around the girl's shoulders. After that, there's the kettle to fill and tea bags to find. Oh, she shouldn't be doing this; it's all wrong. Back to front and inside out. She's supposed to be putting things away this morning, switching the electrics off, emptying the fridge. She stops a moment and holds on to the back of a chair, ready to weep with frustration. Sophie slumps into a seat, her eyes lightly closed.

She's pretty. Or perhaps she's just young? At Virginia's age, youth and beauty look like much the same thing. The old woman has an urge to reach out and brush the wet tangle of hair from the child's face, but she resists.

Virginia finds the whisky bottle on its side at the back of a cupboard, behind a tin of baked beans and a packet of powdered soup. It's three-quarters full — perhaps a bit more — and over the years it's acquired a greasy coating of dust. Virginia's arthritic fingers twist and scrabble at the cork for some time before it comes loose, and when she sniffs at the opening the fumes tickle the back of her nostrils. Goodness knows if it's within its sell-by date or not, but even if it makes the child sick, it'll surely warm her up. Virginia pours a good couple of inches into a teacup and tops it up with hot water from the kettle. On second thought, she pours one for herself as well. The taste is better than she remembered, and she likes the way it scorches her insides; perhaps she'll drink some more tonight before she leaves the house for good.

"Drink that," she says. Sophie opens her eyes and wraps her fingers around the cup.

Her hands are small and white, and thick with rings. Virginia has never seen anyone with such bedecked hands, so the tiny flash inside her brain that feels like recognition can't be anything of the sort, and she ignores her unease.

"Come on, drink up," she says, and Sophie pretends to take a sip, but Virginia isn't fooled. The child will never get warm at this rate. Look at her, quaking beneath that big bundle of a coat, with its goose-down lining and furry hood. She's not even trying. She's got to try, or the day will be gone.

Virginia comes into the big sitting room to fetch the halogen heater. Perhaps now is the time to say farewell to this room: to the straight-backed sofas and tea tables, to Lorna's piano and Clem's bird books. Farewell to the sagging armchair where Max Deering sat one January afternoon near the beginning of the war, when he brought his children to tea and ate scones off a porcelain plate.

Seventy-odd years have passed, and heaven knows this sitting room's been used since, but as Virginia stands in the doorway for the last time, it's the only image she can summon: Max Deering, sunk deep in his chair, a hand outstretched.

Ah-ha, Miss Wrathmell. We meet again.

Virginia's fingers spasm and she drops the heater, startled by the fierceness of her emotions. Over the last few years the wound has begun to close, just a little. She's managed to persuade herself that events as old as these are practically fictive; that the people involved were never quite real.

It's the bird's skull that's concertinaed time and made everything true again. The curlew has reminded her how to hate.

September 1940

The Second World War came home to Salt Winds on a hot September afternoon in 1940. Up until then it had meant next to nothing: a murmuring of voices on the wireless, a gas mask gathering dust in the hall, a shortage of butter. Someone had broken the post office window after it was rumored that the postmistress had a German-sounding maiden name, and Clem had spotted a couple of enemy planes through his binoculars, but even these events felt remote. The nearest dogfight had taken place a long way south of Tollbury Point.

There was something ominous about that September day, even before Mrs. Hill came puffing up from the village, full to bursting with her dreadful news. The weather was hot and heavy, and the wind had dropped for once, leaving a silence that felt like expectation. The birds didn't call across the marsh; the washing didn't stir on the line; the house didn't creak or sigh. Bracken lay on his side in the shade and twitched his ears if someone said his name or stooped to pat him.

Virginia had spent the morning making a den in the back garden, propping the clotheshorse against the flint wall and covering it in old curtains. After lunch she went and sat inside it, cross-legged, with a book and an apple, and tried to persuade herself she was having fun. In the dim and musty heat her eyes were as heavy as lead, and she stopped trying to read before the end of the first page. She felt sticky all over, especially at the backs of her knees where her skin was sore, and the smell of her sweat mingled with the fruity stink of seaweed that had been drifting off the marsh for days, ever since the weather turned warm.

Clem had done a couple of hours of writing after lunch, and he'd just come outdoors for a breather. Virginia could see him through a gap in the curtains, sitting on the bench by the back door with his head tilted back and his eyes closed. Lorna sat beside him with a handkerchief balled in one hand, frowning the way she did when she had a headache coming on.

"Would you like some water?" Lorna

asked her husband, unfastening the top button on her blouse and mopping at her throat with the handkerchief. "Or a cup of tea?"

"I'll get it," Clem murmured, without opening his eyes. "You have a sit-down."

"No, you're all right. You've been working."

Virginia liked it when they discussed everyday things: pots of tea and food prices and what needed doing in the garden. It made them sound peaceful and close. Anything bigger or more personal and they were on edge, like a couple of cats. The various scraps Virginia had overheard — *I wish you'd just say it outright . . . The thing you seem incapable of understanding . . . I know exactly what you think I am* — made her anxious. She tried to tell herself they didn't happen often.

Despite their thoughtful overtures, neither Clem nor Lorna seemed inclined to move. Clem kept his eyes closed, and Lorna stared, dull-eyed, at the new vegetable patch under the scraggly hedge.

"I met Mr. Rosenthal this morning," she said, "pushing his trike through the village."

Clem yawned. "Oh yes?"

"Apparently he's still got your shears. He took them away for mending absolutely ages ago." Lorna dabbed her glistening neck with the handkerchief again. "He was terribly apologetic about it; said he'd drop by before Monday."

"Righto." Clem yawned again, stretching his arms wide, as a ship's horn sounded miles away, beyond the hazy horizon. Lorna dragged herself to her feet and disappeared into the kitchen. Virginia crawled halfway out of the den and flopped onto her stomach with a weary groan.

"Hello there," said Clem.

"I'm hot," she complained, pressing her cheek against the hard earth and plucking at the grass.

"Well, if you spend all morning constructing an oven, and the entire afternoon sitting inside it . . ."

Virginia rolled onto her back and tried not to laugh as she looked at him upside down. "It's not an *oven,* it's a *den,*" she began, but before she could go on Mrs. Hill appeared at the side of the house. Virginia scrambled to her feet and Clem stood up slowly.

There was something unnatural about seeing Mrs. Hill at Salt Winds on a Saturday, her big body trussed up in a flowery dress instead of the usual gingham housecoat. It was even more peculiar to see her running. They stared in confusion as she halted on the grass, red-faced and breathless, her hands pressed hard against her chest. After a moment, Clem took her by the elbow and led her to the bench, setting her gently down.

"Oh Clemmy," she said softly, as she must have done when he was a little boy, and when he made to remove his hands from hers she clung to them, so he sat down beside her. Virginia glanced away, frowning at the oddness of it all. As soon as Mrs. Hill had taken the weight off her feet, her whole body seemed to sag. Even her hair hung in sad strands around her ears, though Virginia knew it'd had a wash and set on Thursday evening.

Virginia didn't dare ask what had happened, and Clem was too patient. He sat still, with his hands trapped, while Mrs. Hill caught her breath and began to cry. Virginia twisted on one foot and wished she'd stayed inside her den.

"Vi will fetch you some water," Clem suggested. "Or maybe something stronger?"

"No, no, just water." Mrs. Hill released Clem's hands in order to dry her eyes. "I'm sorry, I'm all right. I don't know why it's so . . ."

Lorna emerged from the dark kitchen with a jug of water and a tray of glasses, and her eyes widened.

"I thought it was your voice," she exclaimed. "What on earth's the matter?" She set the tray down on the end of the bench and straightened up, drying her hands on the sides of her skirt. Nobody answered, and she looked rapidly from face to face. "Clem? What is it? What's happened?"

Clem poured a glass of water. He did it very slowly, as if he relished the suspense, and placed it in Mrs. Hill's quivery hands.

"Drink that," he said, with a warning glance for his wife, "and take your time." Mrs. Hill gulped the water, and it was as though she were feeding a reservoir of tears, because by the time she lowered the empty glass her cheeks were streaming. Lorna fished in her sleeve for a handkerchief and handed it over without a word.

"I don't know why it's affected me like this," Mrs. Hill wept. "She's not the first to die in this dreadful war and she won't be the last, and it's not as if I knew her, not really, but she was part of the village all the same. And she was such a nice-looking little thing and so terribly young, not yet fifteen —"

"Who?" pleaded Lorna. "Who are you talking about?" But Virginia had guessed, and so had Clem. His shoulders had sunk, and his gaze was turning inward.

"Juliet Deering!" Mrs. Hill was indignant, as though Lorna was being deliberately obtuse. "Max's eldest! It's all over the village."

"But . . ." Lorna knelt down on the paving at Mrs. Hill's feet. "When? How?"

"Yesterday evening." Mrs. Hill leaned forward, twisting the handkerchief in her hands, her sorrow laced with a storyteller's relish. "She was on her way back to school for the start of the new term, and Max had just waved her off at Waterloo. This is straight from the housekeeper up at Thorney Grange, by the way, so practically firsthand. Well, according to Mrs. Bellamy, Juliet's train was just pulling away from the platform when the sirens started up, and a few seconds later the planes were swarming all over, and before you know it, *bang.*" She smacked her hands against her knees. "A direct hit."

Lorna placed her hands flat against her cheeks.

"Juliet's carriage took the worst of it. Completely obliterated. Nothing left at all. No remains to speak of."

Clem frowned and shook his head slowly from side to side.

"It's wicked," Lorna whispered through

her fingers. "Wicked."

Mrs. Hill wiped her eyes and sighed. "Dust we all are, and unto dust we shall return," she observed impressively.

Virginia crawled back inside her den and pulled the curtains shut.

Virginia went to bed early that night because there was an aching lack of anything to say. She tried to help with the drying up after supper, but Clem took the tea towel off her and kissed her on the forehead.

"Up to bed now, go on," he said. "Things'll look brighter in the morning."

Lorna, up to her elbows in soapsuds, shrugged slightly when he said that, as if shaking off a fly, and didn't turn to say goodnight.

The bedroom glowed pink in the evening light, and Virginia knew she'd never sleep. She put her pajamas on and flung the covers back, but there was no point lying down, so she paced the rug instead, following the winding patterns in and out, remembering how she'd jumped out of bed that morning, full of plans for building a den and reading *Black Beauty* and finishing her picture of Bracken.

A *den*. What a pointless thing to have built. What a very childish way to spend an afternoon.

She yanked her hair ribbons out and loosened her plaits. *Black Beauty* was lying on her bedside table, and the horse on the dust jacket watched as she began to brush her hair. She'd thought he had a gentle eye, but now that she looked more closely, she saw how mean and glinting his expression really was.

She didn't cry for Juliet Deering. It wasn't like that. She'd seen Juliet in passing during the school holidays — four or five times in the village, perhaps, and once at the summer fête — but it wasn't as if they were friends. They hadn't even acted like acquaintances, unless they were with their parents, in which case they just about managed a distant *hello.* Like the wind and the war, the Deerings had become a low-level hum at the back of Virginia's mind. She hadn't thought about them much since their visit at the start of the year.

Virginia tugged at a tangle of hair, pulling so hard that some of the strands came out at the root. She couldn't contemplate the bomb itself; that was so faraway and fantastical that her imagination didn't know where to begin. All she could think about was the fact that Juliet had been here, at Salt Winds, in January, and that while she was here she'd eaten scones, bent the corners of her novel, bullied her brother — acted, in short, like someone with both feet in this world, and not like someone marked out by death. She'd been alive — entirely, fearlessly, casually alive — and now she was dead. Again and again, Virginia put the two facts side by side and failed to reconcile them. It was like trying to look in opposite directions at the same time.

The brush was full of hairs and fluff because she hadn't bothered to clean it in ages. She dropped it and went onto the landing, opening other doors, pacing the rooms. Even the attic didn't feel out of bounds today, and she didn't climb the stairs especially quietly. *Lorna's den,* she thought. She'd been up there once before, in the very early days, so she was familiar with the old mattress on the floor, and the hulking shapes of trunks and bedsteads against the walls, and the big round window in the gable end. Now it felt squalid and messy. The old mattress was scattered with bits of torn paper, blankets, and candle stubs, and there were brown stains all over it, which she hadn't noticed before. She picked up a scrap of paper, half expecting to find a love letter in Mr. Deering's handwriting, but there were just a few pencil lines, which might have been anything. The start of a sketch, perhaps? The paper fell from her hand, and she found herself thinking things about Mr. Deering and Lorna; images she didn't want but couldn't shake off. She stared at the mattress a little longer, hoping her thoughts would exhaust themselves, but they just got more and more lurid and started muddling themselves up with Juliet's death. In the end she left rather suddenly and ran downstairs feeling sick and unclean.

She made her way to the spare room, where she knelt by the window and laid her arms on the sill. The sun had just set over Tollbury Point and the village was a gray mass against the dimming sky. Clem had switched the wireless on downstairs, and the Home Service was playing cello music, which made her feel calmer. She gazed at the stubby church spire and the silhouettes of chimneys and treetops, and found that it was hopeless trying to distinguish particular buildings because they'd all melded into one. It occurred to her that every single person in the village was thinking about Juliet Deering at this moment, and wishing they didn't have to.

Virginia's gaze wandered down from Tollbury Point to the white ribbon of road that ran alongside the marsh. She leaned forward with her nose to the glass. There was someone there, emerging from the gloom and heading toward her; a man with his arms swinging free and his head bent low. He was moving quickly, charging along like a wounded bull, weaving from one side of the road to the other, sometimes banging against the flint wall, sometimes tripping and staggering on potholes. He might have looked quite funny in a Charlie Chaplin film, but he didn't look at all funny in real life. When he was halfway along the lane his hat fell off, but though he paused to watch it roll into the verge, he didn't bother to stop and pick it up. That was when Virginia recognized him and drew away from the window.

Virginia ran on tiptoe along the landing. Her first instinct was to warn Clem of Mr. Deering's approach. She didn't want to shout — apart from anything else, Mr. Deering might hear her through the open windows — but there might not be time to run downstairs and back before he began hammering on the door. It was when she heard Lorna whispering across the hallway — "Clem? Where are you? I think I just saw Max in the lane!" and Clem saying, "Max? Oh Lord" — that Virginia remembered he was not Clem's acknowledged enemy but a childhood friend in dire straits. She waited at the top of the stairs, in the shadows, where no one would see her.

In fact, Mr. Deering did not hammer on the front door. He must have gone to the back of the house and come in through the kitchen, because that's where their voices gathered. Virginia knelt on the wooden chest and leaned over the banisters. She could hear a chair scraping across the stone flags, and Clem — as calm and soft as if he were talking to her — saying, "Sit down, Max; easy, old chap." Lorna suggested a cup of sweet tea, and Mr. Deering retorted that he was in the market for something a bit harder than tea, which seemed a rather jaunty thing to say in the circumstances, except that his voice sounded strange and not jaunty at all.

The kitchen door opened and Lorna's voice grew clearer. "I'll have a look in the dining room," she was saying. "I'm sure we can find you a drop of scotch."

"Lorna . . ." Clem's voice followed her like a warning and she hesitated, but he didn't elaborate, so she carried on.

As Lorna entered the dining room, the sound of the wireless flooded the house. It was still a solo cello, singing long, low notes, enough to make anyone cry, and Virginia's eyes prickled. She hated having to pity Mr. Deering; she didn't want to have soft feelings for him. If only he would laugh out loud like a villain and say, "Who cares about Juliet? Thank God it wasn't me!" She would know for sure, then, that he was a bad person, and she could stop worrying about the secret notes in Lorna's sleeve, and the charm of his smile, and the way Clem's expression closed when his name came up. It would be such a relief to dislike him straightforwardly and in good conscience.

Lorna returned with decanter and glasses on a tray. She shut the kitchen door behind her and Virginia stole away.

The stars were starting to poke through the sky, like silver pins through lilac silk, and Virginia could smell the sea. She pushed her bedroom window open, as wide as it would go. It struck her as odd that Mr. Deering — an important man with dozens of friends and acquaintances — had chosen to walk all the way to Salt Winds in the first flush of his bereavement. Perhaps it had something to do with his boyhood, she speculated vaguely. Or perhaps he'd come on the off chance that Clem would be out and he'd find Lorna alone. But that was a mean thing to suppose. The voices in the kitchen must have grown louder, or perhaps everyone had moved to another room, because she began to hear them again, even though her door was shut. When Bracken barked a couple of times, a few minutes later, Mr. Deering shouted and a glass shattered.

All was quiet as Virginia glided downstairs, and she couldn't tell which room they'd moved to.

She pressed her ear against the kitchen door. There were no voices, but she could hear Bracken pattering across the floor and someone rooting through a cupboard. The dining room door stood ajar and light spilled like honey through the gap.

None of them was sitting at the dining table now, though they obviously had been, because she could see the whisky decanter, the silver tray, and a muddle of wet circles where their glasses had stood. She pushed the door and went a little farther in, and saw broken glass on the floor near the fireplace: thousands of tiny shards that glittered like diamonds in the lamplight.

"Mind those pretty feet."

Mr. Deering was in here, all alone, and it was too late to flee. She hadn't spotted him in the high-backed armchair because he'd blended so well with the shadows — all of him except his hands, which were spot-lit by the lamp. His signet ring winked as he raised an empty tumbler to his mouth, tilting it right back and probing with his tongue in search of a last drop.

"Ugh." He glared into the bottom of the glass, a drop of moisture hanging off his lower lip. All his well-groomed elegance had melted away, and his whole face looked wet and swollen. Virginia hoped it was just the heat and alcohol making him sweat, because the thought of Mr. Deering in tears made her squirm. She thought he was going to ask for the decanter, which was still a third full of whisky, but when he looked up he was frowning as if something perplexed him; as if he'd forgotten what exactly he wanted. His bloodshot gaze landed on her and wandered over her body in frank appraisal, like he was making calculations; totting up a price. When he hovered over the area of her navel, she thought one of her pajama buttons must have come undone, and she moved her hand to cover the gap.

"Come and sit on my knee," he mumbled, rubbing his thighs with his free hand, as if to smooth a seat for her. His words kept running into one another, and his head wobbled from side to side as if it had come loose from his neck and needed fixing with a screwdriver.

Virginia swallowed. The fingers of Mr. Deering's other hand kept tightening and untightening around the empty glass, as if he were trying to pump it for more spirits. If he gripped any harder, it would implode in his fist, and there'd be more broken glass on the floor. She crossed her hands over her stomach as if she had an ache, and tried to think of something ordinary to say. She ought, probably, to make some sympathetic remark about Juliet, but she didn't dare.

She fixed her eyes on the green lampshade, slightly to the left of his head. "Don't break it," she said in the end, her tone wavering between resolve and apology.

"Oh?" Mr. Deering held the glass aloft, as if he was about to administer the final squeeze. "Why's that? Is it one of Daddy's heirlooms?"

"I just meant you might cut yourself."

"Aaah," he cooed, swaying forward in his chair.

He began drawing circles on his lap again. "Come on, don't be mean. I'll make you comfy on my knee."

When Virginia shook her head, Mr. Deering lurched to his feet. She thought he was coming after her — perhaps he was — but the whisky decanter diverted his attention.

106

He staggered against the table, catching at the back of a chair to stop himself from falling.

"We should drink a toast," he mumbled, as he began to pour. "I propose a toast."

His hand wavered back and forth over the glass, and the amber liquid pooled on the tabletop.

"To lovely little girls," he said, lifting the half-filled glass to his mouth and draining it in one go. He wiped his moustache on his sleeve, belching softly, and Virginia ran away.

Footsteps in the hall made her think she was being followed. Animal-like, she turned and crouched on the top stair, but it was Lorna, coming out of the kitchen with a steaming mug in one hand and a dustpan in the other.

"Bracken?" she cajoled, without noticing Virginia behind the banisters. "Bracken! Come with me. Come on, good boy." The dog obeyed reluctantly, creeping from the kitchen and sniffing near her ankles for a treat. "That's it," Lorna whispered, squaring her shoulders and pushing the dining-room door wide open.

"Well! What a mess!" Her voice was bright all of a sudden. "Not to worry. You sit down, Max, and drink this tea while it's hot. I'll tidy a bit."

Virginia heard one of the big dining chairs toppling and heavy shoes crunching through the crystal shards. A hollow knocking began to interfere with the music: Mr. Deering was doing something to Clem's wireless. Bracken began one of his deep, sustained growls as Mr. Deering's speech grew louder and more shapeless.

"It's nice, this German music," he slurred. "Isn't it nice? Beethoven, or something. Brahms. One of those Jerry composers, anyway. Very civilized. Don't you think it's most awfully civilized, Lorna?"

A swift click, and the music stopped.

"Lorna! Don't switch it off, just like that. You heard me say I was enjoying it! Don't I deserve a bit of pleasure this evening?"

After that he started saying "Lorna" over and over again, and his voice became muffled, as if he were talking with his mouth full of food. Virginia pictured him eating Lorna up bit by bit, stuffing his cheeks with her flesh and hair.

"Max, please, please." Lorna's voice was desperate; the genteel hostess had cut and run. "Don't. Please get off me. Please, just sit down."

Virginia wondered where Clem had got to, and wished to goodness he would come.

■ ■ ■ ■

When she got back to her room she sat down on the floor with her back against the bed. Something was bumping and jangling across the garden, like an unwieldy bicycle, and she could hear the rumble of a man's voice below her open window. It was Clem. So that was where he was.

"Oh goodness, the shears!" His words floated upward with the smoke from his pipe, and Virginia raised her head to listen. "I'd quite forgotten. Thanks, Rosenthal, you must let me know what I owe you." But before Mr. Rosenthal could reply there was the bang of a door bursting open, and Mr. Deering's voice flooded the twilit garden.

"What's this then?" he slurred. "What's going on here?"

He must have given Mr. Rosenthal's trike an almighty kick, because there was a ringing, grinding crash and the wheels ticked wildly, around and around, like the hands of a crazy clock. Then there were grunts and screams and thuds and shouts of *"Max! Max!"* and a pattering noise, like bits of stone spraying off the wall, and a voice that kept calling on God, only the sound it made was *Gott, Gott!*

The sudden quiet was worse. She had time to picture Clem bleeding his life out on the grass and to wonder what on earth she was supposed to do, when Mr. Deering broke the silence.

"Quite the enemy sympathizer, aren't we, Clement?" he gasped, breathing hard. "With your Jerry music and your fucking Jerry friend?"

"Max, old man." Clem spoke gently, as if cajoling a small child. "Let him alone, now. Come on. Let him alone." Mr. Deering's obscenities rose above all the other noises, flowing like hot breath into Virginia's ear — *bloody hun, bastard, fucking bastard* — on and on and on in a rhythmic chant. Lorna's pleas glided in and out of the din, until finally there was something like a pause, and the clatter of the tricycle being righted, and a series of gasping whispers that Virginia couldn't make out.

Virginia counted to twenty before crawling, cautiously, to the window. Mr. Rosenthal and Lorna had gone, but Mr. Deering was pounding his fists against the earth as if there were still someone there to punish. It couldn't have been very satisfying because his flow of swear words began to dwindle, and eventually they stopped altogether and he just huddled there on his hands and

110

knees with his head hanging low. His shoulders began to convulse, and at first Virginia thought he was crying, but then she realized he was being sick into the grass.

When he'd finished, he crawled to a clean patch of earth and lay down with his head on his arms. Clem sat nearby, like a watchman, with his back against the knobbly flint stones and his pipe — extinguished during the fight — dangling from the corner of his mouth. He had dark stains on his sleeves and all down the front of his shirt.

"Is Mr. Rosenthal all right?" Virginia asked from the kitchen doorway.

She thought she'd find him in here — she'd pictured him lying on the table, half dead in a pool of blood, and had entered warily, ready to fling her hands over her eyes — but there was only Lorna, sitting with her sewing basket and a pile of mending. She'd just picked Virginia's gray pinafore dress off the top of the pile: the hem needed a stitch before school began on Monday morning.

"Why aren't you asleep?" Lorna snapped, but before Virginia could reply she was shaking her head and answering, more patiently, "I don't know. I think he is. He wouldn't stay."

"Where did he go?"

Lorna tried to thread a needle with a length of black cotton, but her fingers were unsteady. When she caught Virginia watching she gave up and lowered the gray pinafore onto her lap.

"I don't know, he just went. His face was bleeding, and I don't know . . . I think it was mostly his lip, but I'm not really sure. He wouldn't let me see. He kept saying 'It's fine, it's fine, it's all right,' but he sounded so upset. Oh Christ."

Lorna dropped the sewing and pressed the heels of her hands against her eyes. Virginia sat down carefully and traced her fingers over a whorl in the wood while she wondered what to say. The old tabletop rolled between them like a parchment map, grainy with longitude lines and knotty islands and uncharted territories. Sometimes she felt she hated Lorna, but other times she felt a funny kind of concern for her, a protectiveness, as if she herself were the real grown-up and Lorna were a little girl.

"It's not your fault," Virginia ventured, at last.

"Clem will say it is. Max was drunk when he arrived, and what did I do but bring out the whisky? I didn't — I wasn't thinking . . ."

Lorna ran her palms over her face, as if rinsing it with water. She must have touched Mr. Rosenthal's wound without realizing it, because a little gobbet of blood came off her cuff and hung in her hair like a jewel.

Virginia stared at the bead of blood. She couldn't think of anything else to say.

"Poor Mr. Rosenthal," sighed Lorna, sinking against the back of the chair. "Poor him. Poor Juliet. Poor Max. Poor everyone. What a mess."

At some point during the night Clem summoned a taxi and took Max Deering home to Thorney Grange, and weeks went by after that without any contact. Of course, they glimpsed him and his son at Juliet's memorial service, but the church was so full that they easily avoided having to speak or shake hands.

In the middle of October, a bouquet arrived at Salt Winds addressed simply *To Mrs. Wrathmell, with warm wishes, M. D.* It was an extravagant confection of roses, carnations, zinnias, and delicate greenery.

"Very seasonal," muttered Clem, but Lorna was resolutely touched. She arranged the flowers in a vase and put them in the dining room, by the cabinet with the Meissen cups. It was Max's way of apologizing, she said, and it drew a line under the whole affair.

Around the same time they heard that Mr. Rosenthal had been arrested as an enemy alien, and that he was going to be interned on the Isle of Man. It was a shame in a way, said Mrs. Hill, because he was a pleasant sort of chap and a bit of a local character. Still, a German is a German, and you can't argue with that.

New Year's Eve 2015

Virginia finds Clem's obituary in the top drawer of his desk, the one from the local newspaper that she defaced as a child. Strange that it's been lying here all these years; stranger still to think of Lorna cutting it out and keeping it, ink-stained gash and all.

They used a nice photograph, she'll give them that. In fact, it's the same as the one on the dust jacket of his last bird book, where he's standing by the flint wall in jacket and tie, his hair tufting up in the wind. Underneath the photograph they'd printed *Clement Gordon John Wrathmell, 5th April 1895 to ?31st December 1940?* but eleven-year-old Vi had taken it upon herself to erase the second date, giving the two question marks on either side a chance to speak for themselves. She remembers doing it, scribbling so hard over the offending words that she ripped a hole in the paper and broke the nib of her fountain pen.

Virginia puts the obituary in her dressing-gown pocket, alongside the wedding photo, and shuts the desk drawer. There are five more drawers full of tobacco-scented relics, and she's got half a mind to carry on exploring. Half a mind. Yes, exactly. That's what's annoying her. The other half of her mind is obsessing about Sophie. It's impossible to concentrate with another person in the house, even when that person is asleep. Twenty minutes ago she heard a squeaking noise and clumped all the way downstairs to find out what it was, only to glimpse Silver streaking along the baseboard with a mouse dangling from his jaws.

Virginia taps her stick impatiently, wondering what to do. The whole point of coming upstairs was to pull away from the girl; from the new magnetic center of the house. The more distance there was between them, she'd calculated, the less distraction there'd be. It sounds silly now.

Virginia stumps to the top of the stairs and peers down at the closed kitchen door. There's not a sound, except for the wind, and Silver has disappeared with his catch. Why can't she just *imagine* she's alone? She, who's been living off imagination and little else for eighty-six years? She's surely capable of pretending that the house is empty?

It's because this day is different; that's the problem. That's what it all boils down to. Ever since last night, when she found the curlew's skull on the doorstep, she's known that this day, more than any other day of her entire life, possesses meaning and weight. Accidental things will not — cannot — happen to Virginia Wrathmell on New Year's Eve 2015. If a half-familiar girl rolls up in the Salt Winds kitchen on this day of all days, it's because she's been sent by Fate, or the Dead, or the Past, or whatever it is that stared back at her, last night, from the bird's hollowed eyes.

Who are you, Sophie? What have you come here for? Spit it out, girl; there's not much time. Virginia curls her claws around the banister and thinks about going downstairs — again — and shaking the child awake. But she's lived long enough, and has read enough stories, to know that Fate and the Dead and the Past won't give straight answers to straight questions. She'll have to be patient. Besides, she can't face staggering down those blasted stairs for the second time in half an hour.

There's a wooden chest on the landing where spare blankets and pillows are stored.

Virginia sits down on the lid to rest her hurting bones and enjoy a proper cough. Her chest is bad this winter, worse than in previous years; every time she wakes up, it's as though her lungs have shrunk overnight, and there's a little less room for breathing. It's a shame the whisky bottle is downstairs, because she could do with another draft of that liquid smoke. She could do with a bite to eat as well; her head feels light.

The church clock hasn't struck for a while, or at any rate she hasn't heard it, and she wonders what time it is. The morning's getting on, and there's still so much to do. All those boxes and drawers to look through; all those notebooks and letters and photos; all those rooms. There won't be time for them all. Not now.

Virginia strokes her palm over the lid of the chest. It's a dark, tomb-sized Victorian monstrosity, and it fits nicely at this end of the landing, against the banisters. This is its proper place. This is where it stood before Clem was born, and this is where it stood throughout his life. Virginia remembers him on his last day, sitting on the lid while he talked to her and laced his walking boots.

It was Lorna who moved the chest, of course, in the spring of '42. She shifted it in front of the attic door, even though it looked all wrong there, and they both bashed their shins on it whenever they walked past. Not that Virginia argued at the time; she wouldn't have dared. She just waited, and after Lorna's death Joe helped her move it down the landing again, back here, to its rightful place. Joe never questioned the ins and outs of these maneuvers; he just did as he was told. He was good like that.

And now Virginia's got herself thinking about the attic again. She sighs heavily and looks down the landing toward the hidden door. The velvet curtain is still swaying in a draft. It was moss green when Lorna hung it, but now it's the color of dust.

It's seventy-four years to the day since Virginia last went through that door and up the winding stairs to the top of the house. She knows she must face it again before tonight, but she's not sure she's ready. For years and years she's pictured herself in the twilight of her last day, climbing up to the attic, the rest of the house already shut up and in darkness. She'd sit on the broken settee for a while, closing her eyes while the ghosts gathered, and then she'd go. Flashlight in hand, straight downstairs, from the attic to the marsh in a simple, swooping trajectory. Yes, that has been the plan, but now the girl is here. She's forced to consider Sophie.

The attic is cold and dark. That's the first thing. In her mind's eye the attic is hot and golden, with a sun-shaped window in the east-facing gable, and needles of light piercing the roof slates here and there. But decades of polluted rain and spiders' webs have dulled the round window, and the only thing that penetrates the roof is the *drip-drip* of water.

Virginia walks on bird droppings to reach the window. The wood feels spongy under her feet — no wonder, when you start counting the number of missing slates — and she ponders how long it will be before it caves in and the rain falls straight through to the bedrooms, and Salt Winds really starts to die. Because Joe won't try to rescue the place; he knows how Lorna felt about it. Perhaps he'll sell up.

She unlatches the window and tries to pull it open, but the mechanism has warped and corroded over the years and she's too weak to shift it. Not to worry. There won't be much of a view over the marsh today, even from up here, not with the weather like this. That's what she tells herself, but she continues to stand and stare at the opaque glass.

When at last she turns around, she finds herself face-to-face with the old rocking chair. Rain or mice, or both, have nibbled away at the wicker seat, and its legs are speckled with mold, but it's still in position — of course it is, why wouldn't it be? — and Clem's binoculars are hanging off the back, cobweb-gray and dilapidated. She touches the rocker with her foot and it moves as smoothly as it ever did, rumbling over the floorboards. Clem's shotgun is there too, a few feet from the chair, its muzzle fuzzy with dust. And there's the wireless, and the typewriter under its canvas cover; and there's a dried-up bottle of printer's ink with *Samphire Green* on the label, though all that's left is a gray crust where the lid ought to be. And there, right by her left slipper, despite all Lorna's desperate scrubbing, is the stain.

It's bigger than Virginia remembered, as though it's been spreading all these years instead of drying as it should. She touches the edge of it with her slipper. It's big and spattery and black, and if she didn't know it was blood, she wouldn't guess. She'd think someone had hurled a bottle of ink across the room and shattered it on the floor. Virginia has to remind herself that none of this is really unexpected.

All the same, she should have allowed herself longer to prepare; should have waited until this evening. To come up here on a sudden whim, after seventy-four years . . . She looks for somewhere to sit, but there's nowhere. The trestle tables are all folded away and she couldn't use the rocking chair, even if the seat were still intact. As for the settee, it was on its last legs back then, in the early forties, and now it's just a mound of wet sponge and rusted springs. And she can hardly bring herself to look at the mattress. It used to be yellowy white, but now it's brownish black and there are mushrooms growing out of the stuffing. She shivers. The whole attic smells of fungus and droppings and rain. It smells of darkness.

Lorna was conscious of this attic, moldering away above the rest of the house, year in, year out. Virginia managed to pretend it wasn't there and made an uneasy peace with the place, but Lorna never did. Sometimes she used to threaten to sell Salt Winds and move them away for good, and she meant it — though she never did it.

Virginia is shivering persistently now. She's had enough already, and steels herself for the descent, but then she stops and the hairs on her neck rise like hackles. Salt

Winds is creaking — somewhere nearby, beside her, below her — and this time it isn't the cat, or the weather. It's the sound of feet on aching boards. Light, stealthy, human feet, making their way up from the ground floor and along the landing.

She had not thought to shut the door behind her. Or even pull the curtain across. The feet pause at the foot of the attic stairs and a small voice calls, "Hello?"

December 1940

At Salt Winds, as at the orphanage, there was a proper time to bathe, and a proper time to do homework, and a proper time to go to bed. It was Virginia's job to lay the table for supper every evening and to do the drying-up afterward, and on Saturday mornings she helped Lorna change the sheets on the beds.

All the boring routines were instigated by Lorna or Mrs. Hill, and all the best ones involved Clem. Virginia used to go along the lane with him and Bracken every morning, early, while Lorna got breakfast ready. He would hang his binoculars around her neck and let her walk on the wall.

"There's Mrs. Hill, turning into the lane," he said, a week or two before Christmas, as they trudged toward Tollbury Point with their collars turned up. Virginia squinted into the wind and Bracken yapped.

"All right," said Clem, "here's a challenge for you. How many birds can you spot before Mrs. Hill draws level? And you can't just say you've seen one; you have to name it properly. If you get five or more, I'll give you the top off my egg. Ready? *Go!*"

"No, no, no, I'm not ready! The binoculars are still in their case!" Virginia had already whipped her mittens off, but she was all fingers and thumbs in the cold, and she couldn't open the clasp. She jumped up and down and laughed giddily, as if he were going to tickle her. Clem hauled himself onto the wall and stood beside her in the blustery cold, and although his gloved hands looked clumsy, he removed the binoculars from their leather case in no time at all, deftly pocketing the lens caps.

"Now," he said, as she lifted the binoculars and swept her gaze across the marsh.

"Herring gull," she squeaked, pointing with her free arm. "*Two* of them."

"Oh, all right, but you score half marks for herring gulls."

"That's not fair," she protested, half-indignant, half-amused. Mrs. Hill was almost upon them — she could hear the squeak of the pedals on the wind — and there wasn't time to argue.

"Oh, oh, oh! There! An oystercatcher!"

"Let's see . . . Very good!"

Virginia swung the binoculars slowly from side to side.

"Oh, over there! Look! Starlings! Thousands of them! I think I just got about a million points."

She lowered the binoculars and he clapped his hands to his cheeks in mock despair. "Blimey, Vi, I can't be having that! I'll be owing you egg tops for the rest of my days."

Virginia twirled delightedly on her toes. Clem threw his arm around her shoulders, and she had to grab on to his coat to keep her balance. Side by side they watched the cloud of starlings as it rode the wind, twisting and curling over the marsh like smoke.

"Bonus question for an extra million points," said Clem. "What's the name for a flock of starlings?"

"Murmuration," she shot back, before he'd finished asking, and it was his turn to laugh. He pulled her closer and she huddled against the rough wool of his coat.

Mrs. Hill bustled in and out of the dining room as they ate their breakfast. She was full of chatter that morning: there'd been yet more air raids on London, and there was something wrong with the back tire on her bike, and the wind was like a knife today

— oh, and she'd met the postman on her way from the village and he'd given her the mail for Salt Winds.

Virginia had never received a letter in her life, so she was puzzled, as much as excited, to receive a cream envelope with a stamp and a postmark, and her name and address in fancy copperplate. It looked too expensive to rip, so Mrs. Hill helped her to slit it open with a clean knife.

Master Theodore Deering requests the pleasure of your company on the occasion of his eleventh birthday.
Tuesday, 31st December, 2 o'clock till 5.
Thorney Grange, Tollbury Point.
RSVP

"Oh," she said. If she could have pocketed it discreetly and burnt it in secret later on she would have done so, but the others were waiting. She handed the card to Clem, who glanced over it and passed it to Lorna.

"Requests the pleasure," he muttered, slicing the top off his soft-boiled egg and sneaking it onto Virginia's plate. "Typical Deering. You'd think the boy was being knighted. Or married."

Lorna set her teacup down and read the invitation studiously, as if there might be more to it than met the eye. She flipped it over to make sure the reverse side was blank before reading it through again.

Virginia watched and waited, knotting and unknotting her fingers, but nobody seemed inclined to speak. Clem went back to his newspaper.

"I don't have to go, do I? Please?"

She was so vehement that Clem raised his eyes from the *Times* and stopped chewing. A question began to form in his expression, but he didn't have time to phrase it.

"Yes, you absolutely do," Lorna replied, pocketing the card. "Pass the marmalade, would you? And don't pout." She began spreading margarine over her toast with brisk strokes of her knife. The decision had been made, and now they were going to eat their breakfast and talk about something else.

Virginia picked up the marmalade jar and affected an interest in the handwritten label. She'd penned it herself back in February, while Mrs. Hill padded about the kitchen, stirring the preserving pan and grumbling about the shortage of oranges.

"Hello?" Lorna was waiting.

Virginia wasn't a natural rebel, and her heart thundered as her fingers closed over the lid of the jar.

"I just . . . I don't see why I *have* to go."

"Don't you?" When Lorna shut her eyes like that she became cold and untouchable, like a statue in a fancy garden.

"It's not going to make any difference to Juliet," Virginia mumbled, addressing the butter dish.

Clem let slip a quick smile.

"Please don't be stupid," Lorna retorted, reaching across the table and prizing the marmalade from Virginia's grasp. "It doesn't suit you." Her voice was languid, but her fingers felt strong and cruel, as if she had it in her to smash the jar against the wall.

A small difficulty arose when Lorna remembered that the Women's Institute was holding a New Year's Eve party too, and that she'd volunteered to spend the day making preparations at the church hall. A few days after Christmas the chairwoman rang to remind her, and after she'd put the telephone down she tutted, but couldn't see a way around it. She couldn't let the committee down, and therefore she couldn't deliver Virginia to the Deerings' house in person. Clem would have to do it.

"Clem?" she called out, on the morning of the thirty-first. She already had her coat on and was stuffing extra pins into her wayward hair: no easy feat with a mock-apricot flan in one hand and a bag of bunting in the other. "You promise you won't forget about Theodore's party this afternoon?"

"No."

"What do you mean, *no*?"

"No, I won't forget."

Lorna's eyebrows rose fractionally and she scooped her handbag off the hall table. "It starts at two o'clock. His birthday present is on the kitchen table, as is your lunch. Virginia, I never got to lengthening the hem on your red frock, but I think it'll look all right. At least it's clean."

Virginia nodded. She wished she had trouser pockets, like Clem, so she could stuff her hands inside them the way he did, and lean against the doorframe looking bored.

"Bye," Lorna called over her shoulder. Sometimes she thought to blow a kiss when she was on her way out, but she didn't have a free hand that day.

The sky looked hard, like a sheet of hammered metal, and the wind sounded tired, as if it were looking for somewhere warm to rest. After an early lunch, Virginia stole up to her room, lit the gas fire, and curled up on her bed with a pile of books. Even though she was on her own, all her movements were slow and soft, as if by making herself inconspicuous, Theodore's party would pass her by.

It was no use. She'd just found her place in *Tales from the Arabian Nights* when Clem arrived, carrying her coat and scarf over one arm. She turned the page, pointedly, but he didn't go away.

"I suppose we'd better go," he said apologetically.

Virginia sighed and closed the book, but made no further move. Clem came in and sat on the end of the bed.

"What is it, Vi?" he wondered. "Why don't you want to go?"

She frowned and leafed unseeingly through her book. If there was anyone she could tell the truth to, she supposed it was Clem, but how could she say it without saying *Mr. Deering saw me in my pajamas and made me feel like I wasn't wearing anything at all?* She blushed hotly, but Clem was waiting for an answer and his eyes were on her face.

"I just don't like him much."

"Theodore?"

". . . Hmm."

"No. Well, that's fair enough. He is a bit

of a tick."

Virginia smiled dutifully, but Clem was still watching, and he was so attentive that for a moment she thought he'd understood; actually understood, without being told. She ran her damp hands over her skirt. There was a sour stain on one of the pleats where she'd dripped milk at breakfast, and she fixed her gaze on it while she waited for his reply.

"Look, Vi, I know it's a bore, but it's only a few hours. You'll survive, won't you? Make believe it's for king and country. I'll never hear the end of it if I let you stay home." He smiled half-heartedly, without quite meeting her eye. "Pop your smart dress on and run a comb through your hair, there's a good girl. Look sharp, though; we really do need to get going."

He shook the coat out and laid it over the bedstead. Virginia tried to imagine herself saying no, but it was impossible. She would never be able to refuse Clem anything; there was always going to be too much at stake. You couldn't be too careful. Sometimes things were lost in the blink of an eye; in the slippage of a second. These things happened. She already knew that, before the plane fell from the sky.

■ ■ ■ ■

It was merely because she was crossing the room to fetch her dress that she noticed the airplane. The whole thing was over in thirty seconds, and she would have missed it from the bed or the wardrobe.

"Look!" she cried. Clem turned back from the landing and crossed her room to look.

It was the grace of the thing that astonished her in retrospect. You'd expect a burning fighter plane to make a great hullabaloo: howling engines, roaring flames, a great boom as it hit the ground nose first. But if this one made any noise at all, Virginia didn't notice. All she recalled, later on, was the slow arc it traced through the sky on its way down, like a spark floating from a bonfire. Even the explosion was gentle from their vantage point: a little orange flower that budded, bloomed, and withered, all in a moment, far away on the edge of the marsh.

She thought it was over and turned to Clem, full of astonished questions, but he was shaking her by the shoulder and pointing.

"There!" he whispered. "Over there!"

She looked and saw another bit of bonfire

ash, but this one was smaller and blacker than the first, and it drifted very slowly onto the marsh. It didn't explode as it touched the ground, but disappeared among the long shadows and reedbeds.

"A parachute," he said.

Virginia stared, and Clem was gone. By the time he returned with his binoculars there was nothing left for the naked eye to see except a thread of smoke and a twisted bit of metal, which might easily be a shrub, or a wooden post, or a bit of flotsam that the tide had left behind.

"I thought so!" he said, lowering the binoculars and passing them to her. "It's an enemy plane. A Messerschmitt."

Virginia swung the lenses back and forth over a blur of greens, grays, and browns until she found the piece of metal. It was part of a wing, and it was marked with a black-and-white cross. She searched for some sign of the airman, but there was no movement. There weren't even any birds cascading through the sky or ruffling the waters. The whole stretch of marshland had an innocent air, as if nothing had happened.

Clem took the binoculars again and stood for a long time, scanning the scene.

"Poor bastard," he muttered under his breath.

"Do you think he'll drown?" Virginia asked, noting how grown-up and unperturbed she sounded. This was partly because he was a German airman — not a Mr. Rosenthal, but a proper, uncomplicated, enemy German — and partly because she didn't quite believe he was real. The plane had swooned so gracefully, from her point of view, and the marsh looked so tranquil, that it was hard to imagine a real man out there, flailing in mud and sweat and parachute silk.

"He must be two miles out, at least," Clem replied, which was as much as to say, "Yes."

"Will anyone go to him, do you suppose?"

Clem swept the scene from left to right and back again, as if searching for an answer to her question. "Who, though?"

Looking back, she realized that this was the moment in which everything started to decelerate. Time slipped into a heavier gear the second Clem frowned and scratched the back of his neck and wondered "Who?" He began to pace up and down the room, and she was too slow to follow the direction of his thoughts. She was simply glad that he seemed to have forgotten about Theodore Deering's party.

The wardrobe door swung open of its own

accord, and Virginia remembered she was meant to be getting changed. She hoped Clem wouldn't spot the red dress and was relieved that he didn't seem inclined to. He didn't give the wardrobe a second glance, even when he nearly walked into it, but every time he passed the window he stopped and frowned at the view. He kept taking his pipe out of his pocket and tapping it against his chin.

"You're right," he announced suddenly, stopping in the middle of the floor.

"What about?" Virginia was half thinking about the crashed plane. The red dress was dimly visible in the wardrobe behind him, and she was trying hard not to look at it. It was hateful, with its tight collar and sash and fancy sleeves. Worst of all it was too short, which was all right when you still looked like a child, but not when you were starting not to.

"You're right," Clem repeated. "Of course you are. No one else is going to risk their necks for some Jerry."

Virginia tore her eyes from the wardrobe and stared at Clem.

"What . . . ?" She'd let her attention wander and missed the crucial moment — the link, the key — that would make sense of what he was telling her. He darted from the room and Virginia followed with her mouth open, feeling stupid. By the time she caught up he was sitting on the wooden chest at the top of the stairs, tightening the laces on his walking boots.

"Where does Lorna keep the flashlight these days?" he puffed as he leaned over, tugging on the rusty strings.

"The bottom drawer in the kitchen," said Virginia. "But —"

"Go and fetch it. And there's a length of rope in the toolshed: bring that too."

Virginia hovered uncertainly.

"Go, go! Quickly!"

She obeyed because he was Clem, and because he seemed so certain. As she went downstairs and rummaged in the kitchen drawer, she tried to marshal her own ideas in opposition to his, but it was hard — very hard — like trying to sprint underwater. The coil of rope was hanging on a nail in the shed, and she wondered about thrusting it under the hedge and telling him she couldn't find it, but even as she wondered, she was unhooking it and running back to the house with it.

Clem was in the hall, buttoning up his coat — the big gray one that went all the way down to his shins — and Bracken was prancing about in expectation of a walk, his stubby tail aquiver. Virginia stood and watched as Clem pocketed the flashlight and slung the rope over his shoulder. All of his movements were quick and calm, but he was breathing rather heavily, more like someone returning from a long walk than someone about to set out on one. "Rope, flashlight, brandy . . ." he muttered, patting his pockets.

"Don't go," Virginia pleaded, pointlessly, when the time for protest was long gone. He ruffled her hair, smiling faintly, and reached for his hat and gloves. She looked up at the folds of skin at his jaw and the graying hair at his temples and felt love rising like sickness from her stomach. If she opened her mouth to speak again she thought she might retch, so she didn't risk it.

"Now listen," said Clem, as he batted the dog away. "If I do find this poor chap alive, he's likely to be in a bad way, so you'll need to be ready when we get back. Can you see to it?"

Virginia stared at him dumbly.

"Can you see to it, Vi? Light a fire in the spare room, put some blankets on the bed, boil up a big kettle of water . . . that sort of thing? Maybe root out the first aid kit; I think it's in the bathroom cupboard."

She nodded.

"If I'm not back before your mother, she's not to fret. Just tell her —"

"Can't I come with you?" She had to ask, although it wasn't what she really wanted. What she really wanted was to wind the clock back ten minutes so that she could watch in absolute silence as the Messerschmitt crashed and Clem — none the wiser — wandered off down the landing. There'd be no jumping up and down this time; no childish "Look what I can see!" She'd delve inside her wardrobe while the explosion flowered and wouldn't breathe a word.

"Don't be soft," Clem replied. There was an edge to his gentleness; a testy reminder of all he'd ever told her about the dangers of Tollbury Marsh. "Off you go now, and do as I say. Tell your mother I won't be long. If there isn't any sign of the poor devil after —" he looked at his watch "— after an hour, I'll give it up and come straight home. All right?"

Virginia followed him outside, shivering in her pleated skirt and cardigan. They both lowered their heads against the wind before setting off down the lane, Bracken bounding back and forth between them. Clem's boots made prints in the thin mud, so she placed her feet in them, like the page boy in

"Good King Wenceslas," and tried to imagine a miraculous warmth coming up through the soles of her shoes. It didn't work. Her legs were bare above her ankle socks, and she could feel the goose pimples on her thighs where they brushed against one another.

A little way along the lane there was a break in the flint wall and a flight of steps — the old harbor steps, as they were known — that led down to the marsh. Clem stopped and turned.

"Listen, Vi, I'll be fine. The marsh is in a good mood this afternoon."

She glared at her shoes and nodded.

"Go back now," he said, putting his hands on her shoulders. He looked huge in his coat and boots, and Virginia was suddenly afraid of him. Everything around them looked dead: the empty lane, the church tower, the treeless horizon. She wondered whether anyone else had seen the German airplane. She half wondered whether she and Clem had made it up between them, but she could still see the wing, like a deep dent in the steel sky, and a twist of smoke above it.

"Theodore's party will be starting," she observed wanly.

Clem held her at arm's length and

squeezed her shoulders. They stood like that for a moment and looked at one another, while Bracken scuttled through the dry grasses and weeds at the foot of the wall, urgently sniffing and cocking his leg.

"Take Bracken back with you," Clem said, as he let her go. "I could do without him under my feet."

They hadn't brought a lead, so Virginia had to pick the dog up, and by the time she'd done it Clem was several yards out from the wall. Bracken whimpered and scrabbled and twisted in her arms all the way back to Salt Winds, and she kept thinking she was going to drop him. When they got home she gave him a biscuit from the tin. He wasn't supposed to have them at odd times, but he sounded so unhappy and she wanted to cheer him up.

Bracken took the biscuit and carried it to his bed, where he set it down between his front paws and licked it. Virginia leaned against the stove and tried to massage some warmth back into her ears. "Hot water," she said aloud. "Hot water, blankets, and a fire."

Theodore's birthday present was lying, neatly wrapped, on the kitchen table. It was obviously a book. Virginia picked it up and turned it over in her hands, and hid it behind the flour bin so that it wouldn't be the first thing Lorna saw when she came in. Lorna was going to be livid about the party, and no doubt Mr. Deering would make sure they felt awkward about it too. It was hard to worry about all that and at the same time remember everything Clem had asked her to do. Hot water and blankets, and a fire in the spare room. And where did he say the first aid kit was kept? And when would Lorna be back? And how was she going to explain what had happened?

She found the first aid kit and put the kettle on the range to heat, but then she lost track of what she was meant to be doing and wandered back to her bedroom. The gas fire had been blazing all this time, so she turned it off and let the chilly colors of the marsh invade her room, changing all the pinks into grays and blues. Clem had left his binoculars on the windowsill and she picked them up, but just to hold them on her lap and mess about with the focus.

She shut the wardrobe door but it swung open again, and she kept glimpsing the red dress inside, turning gently on its hanger.

When the front door banged Virginia lifted her head and dug her nails into her palms. "Clem?" she said, quietly inquiring. She hadn't realized how dark it had gotten: the marsh and sky were almost merged.

"Clem?" Lorna cried, leaping up the stairs two at a time. "Clem? Where are you? Did you hear about the German plane?"

Lorna ran along the landing and burst into his study, but then her footsteps halted.

Virginia heard uncertainty in the sudden stillness. She stole along the landing and watched from the doorway as Lorna unwound her scarf and dropped it, absent-mindedly, over the back of Clem's chair. Downstairs, the sitting-room clock began to strike, and Virginia counted all five of the chimes in her head before Lorna sensed her presence and turned.

"What on earth —" Lorna reached for the light switch and they both screwed up their eyes against the dazzle. "What's going on? I thought you were at Theodore's party?"

Virginia didn't reply.

"Why are you in your old clothes? Where's Clem?"

Virginia had been calm up until then — almost lethargic — but now her heart began to flounder like a fish caught in a net.

"He felt sorry for the airman," she said. She wanted to sound cool and reasonable about it, but her voice had taken on a breathy vibrato that she couldn't seem to control. "I tried to stop him. He said not to worry if you were back first; honestly and truly he said not to worry —"

Lorna took Virginia by the shoulders and sat her down in the desk chair. It was obvious she felt frightened, but her hands didn't shake as some people's might; they gripped very tightly.

"Look at me," Lorna said, but Virginia couldn't raise her eyes beyond the pale green collar of Lorna's blouse and the silver necklace that dangled in the shadow between her breasts. When she breathed in, she could smell the cold outdoors on Lorna's skin and clothes.

"Tell me exactly what you mean," Lorna went on. "What did you try to stop him from doing?"

"From going out on the marsh. He went to help the German pilot."

Lorna didn't ask anything else, but Virginia could see the pulse flickering in her neck and feel her grip growing ever more rigid.

Lorna made a telephone call and people began arriving at the house: a police constable on his bike, several neighbors from the village, a woman with an apple cake, the vicar. Mrs. Hill came, ashen-faced, in a taxi.

Virginia weighted the front door open

with the umbrella stand and people drifted in apologetically, glancing at one another and whispering — if they dared to talk at all. Lorna paced up and down the kitchen, fiddling restively with an unlit cigarette, and barely seemed to register their arrival. She kept picking at her lower lip, and it started to bleed.

Mrs. Hill slumped at the table and wept into a red handkerchief, while the woman with the apple cake wondered aloud where she should put it. The young policeman fumbled in his pocket for a strip of matches, cleared his throat, and asked Lorna if she needed a light, but she stared back at him as if he were speaking in Chinese and carried on pacing.

The vicar opened the back door and a few people, including Virginia, went outside and leaned over the wall. The wind had got up, and the stinging smell of the sea blew in their faces. One of the men had brought a flashlight, and he broke the blackout rules by switching it on, but there was nothing to see except a few bleak yards of grass. "Clem!" he shouted, and the others joined in — "Clem! Cleem!" — but their voices were guzzled up by the wind, and after a couple of minutes they gave up and trooped inside again.

Mr. Deering rolled up to the house eventually, with a smooth crunch of tires, and Lorna went outside to meet him. She let him kiss her on the cheek, and they talked for a few minutes on the doorstep. A few people got to their feet when he entered the kitchen, and the vicar shook his hand. He sat down at the table, his fingers steepled against his lips, and everyone grew more alert. The policeman took out a notebook and licked the lead of his pencil.

"So," said Mr. Deering, his eyes falling on Virginia. Someone pulled out a chair and pressed her into it, and she thought how sleek and sober he seemed tonight, with his black eyes gleaming like shards of coal. She tried to picture him the way he had been in September, dissolute with grief and vomiting on their lawn, but all that was gone; it seemed impossible, unthinkable — a delirious dream. He stretched his legs under the table and crossed them at the ankle, and as he did so his shoes brushed her bare legs. He sighed, as if weighed down with anxieties, but Virginia saw the minute smile that lurked beneath his heavy eyelids and under his moustache.

"So, Vi, Clement left you on your own while he set off on this 'mercy mission'? Is that correct?"

Nobody called her "Vi," except for Clem. Virginia wasn't going to answer, but Mr. Deering seemed prepared to wait, so in the end she nodded briefly. The policeman began making notes in a laborious long-hand.

"I must say I'm surprised," Deering remarked, accepting a cigarette from Lorna. "I know Tollbury Marsh as well as he does, and I wouldn't have risked it today, with the tides as they are." He put the cigarette between his lips and removed it again. "Not without exceptionally good cause."

"Oh, but that's not true!" Virginia leapt from her chair. "Clem said the tides were all right today; he said the marsh was in a good mood."

Mr. Deering laughed bleakly and shook his head.

"Mr. Deering knows the marsh better than most," someone said, reprimanding her, and there was a murmur of agreement around the table.

"*Clem* knows the marsh," Virginia retorted, gripping the sides of her chair. "And he promised he'd be back. He said we absolutely mustn't worry, even if Lorna — I mean, Mother — even if she got back before him, and she's barely been back an hour, so . . ."

Her voice petered out and she shrugged. She'd offered exactly the same reassurance when everyone was arriving, and she was aggrieved that nobody seemed inclined to give it weight. The apple-cake woman shuffled uneasily, as she had done before, and the vicar smiled at Virginia without quite meeting her eye. The police constable stroked his moustache and made a half-hearted note in his pad.

"Right enough, Vi," said Mr. Deering, the words drifting lightly from his lips and twining with the cigarette smoke. "Hope springs eternal."

The police constable cleared his throat and put forward a few questions of his own — "What time did Clem leave? Which direction did he take? Was he carrying anything with him?" — which Virginia answered as best she could, although she hesitated over the question of time.

"It was after one o'clock and before two, but I'm not exactly sure . . ."

The policeman rattled the pencil against his teeth and told her to think carefully and try her best to remember. He wrote down everything she said, read it out loud, reread it in silence, and closed his notebook.

"Well," he sighed, sitting down and accepting a slice of apple cake. "I think we've done what we can for now?" He shot Mr. Deering a querying glance, and Mr. Deering nodded his assent.

Virginia looked at them all: the familiar, the semifamiliar, the strange. They seemed large and looming, like creatures of a different order whose ways she'd never understand. She sought the plainest English words she knew.

"Aren't we going to go and look for him?"

A burst of wind made the kitchen window shudder, and the pulsating orange embers inside the range glowed red. A piece of coal crumbled and fell. Nobody looked at Virginia, not even Mr. Deering. He just smoked and scattered ash on the tabletop and gazed into space.

"You heard what Mr. Deering said." The vicar looked at her over the top of his glasses, as if he thought her impertinent. Mrs. Hill mopped her cheeks and took a long, shaky breath. "It's too risky, love." She screwed the handkerchief into a ball and pressed it against her mouth.

Virginia narrowed her eyes and berated them soundlessly, barely moving her lips. *What did you come for then?* She stared at one of the whorls in the wooden tabletop and made it into an island, a solid fragment amid miles of sliding sands and waters.

"Will you excuse me?" Lorna stood up very suddenly and her chair rocked backward. "Sorry."

Mr. Deering glanced around and started to stand, but Lorna walked out of the room and ran upstairs before he could even say her name, or try to stop her.

"You can come home with me tonight, if you'd rather," said Mrs. Hill as she and Virginia stood by the open front door. She'd folded the red handkerchief into a tidy square and put it in her pocket, as if to say *enough is enough,* but she couldn't stop her eyes and nose from watering, and she kept swatting irritably at the drips.

"No." Virginia hugged herself and shivered. "Thank you." People were starting to drift away now, and they all seemed to want to touch her as they squeezed past. Some of them patted her on the back or the head; others squeezed her shoulder.

"Are you quite sure?" Mrs. Hill peered back inside the house as she knotted her headscarf. Mr. Deering was making himself at home, strolling about the downstairs rooms with his hands in his pockets and a freshly lit cigarette in the corner of his lips. His hat and coat were still hanging in the hall. Virginia listened to his silky tread for a moment and pulled her cardigan tight, but in the end she shook her head.

"I can't. I promised Clem I'd be here when he gets back."

Mrs. Hill stared at her, and slowly nodded.

"All right," she said, placing her damp palm against Virginia's cheek.

Virginia left the front door on the latch so that Clem could get in without knocking. She scurried upstairs, keeping close to the wall where the shadows were deepest, and didn't stop to spy on Mr. Deering until she was almost at the top.

As soon as the neighbors were gone he went back to the kitchen to cut himself a second wedge of apple cake, and then he resumed his tour of the ground floor, dropping a trail of crumbs and ash behind him. He paused every now and then to look at the photos, or the Meissen teacups, or the sliver of night between a pair of half-closed curtains. Of course people eat and smoke and fidget when they're on edge, but all the same he didn't look like a man whose oldest friend was lost on Tollbury Marsh. She wished Clem would burst in now and catch him at it.

Mr. Deering popped the final piece of

apple cake into his mouth and unstoppered the whisky decanter, emptying what was left into a clean glass. Something squeaked and bumped upstairs in the bathroom, and Virginia heard the slosh and spill of water. It happened again — the squeaking, bumping noise — and she recognized the sound of enamel pulling on skin. Lorna must be taking a bath.

He'd heard it too; she could tell by the way he looked upward, toward the noise, as he drained his whisky. *Oh God,* thought Virginia, crossing her fingers. *Come back, Clem; come now.* Perhaps she said part of her prayer out loud, or perhaps she moved too quickly, because all at once Mr. Deering was gazing at her over the rim of his glass. He raised it a little, as if to drink to her good health, and smiled like a man who's been gifted with good fortune.

The bolt on the bathroom door was inadequate; she'd always thought so. She'd point it out to Clem just as soon as he got back. It was tiny, and the screws on the bracket were loose, too; anyone trying to break in from the landing could do so with a modest shove — as she had just done. All the same, she wiggled it across as far as it would go and leaned back against the door.

She thought Lorna would be angered by the intrusion; that she'd bring her knees up to her chest in a swirling flurry and hide her nakedness as best she could. But she just lay in the bath with her legs straight out in front of her, her hair floating around her shoulders like pale seaweed, and said, simply, "Have they gone?"

Virginia had never seen Lorna so unguarded; so lacking in ceremony. It unsettled her because she wasn't sure what it meant.

"You're having a bath."

Lorna closed her reddened eyes. "Sorry. I just had to get away. Have they all gone now?"

"All except Mr. Deering."

"Oh." Lorna fished a cloth out of the water and laid it, dripping, across her face, so that nothing was visible but her mouth. "Oh, hell."

Virginia stared at the pliable pallor of Lorna's grown-up flesh. She couldn't envy it — not exactly — but even in the midst of this crisis it caught her interest. Lorna's legs seemed completely different in substance from her own. They were like the soft white lumps of wax you pick off the side of a burning candle and mold between your thumb and forefinger. She wondered whether Mr. Deering had ever molded them between his fingers, and then she caught her tongue between her teeth, as if to bite the thought away and spit it out.

Lorna dragged the cloth from her face and stared back at Virginia.

"Are you staying?"

"I'm not going downstairs again while *he's* here. Not until Clem gets back."

"Stay, then. I don't mind."

So Virginia sat down on the linoleum floor with her back against the tub and her feet pressed against the door. Puddles of cold water soaked through her skirt.

"You'll get wet," Lorna murmured, and Virginia could tell she had her eyes shut.

"It doesn't matter. What will we do about Clem?"

Dripping fingers touched her softly on the head and played with her hair. For a long time Lorna made no reply, and Virginia thought she hadn't heard, but then she said, "You're very fond of him, aren't you?" as if it were something she'd just realized.

Virginia dropped her chin onto her knees and they sat together in silence while the bath went cold. The water from Lorna's hand filtered through her hair and dribbled down her neck, but she didn't move away. She listened to the dripping tap and improvised little bargains with fate. *If I can count*

154

to ten in French between two drips then he'll come . . . If I can say my twelve times table without a single mistake, one sum per drip, then he'll come . . . Eventually, as if granting a concession at the end of a hard-fought inner argument, Lorna said, "He loved you too. He loved you for your gratitude."

The past tense felt like a kick in the stomach, and for a few moments Virginia could hardly breathe, let alone move. As soon as she was able, she staggered to her feet and flung the bathroom door wide open.

"Oh." Lorna sat forward, her hair trailing over her face like a tangle of fine wires, and held out a spongy hand. "Listen, Virginia, I didn't mean it badly —"

Virginia hovered in the doorway, ignoring the outstretched hand. Outside the house a motor coughed and rumbled into life, and they turned their heads in unison toward the sound.

"Is that Max?" Lorna whispered. "Is he leaving?"

Virginia went to the spare room and peered down at the driveway. She could just make out the majestic bulk of the Austin 12 as it maneuvered in front of the house before inching its way down the potholed lane and disappearing into the darkness. She waited a couple of minutes, and even then she ventured downstairs with caution. He'd left a folded note on the hall table.

There was a wild lumbering and sloshing from upstairs as Lorna climbed out of the bath.

"Has he gone?" she shouted.

Ladies, I hate to leave you alone at such a time, but Theo will be missing me. I'll drop by first thing. In the meantime, if there is any news — or should you want me for whatever reason — don't hesitate to call. You know I'm at your service, day and night. M. D.

Lorna appeared on the landing, tall and dripping in a gray towel. She looked like something out of a myth; a river goddess in a sleeveless gown.

"Yes, he's gone."

Lorna nodded slowly.

"For now," she murmured, as if she'd read the note, word for word, right from the top of the stairs.

Midnight came and went, but they forgot about the New Year — or if they remembered, neither thought it worth mentioning. Lorna sat at the kitchen table, shivering in her dressing gown, while Virginia paced about in search of things to do. She boiled the kettle and stoked the range and hung Clem's pajamas on the rail to warm. She took Bracken outside. She brought the kettle back to the boil and then did nothing with it. Neither of them said much.

When Virginia was drying up she found a tin at the back of the cutlery drawer, full of string and drawing pins and candle stubs. She took out all the candles — some were an inch high, with black pimples for wicks, but they were better than nothing — and proceeded to place them in all the marsh-facing windows of the house. She was breaking the blackout regulations, but she didn't care.

When all the windows were lit, upstairs and downstairs, there was one candle remaining. Virginia melted the base and stuck it inside an empty jam jar, pressing it down until it stood unsupported. Then she thought for a moment, before lighting the wick and starting up the attic stairs.

The round window was like an eye in the east-facing gable, staring blindly over miles of bare darkness. Virginia placed the jar on the sill and knelt beside it for a while. It was cold in the attic, with the wind creeping under the slates, and her cardigan was thin. She wanted to look out into the night, but all she could see when she tried was her own face reflected in the glass.

New Year's Eve 2015

Sophie pokes her head up the stairwell and calls again. "Hello?" There's a moment of quiet during which, no doubt, she peers timidly into the gloom and wonders what's lurking, but before you know it she's pulled herself together and started the ascent.

Virginia is too appalled to move. She feels like a spider whose web has caught the interest of a curious cat. If she were younger and stronger she would run down and shoo the girl back to the landing, but she can't do that anymore. She tries to stand more squarely and breathe more deeply, but it ends in a coughing fit.

Sophie jumps when she catches sight of Virginia, but she doesn't retreat. She hovers inside the doorway, pulling her sleeves down over her hands and trying not to look curious.

"Sorry," she mutters. Virginia nearly

retorts, *sorry for what?* but it's obvious the girl won't understand what she means. It was a diffident greeting, not an apology.

Virginia shuffles and clears her throat, and Sophie seems to take that as an invitation, because she sticks her hands in the back pockets of her jeans and comes right in. Her glance takes in the rocking chair — it's a not-unattractive antique, apart from any-thing else, or it would be if the wicker seat were repaired — and Virginia moves side-ways in a half-baked attempt to shield it from innocent eyes. At least she hasn't spot-ted the shotgun.

There's one thing in Sophie's favor: she doesn't act as if Salt Winds appalls her. As she ventures across the attic floor, crunch-ing through dead wood lice and catching cobwebs in her hair, Virginia is alert for any sign of distaste. But the girl is wide-eyed, and when she reaches the center of the whole space — which is impressive, when you remember to think about it — she turns and mouths a discreet "Wow," and the old woman can't help feeling touched.

"You've called your parents?" Virginia says. It's a question, but she makes it sound like an observation.

"I can't." The girl touches the rectangular shape inside her pocket as she continues to survey the room. "The battery's dead."

Her eyes are still pink, but she's not shivering much, and she looks more sensible than she did before. She talks quietly and avoids eye contact, but she holds her head up with a conscious firmness as if telling herself, inwardly, *Courage!*

"You'll have to use my phone, then," says Virginia, leaning on the stick with a faint wince and heading for the door. "Come. I'll show you where it is."

Perhaps Sophie is not so sensible after all, because she makes no move to follow. She touches the mattress with the toe of her shoe and a cloud of spores puffs up. Her eyes fill, and the corners of her mouth waver, and all the spores have settled before she risks a reply.

"No, it's OK," she says. "I don't want to call anyone."

Virginia catches hold of Sophie's arm and they both stagger slightly.

"Oh, but you have to," she cries. "They'll be worrying."

"Will they?" Sophie shrugs and gives a little pout. "Good."

Virginia's hand drops as the child moves away from her and wanders toward the window. As she passes the rocking chair, her thigh brushes against the armrest and

161

sets the whole thing in motion. *Rumble, rumble* go the stately wooden runners, back and forth, and suddenly Virginia is faint. She's going to be sick; she's going to fall — but the rocking chair slows and stops, and the feeling passes. So much for whisky on an empty stomach. She draws a shaky breath and the nausea washes over her, and away, like a wave.

Sophie hasn't noticed anything.

"I've run away from home," she confesses, without a trace of self-mockery. A tear trickles down her cheek and in through the corner of her mouth.

Virginia sighs. If she were sitting down she might feel more indulgent, but as things are, she can only snipe.

"Ah," she says. "I think I can guess why. They're all stupid and none of them understands you. Is that it?"

Sophie draws a long, curved line down the window, dispersing seventy-four years' worth of dust. She is nodding gratefully and her mouth is firm again, for the time being.

"Exactly," she says with a watery sniff. "That's exactly it. I just want to be myself — that's all it is — and they won't let me. They have all these plans . . ."

"Hmm." It's as much as Virginia can do to half listen. She's surprised at how hungry she feels, given this is her last day on earth. When they get downstairs she'll put some toast on and open a tin of baked beans, but not before giving Joe a ring and asking him to pop round. He'll know what to do about Sophie. She should have phoned him in the first place.

It's so difficult to gauge the time, but say it's noon now . . . Virginia screws her eyes shut and calculates in silence. It seems reasonable to hope she'll have the house to herself by half past one — say two o'clock to be on the safe side — which still leaves a couple of hours of daylight. And of course, she doesn't have to set out across the marsh the moment darkness falls. She can have all evening at home, if she wants, as long as it's all over by midnight.

"Do you think going to art school is a cop-out?"

"Pardon?"

"Art school. Do you think it'd be a soft option? For me? My dad says so. His family all read law at Oxford — I mean literally *all* of them, dating back to the dinosaurs — and he treats it like it's a kind of inheritance or something, and if you don't want to you're just, like, a traitor to the family name or something."

Sophie scrubs the tears off her face until

her skin is burnished red, and Virginia is drawn in, despite herself.

"I've nothing against artists," she remarks. "I used to work for one."

"Oh?" There's something rather endearing about the way Sophie looks up, her eyes round and hopeful, like a puppy's.

"You've heard of F. L. Leonard?" Virginia continues, suppressing a very slight — very natural — smirk of pride.

Sophie considers for a moment. "No, I don't think so . . ." It's obvious she's disappointed, but she's nice enough to ask, "What was your job?"

Virginia shrugs. "Oh, I was a jack-of-all-trades, really," she says, though she regrets her modesty immediately, as the girl turns back to the window and resumes her finger drawing. "Well, I suppose you might say I was a secretary, or — what would you call it these days? — a personal assistant. It was a good life. We traveled a good deal. There was a lot of interest in the States."

But Sophie isn't listening. She's drawing a face in the dust, but she can't get the nose right. Impatiently, she wipes her palm through the whole thing, clearing a space in the glass, and suddenly they're no longer looking at spiders' webs and dirt-filtered light. They're looking, instead, at a grand vista.

The clouds have moved away, leaving a smattering of snow behind, and the horizon is visible for the first time all day — though whether that daub of crushed pearl belongs to sea or sky or both is anyone's guess. Aside from the tracery of snow, all the colors are dark and strong, smeared straight from the tube in immense swathes of yellow ochre and Prussian green and Payne's gray. It's vast and simple. *It would take a bold artist to paint Tollbury Marsh in this mood,* thinks Virginia. There's no charm in it. Nothing to break it up, except the quick flit of a bird here and there, and the odd wooden post.

"Oh!" Sophie exclaims. "It's so . . . It's beautiful." She wipes a larger circle in the dust and kneels down so that she can get closer to the glass and take in more of the view. Underneath all the vestiges of distress — the wet face, the pink eyes, the liquid sniffs — there is a core of joy. You can see it in the way she bites her lower lip as she leans this way and that to get a better angle.

"It is beautiful," Virginia agrees reluctantly. After a moment she gives up on the marsh and watches Sophie instead.

"I knew I was right to come here," Sophie says, looking at Virginia and then back at the marsh. "I knew it, just from the name. *Salt Winds.* It's just so . . . I don't know. Every time they said it, it was kind of like it was speaking to me. Does that sound really lame?"

Virginia's eyes come back into focus and she leans forward on the stick. Several questions present themselves, but she's not sure where to start. Sophie is busy cleaning the window again; her question was rhetorical, and she's not expecting an answer.

"You came here on purpose?" Virginia asks. "You came especially to look at Salt Winds? But I thought you just — well, I don't know."

The girl is half listening as she spits exultingly on her cuff and polishes the glass.

"And where exactly did you come from?" Virginia goes on, more briskly. It occurs to her that Joe can run the girl home in his car. In fact, if he's agreeable, that might be for the best. It'll save getting the parents involved.

"London."

"London?"

"Mm." Sophie is surprised by Virginia's surprise. She sniffs again, and wipes her dusty sleeve across her nose. "Putney," she clarifies, before sneezing wetly into her cupped hands.

"Putney?" Virginia rummages in her dressing-gown pocket for a handkerchief. "You came all the way to Tollbury Point from *Putney*?"

She pulls a balled-up tissue from her pocket and the old wedding photograph comes with it. Sophie wipes her palms and blows her nose as Clem and Lorna flutter to the floor with their posy of gray flowers and their gray half smiles.

"Oh my God!" Sophie exclaims, as she stoops to pick it up. The joy, or excitement, or whatever it is, has got inside her voice now.

"What?" Virginia urges, clutching the handle of her stick with both hands. "What is it?"

Sophie points at the photo and smiles.

"I knew it," she says. "I knew it! Look. That's my great-granddad."

January 1941

True to his word, Mr. Deering dropped by first thing on New Year's Day, and Virginia had to let him in because Lorna wasn't ready. In fact, neither of them was ready, but Virginia was at least dressed, albeit in yesterday's grubby skirt and cardigan. Lorna was still in her dressing gown, her uncombed hair straggling down her back.

Virginia admired that dressing gown of Lorna's enormously. It was slate green, like a stormy sea, almost long enough to sweep the floor. And yet that morning it seemed to have lost all its film-star glamour. It made Lorna look chilly and tired and definitely not what Mrs. Hill — or Clem, for that matter — would call *proper.*

Virginia would have ignored Mr. Deering's knock altogether, but Lorna kept hissing, "Hurry up and open the door! He doesn't like to wait!" and she sounded so urgent about it that Virginia didn't dare argue. She was too tired to care much, anyway. The whole scenario — like the preceding night — felt as slow and detached as a dream; the foggy interlude between Clem's departure and his eventual return. She held the door open a couple of inches and Mr. Deering sidled in. His arms were full of flowers — great perfumed blooms that seemed out of place in a wartime winter — and he tossed them onto the hall table, as if they were nothing much.

"Any news?" he asked as he shrugged off his coat. Virginia stared at the white lilies and shook her head. The flowers made the hall smell of funerals. Lorna was creeping upstairs, but Mr. Deering caught sight of her before she made it to the landing, and when he said her name she turned and came to meet him.

"Hello, Max!" she said, as if this was a nice surprise, at the same time pulling the dressing gown tight about her throat. "I was just going to get dressed. Give me five minutes?"

He shook his head.

"Less than that," she pleaded. "Two."

But Mr. Deering shook his head again and placed his fingers under her chin, tilting it ever so slightly upward. He looked especially glossy this morning, as if he'd rubbed his skin and hair with the same wax polish he used on his car. He stood still for a good minute, studying Lorna's bare face at arm's length, and all the time his lips moved playfully without quite breaking into a smile.

"No," he said, eventually. "Don't go. You're lovely as you are. Besides, I'm gasping for my cup of tea."

"I expect we all are." Lorna pushed a tangle of hair out of her eyes and tried to smile, but it was difficult to look bright and breezy with someone's fingertips pressing up against your jaw. "I'll put the kettle on."

He ran his thumb down her cheek, touching the corner of her mouth, and dropped his hand.

"Vi can do that." He turned to Virginia and slipped her a private wink. "You can make us all a cuppa, can't you?"

Virginia nodded, but she was only half-relieved to escape to the kitchen while they made their way to the sitting room. She stoked the range impatiently — pushing Bracken away when he ambled over in search of his breakfast — and slammed the half-filled kettle down on top. *Hurry up, hurry up,* she muttered inwardly, as she dusted biscuit crumbs off the tray and grabbed three cups from the draining board, shaking them dry. The milk had been out all night and it smelled like cheese, but it would have to do.

While the water began heaving its way toward the boil she leaned into the hall and listened. After a long time, she heard Mr. Deering speak from behind the sitting-room door. A minute passed — two minutes — and Lorna replied. Armchair springs creaked as someone sat down, and then there was silence. Virginia glanced urgently at the kettle and took the teapot down from the shelf. She wondered what Clem would have her do.

Two hours Mr. Deering stayed, although he must have known he wasn't wanted. Lorna perched on the sofa, her untasted tea going cold in her hands, and Virginia sat beside her, stone-faced, like a middle-aged chaperone from Victorian times. It was damp and cold in the sitting room — it was rarely used, except for visitors — but Lorna didn't offer to light the fire. Her gaze strayed, now and then, to the window and the lowering clouds.

Virginia wondered what it would take to embarrass Mr. Deering. He sank back in the old armchair, slurping his tea and making trite observations like "Damned Germans . . ." and "If anyone can get the better of that old marsh, it's Clem." When no one replied he just smoked and smiled and watched them through half-closed eyes.

"Looks like we might have snow," he remarked at one point, following Lorna's gaze to the window. "That'll please Theo, I hope."

Lorna straightened her shoulders and fixed her smile, as if she'd just remembered she had a guest. "And how is Theo?"

Mr. Deering frowned and ran his finger slowly around the rim of the cup. "Oh, well. He's fine, all things considered. Doesn't say much. I think he enjoyed his birthday party yesterday."

Virginia watched him as he was speaking and thought she glimpsed his dead daughter lurking, like a delicate pencil sketch, beneath the coarsely painted lines of his day-to-day face. So that's what it took to discomfit him. Of course. Well, it was a relief to know there was something. She relaxed ever so slightly, but when he looked up she saw he'd gone all misty about the eyes and that seemed to make him worse — more dangerous — than before.

"It's easier for me, in a way, than it is for you," he said softly, setting the empty cup on the tray. "At least, with Jules, I *knew.*

There was never this dreadful uncertainty."

When he said that, Lorna had no choice but to look up, and it was as if he'd caught her in a spell, because he held her gaze for ages and ages and ages. Seconds ticked by on the clock — Virginia counted twenty-three — before he sighed and ran his hands over his face. Lorna sat very still, her fingers knotted in her lap.

They all jumped when the front door opened and footsteps crossed the hall. Mr. Deering shot to his feet but Lorna said, "It's Mrs. Hill."

"Mrs. Hill? Oh, yes." Mr. Deering clasped his fidgety hands behind his back and took a turn of the room, stopping at the mantelpiece mirror to slick his hair and study his moustache. "Yes. Well, I'd best be making a move, if you're sure you can manage."

Virginia watched him discreetly from under her eyelids, and saw the way his forefinger trembled as it slid over the line of hair on his upper lip. *What a fright he'll have,* she thought, *when Clem really does come back.*

He caught her eye in the mirror and smiled. "I'll drop in again, sometime this evening."

"Oh, but really —" Lorna protested weakly, getting to her feet. Mr. Deering took hold of her chin again, and this time he didn't just prop it up — he gripped it between his thumb and his knuckle.

"But of course I will, Lorna," he said. "It's natural I should worry about you. Isn't it, though?"

As soon as he'd released her she nodded, and a split second later she remembered to smile as well. His thumbnail had made a pink crescent moon on her skin.

When he'd gone, Lorna picked up the bouquet from the hall table and handed it to Virginia.

"Put these in some water, would you?" she said, wearily. "There's a vase under the kitchen sink. And just check Mrs. Hill's all right. I'm not sure I can face her, on top of everything else."

Virginia wasn't especially keen to face her either; there was a lot of angry clattering going on behind the kitchen door. It sounded as though Mrs. Hill had decided to clean the cupboards in Clem's absence. Bracken was scratching diffidently on the back door while saucepan lids crashed and spun like cymbals.

"No, wait!" Virginia bounded up the stairs after Lorna, scattering yellow pollen in her wake. "Wait!"

"Oh, for goodness' sake, *what*?" Lorna wheeled around, just inside her bedroom door. "If it's all the same to you, I'd like to get dressed."

Virginia pushed the flowers away, crushing them against the V-neck of Lorna's dressing gown and staining the lapels with gold-brown dust. Lorna hadn't much choice but to take them in her arms, though a couple of stalks missed and tumbled to the floor.

"What — ?"

"They're your flowers; *you* put them in water." Virginia had to fight so hard for breath between each word, she thought she must be having some sort of fit. "You're married to Cl— to Clem; you've no business taking flowers off another man. It's disgusting."

She hadn't meant, when she started, to use a word like *disgusting;* neither had she meant her voice to waver up and down. She half expected a slap on the cheek and braced herself, tight-jawed, but Lorna sighed and leaned against the doorframe. Two more lilies dropped from her hands while she considered how to reply.

"He'll want to know where I've put them," she explained, eventually. You could tell from her voice that she hadn't slept all night; she sounded as though she'd keel over if the wall weren't propping her up. "That's all it is. He's one of those people who always ask after their own gifts. He likes to make sure they're being enjoyed."

"So?" Virginia wept. "Tell him you put them straight in the dustbin! We don't want his stinking flowers! Why do you have to do whatever he wants?"

Lorna's shoulders drooped. She drifted into the bedroom and stood in front of the mirror. Virginia followed, grinding the flowers into the rug with her shoes.

"Why?" she persisted.

Lorna placed a couple of hairpins between her teeth and began brushing her hair with long, languid strokes. Virginia stood behind and glared at her reflection.

"Tell me why."

"I feel sorry for him," Lorna shrugged. "Of course I do. His wife's dead, his daughter . . ."

"Are you in love with him?"

Lorna closed her eyes. She rolled her hair up to the nape of her neck and stabbed it with one of the pins. "No, I am not."

"Then why act like you are?"

The pin dropped, spilling hair all the way down Lorna's back again. She growled and threw the brush across the dressing table.

"I'm thinking of you, aren't I?" Lorna said, pressing her hands to her temples. "Of you and me. We're alone, Virginia, do you understand me? We are two women alone in this big, empty house. We cannot afford to make an enemy of Max Deering."

"But Clem —"

"Clem is not here."

They stared at one another. Lorna said it again, but this time she said it slowly and roundly, as if she were talking to a simpleton.

"Clem. Is. Not. Here."

When Lorna began to dress, Virginia just stood in the middle of the room and watched through the blur, unable to move away because of the shuddering in her knees. She tried to say *I hate you,* but it came out as a small, blubbery noise, which Lorna affected not to hear.

Lorna got ready with uncharacteristic haste, leaving the dressing gown in a slippery heap on the floor and laddering her first stocking on a toenail. Normally she'd have folded it up and put it in the mending basket, but on this occasion she tossed it to the end of the bed with a curse. She didn't choose her clothes, she just grabbed them from the cupboard — a gray tartan skirt and a holly-green sweater darned at the elbows. When she was done, she had another stab at fixing her hair, but the pins kept falling out, so she bundled it up inside a headscarf and left it at that.

Virginia watched as Lorna picked up a lipstick and unscrewed the cap, staring at the greasy red tip as if she'd forgotten what to do with it. She seemed dreamy and tired again.

"The thing is, you see . . ." She put the lipstick down, unused. "Max and I were engaged once. But then I married Clem instead, and Max was — well, you can imagine. He doesn't like to be crossed. Nor will he admit defeat."

Lorna lifted a pearl necklace from her jewelry box and began to fasten it at the back of her neck. Virginia watched her. The scene in the mirror was so peaceful that she was almost taken in by it. They looked like two girls in an old Dutch painting, with all the even light and stillness that implied. *A Lady with Her Maid,* or something along those lines. As Lorna lowered her arms, snowflake shadows began sliding down the bare wall opposite the window.

"It's probably the bravest thing I've ever done in my whole life," Lorna observed.

"What is?"

"Breaking it off with Max."

Virginia looked up hopefully. "And you did it because you were in love with Clem?"

Lorna closed the lid of her jewelry box and rested her fingertips on the lid. "I suppose that's what I told myself at the time. It's what I told everyone else." She hesitated before pushing the box away. "I don't know why I'm telling you, though. What are you — twelve? Too young for such nonsense."

I'm eleven, Virginia thought, but she didn't say so. She went to the window to watch the snow fall and thought of Clem out there on the marsh, waiting for the conditions to come right so that he could walk safely home. He must be starving by now. At least he wouldn't be thirsty, because there'd be snow to eat. She pictured him sitting on a tussock of grass and sticking out his tongue to catch the falling flakes.

The encroaching snowstorm turned the bedroom darker by the second, as if night were coming on at reckless speed. A knock on the half-open door made them both jump.

"Who is it?" Lorna called breathlessly. It was Mrs. Hill, stepping over the broken lilies.

"Pardon me, Mrs. Wrathmell." Mrs. Hill's face was lined with sorrow, as if she'd been crying for years. She peered at the silky tumble of dressing gown, the open lipstick, the carpet of lilies, the pearls around Lorna's neck. "I was wondering how many there'd be for lunch?"

The question was loaded with a hostility that made Lorna stare. She began pointing from person to person. "One . . . two . . . three," she counted leadenly, like someone teaching numbers to a child. "There would appear to be three of us at home today."

"Oh, don't include me. *I* won't eat a thing," Mrs. Hill retorted. "I wondered whether you were expecting any gentlemen friends? Max Deering . . . ?"

Virginia looked fearfully from Lorna to Mrs. Hill. It struck her that the household had no meaning without Clem; until he returned, Salt Winds was nothing but a big, cold structure and three strangers standing in a room.

"Oh, for pity's sake!" Lorna elbowed past Mrs. Hill and broke into a run on the landing. Virginia listened to her flying up the attic stairs and pacing about overhead. Her steps were bolder — fiercer — than they used to be when she went up there at night.

"Slut!" Mrs. Hill muttered, under her breath.

"Don't speak about her like that!" Virginia wiped her wet face on her cardigan sleeve.

"You wouldn't say things like that if Clem were here!"

"No, I'd just think it, and so would he." Mrs. Hill began picking lilies off the floor. "He knew, all right. He knew what he'd married."

"Stop!" When Virginia stamped her foot she felt as though the house was about to collapse on top of them; she could almost hear the fractures spreading out from under her shoe, over all the floors and walls. "Stop! You've no right to say such awful things! Who do you think you are?"

"Who do *I* . . .?" Mrs. Hill laughed shortly and straightened up. "Who do *I* think *I* am?"

She stared at Virginia, and Virginia stared right back.

"Forty-eight years," Mrs. Hill quavered. "Forty-eight years I've served this family, and look what's left . . ." Her eyes filled and she threw the flowers at Virginia's feet, like a sarcastic tribute.

"You can get your own lunch," she said, and five minutes later she marched from the house and slammed the front door hard behind her.

Even so, Virginia needn't have been lonely. People were calling at the house all after-noon — not just the young police constable

181

and neighbors from last night, but friends and official-looking men from farther afield. The first few times Virginia went downstairs and told them Lorna was asleep, and they went away again, having nothing urgent to say or do. After a while she stopped answering the door.

It wasn't until dusk that the strange man appeared in the back garden. Virginia was sitting on the windowsill when his moving shadow caught her eye. Bracken pricked up his ears and gave a low growl, but after a moment's thought he seemed to doubt his instincts and went back to sleep on the bed. Virginia made herself small and still and kept watching.

The snow made such a whirl against the window, and the light was so poor, and she'd been willing Clem to appear for so long that at first she thought she'd conjured a phantom. She glimpsed the man for a moment as he staggered across the grass, back bent, and slipped inside the toolshed, but even so, phantom or not, it obviously wasn't Clem. True, their gray coats were practically identical, but this coat was plastered with mud, and the body inside it was nothing like Clem's: it was too tall and slim, and too guarded in its movements.

Virginia waited for the next thing to happen — after all, he couldn't mean to stay in the toolshed — but the light thickened, and nothing moved. After five minutes had passed, she slid to her feet. She was oddly glad, because at least it gave her an excuse to find Lorna.

Lorna was just visible through the crack in the attic door, lying on the old mattress with her hands behind her head. It was too dark to tell whether she had her eyes closed, or whether she was staring up at the rafters. There was a pile of papers on the floor beside her with a packet of cigarettes on top, and the air tasted sharply of smoke. It was freezing up here, and the round window was spattered with snow, but Lorna had wrapped herself up in a couple of moth-eaten blankets, and she looked comfortable enough. The shape of her head and arms reminded Virginia of that faraway look she'd had, last night, in the bath.

She jumped up when Virginia knocked, and shoved the papers under the mattress.

"Sorry," she said. "Sorry, Virginia, I've left you alone too long . . ."

"There's a man in the garden."

Lorna stopped fidgeting with her hair and lowered her arms.

"Clem?" she whispered, following Virginia's example.

"No, not Clem, just this strange man. I don't know . . . he ran across the grass into the shed."

They started down the stairs together, quickly and quietly, Lorna leading the way. A sudden inspiration made Virginia raise her voice.

"Maybe it's Mr. Rosenthal?"

"Mr. Rosenthal? You mean the knife grinder?" Lorna sounded less than convinced. "What would he be doing in our shed?"

"Maybe he's escaped from the police. That would explain why he looked so furtive: he's looking for somewhere to hide."

Lorna didn't say anything. Virginia followed her to Clem's study and watched as she rummaged in his desk for a key before unlocking the corner cupboard. The twilight was heavier in here than in her bedroom because the furnishings were dark and the walls were lined with leather books.

"What are you doing?"

Taking the weight in both hands, Lorna lifted a long cloth bundle from the cupboard and laid it gently on the rug. There was a peculiar smell — an exciting smell — as the cloth fell away, a bit like the whiff of sulfur you get when you strike a match.

Virginia crouched down as Lorna drew back the last fold.

"I didn't know Clem kept a shotgun."

"It's not loaded," Lorna whispered. "But it looks the part. We may as well take it."

They didn't bother with hats and coats — it seemed a bit fussy in the circumstances — but the rubber boots were standing in a row by the back door, so they put them on. Virginia waited to be told to return to her room — Clem would have insisted on it ages ago — but it never seemed to cross Lorna's mind. She even asked Virginia to hold the shotgun while she shook a stone from one of her boots.

"Ready?" Lorna whispered, taking the weapon back and crooking her finger around the trigger. Virginia nodded, caught halfway between gratitude and mild resentment. This wasn't the sort of thing proper mothers got up to with their daughters. On the other hand, it was exciting.

The wet snow flew in their faces, as if it were coming up off the marsh instead of down from the sky. The flakes were beginning to collect on top of the flint wall and alongside the house, but the lawn was still pulpy with mud. Side by side they plowed the few yards to the shed, their heads bowed, while the wind whipped their hair and clothes. Virginia almost took hold of Lorna's hand — she would have taken hold of Clem's in much less dramatic circumstances — but she decided not to, for fear of seeming childish. Besides, Lorna needed both hands for the gun.

There was no temptation to dither in such wild weather. Whoever was — or wasn't — lurking in the shed, they needed to find out quickly. Lorna gestured to Virginia to unlatch the door, and as soon as it was done she swung it open with the toe of her boot.

It may have been dark, but there was undoubtedly someone there; the air was vibrating with his efforts to shiver quietly. There was a moment of stillness before the hoe fell off its nail in the wall and something else clattered against the wheelbarrow, and Lorna swallowed, raising the shotgun higher. Virginia saw a tall shape against the back wall, and the gleam of an eye, and two pale palms held up in surrender.

"Please," he said. "Please."

He definitely wasn't English. His teeth were chattering so violently that it was difficult to glean much else from his voice, beyond the obvious fact he was cold. He smelled of wet wool and mud. Normally the shed smelled of dry compost and tarpaulin.

"Is it Mr. Rosenthal?" Virginia murmured, standing on tiptoe to look over Lorna's shoulder. There was something about him — his accent, and the shadowy shape of his body — that convinced her. "It is, isn't it?"

Lorna's fingers tightened around the gun. "Virginia?" she said, in a shaky approximation of her usual voice. "I want you to run back to the house and telephone the police."

"Please, no," said the man, stepping forward. "Please wait." His hands were still raised, but he was opening them out in a pleading gesture instead of holding them up on either side of his head.

"Oh God." Lorna spoke so quietly that the words were more like shapes in the darkness than actual sounds. As she readjusted her hold on the shotgun, her wedding ring clinked against the hollow barrel.

"Virginia, do as I say."

Virginia trudged back to the house, but she didn't go straight in. She stood on the back step for several minutes, rubbing her arms and peering out in the direction of the marsh. The snowflakes hurtled toward her face, and she stared at them for so long that she lost her bearings and began to feel as though it were she who was hurtling toward them.

"Clem," she whispered, in case that was the magic word that would bring him back, but the wind blotted it against her lips instead of carrying it out to sea. She waited a minute, repeating the spell, but he didn't materialize, so she turned into the kitchen. Her socks were wet and she couldn't get her boots off by herself, so she kept them on and made a trail of watery footprints across Mrs. Hill's clean floors.

The telephone table was underneath the window by the front door. Virginia went to it — she even picked up the receiver — but she didn't dial. She kept picturing the black police van that would take Mr. Rosenthal away. Mr. Deering was bound to be on the scene — one way or another he'd come, even if it wasn't any of his business — and what if he started stamping and screaming like last time? What if the police let him? With Clem away, there'd be nobody to intervene. She set the phone down and tried to stop shivering.

The back door opened again and a flurry of wind moved through the house, stirring curtains and banging doors. Lorna must be bringing him inside, because there was a brief exchange of voices and the sound of a chair being pulled back. A few seconds later the curtains were drawn with a rackety noise and the kitchen light came on.

Virginia kept her fingers tight around the black receiver, listening as the door of the range clanged open and new coal was scattered over the fire. Lorna asked a short question, which was followed — inexplicably — by a swishing sound, like scissors cutting through cloth. Now the visitor was talking, quietly and rapidly, and Lorna was saying, "Hush, hush." Virginia let go of the telephone and crept up to the kitchen door.

The man was sitting at the kitchen table, wrapped up in Bracken's hairy blanket. His coat was heaped in Lorna's arms, a dripping mess of mud and snow, one of its sleeves slashed open and hanging down. He did not match Virginia's mental image of Mr. Rosenthal. For some reason she'd had him down as long-faced and gray, with bony cheeks and wise eyes. She'd never have guessed he was beautiful.

He watched Lorna as she dumped the coat's filthy remains by the back door and crossed the kitchen to the sink. He was cradling one of his hands against his chest, and Virginia noticed that the fingers were all purple and swollen, which at least explained the scissored coat sleeve. Lorna spent a long time washing her hands under the tap without saying anything. Virginia was glad she'd abandoned the shotgun; perhaps it implied a change of heart. The weapon was propped up against the dresser, with drops of snow rolling down its muzzle, and Bracken was giving it a good sniff. He didn't seem remotely interested in the visitor. Virginia pictured the yapping, wheeling, scrabbling madness there would be when Clem came home at last.

"I'll try and bind it, if you want," Lorna said, turning off the tap but continuing to face the sink. "You ought to see a doctor, though."

The man couldn't seem to take his eyes off the back of Lorna's head, although there was nothing unusual — as far as Virginia could see — about her knotted scarf and the few stray corkscrews of hair. Lorna held on to the edge of the sink as she waited for him to reply, but he remained silent. In the end she turned to face him and, in doing so, spotted Virginia lurking in the doorway.

"Well?" she demanded briskly, drying her hands on a tea towel. Her face was so rosy you'd think she'd been sitting right next to a fire. "Have you telephoned?"

Virginia shook her head and Lorna raised her eyebrows a fraction. She came out to the hall, closing the door behind her.

"You haven't?" she whispered. "Why ever not?"

"I couldn't." Virginia twined her fingers nervously. "Clem likes Mr. Rosenthal."

They were standing face-to-face, almost touching, but Lorna was no more than a silhouette against the dim wallpaper. Virginia readied herself for an argument — Lorna and the law versus Mr. Rosenthal — but before anything was said, something cold touched her wrist. Lorna had taken hold of her hand.

"Vi?" she said softly. "Listen. I have to tell you something about that man. It's —"

She stopped. Virginia wasn't interested in grown-up generalizations, and didn't want to hear Lorna's thoughts on enemy aliens and internment camps, but she waited anyway, out of polite habit. The silence went on. Lorna seemed to be staring toward the front door, as if she'd lost her train of thought.

"Oh no," she muttered, dropping Virginia's hand and walking swiftly to the window. "Oh no, no, no. Not now. Not now!"

Virginia hardly needed to look, but she turned anyway and watched Mr. Deering's car approach the house.

New Year's Eve 2015

For a brief, giddying moment Virginia thinks the girl is trying to claim Clem as her great-granddad. But Sophie isn't looking at Clem. She's pointing at a blur in the upper right-hand corner of the photograph, a figure that consists of little more than a jacket collar and a slice of trilby hat.

"You can't see him very well," Sophie says. "But it's definitely him."

Virginia can also tell, now that Sophie has pointed him out. There are a dozen people milling in the door of the church, and he's right at the back of the group, turning away, half obscured by someone's fox-fur stole. Virginia takes the photo out of Sophie's hand and stares. She must have known already, and mentally blocked it out. She must. How many years is it, after all, since she really studied this picture?

"Let me think. He's my dad's . . . dad's . . .

dad," Sophie explains. There's something rather sweet about her pride, but it vanishes in a blink and she looks much older as she says, "It's his fault about the Oxford thing, really. He was the first to go and read law, and then he made his son go too, and then my dad. And now Dad and Granddad Theo are both on at me."

Sophie reaches for the photo again and Virginia hands it back, unthinkingly. She shifts her aching weight from foot to foot, and tries to focus on the framing of a question.

"So . . ." It's all so simple, but at the same time terribly difficult, like trying to think straight when you're emerging from a dream. "So your surname . . . ?"

Sophie is poring over the photograph. "It's Deering," she says, without looking up. "Same as him."

"Deering." Virginia repeats the name and the whole day is realigned, like a jigsaw that's suddenly slotted into place.

"Oh my gosh, so this person here — the bride — what was her name?"

"Lorna."

And now Sophie is full of questions. "How old was she? She hardly looks old enough to get married. And what was his name? What year was this photo? How are they

193

related to you?" Virginia feels compelled to answer, although her mind is busy with its own obsessions.

Now that the truth is out, Virginia can't see anything but Deering in the girl's moon-like pallor and satin-black hair. She wonders how she ever missed it. And it's not just the way she looks, either. There's something very Deering about a gentle voice that persists with questions, even when the questionee is patently flagging. "So when did they adopt you? Was it because they couldn't have children of their own? Did you look for your real parents? Did you know my great-granddad? Did you know him well?" Perhaps she is cut out to be a lawyer after all. Perhaps it's in the blood, whether she likes it or not.

Admittedly the girl has a milky, childish scent, which bears no resemblance to her forbear's hair oils and masculine soaps. Nevertheless her scent is, by definition, the scent of a Deering, and Virginia can't bear to breathe it in, so she twists away — pins and needles or no — and tries to rest her gaze on something neutral. But there is nothing neutral in the attic at Salt Winds. She turns in desperation to the window and sees the rocking chair, stark black against the winter light.

"You're probably cold," says Sophie, touching her on the arm. "Sorry if I'm babbling."

Virginia flinches when those sharp white fingernails press into her sleeve, but she doesn't shake them off, and when Sophie asks if she'd like help going down the stairs, she doesn't protest. She's not entirely lacking in pragmatism. If Sophie doesn't maneuver her down those winding attic stairs, she won't be going anywhere today; she's too stiff and weak to make it on her own. She has to get downstairs for something to eat and a good rest before she can face the evening's walk.

Halfway down, Virginia stumbles on her own stick, but Sophie catches her around the waist and keeps her from falling. The child may be slight, but she's sinewy, and Virginia leans into her. She doesn't want to, but she has to.

"Your great-grandfather was strong," Virginia hears herself say. "Not a big man, like Clem, but strong. Wiry."

Sophie is frowning with concentration and doesn't reply until they reach the landing.

"It's amazing to think you actually knew him," she exclaims once they're safe, her face clearing as Virginia extricates herself and her stick. "He's like this mythical figure in our family that we're all meant to live up to, and I hardly know anything about him."

"What do you know?"

Sophie meanders down the landing, peering through half-open doors, and Virginia wishes she would stand still while she answers the question.

"Well, I know he had all these terrible things happen to him," Sophie says, and she enumerates, on her fingers, the trials of Max Deering. "First his wife died when their children were really small; then he got engaged to this woman who left him for his best friend; and *then* his daughter got killed in the Blitz."

Virginia gives a noncommittal nod. Put like that, how diminished his losses become. What a fuss about nothing. Sophie obviously agrees, because she looks quite cheerful now, as she contemplates the three acknowledged tragedies of Great-Granddad Max. Virginia's mouth curls into something like a smile. What a lost soul the girl was, just a few hours before, when she was sitting on the flint wall and thinking about her chances of getting to art school.

"But then something else happened," Sophie goes on. "I don't know what it was, but it had something to do with Salt Winds."

The smile — such as it is — freezes on

Virginia's lips. *Something else happened.* Yes, indeed it did, but Sophie is too distracted to notice the effect of her words. She's flitted into Virginia's bedroom now, and Virginia is forced to limp in pursuit. Briefly she fears for her privacy and all her precious things — the curlew's skull, in particular — but then she remembers her fatalistic new creed and relaxes a little. Whatever is meant to happen today will happen. If the child drops the bird's head on the floor and treads the pieces into the rug, it doesn't matter. Nothing will have changed.

"How do you know it had to do with Salt Winds?" Virginia demands, as she reaches the bedroom door. Sophie has, indeed, spotted the curlew's skull and is crouching down to study it more closely. She doesn't touch it, though.

"I just do. In our family, the name 'Salt Winds' has got this kind of aura of horror about it." She chooses the word *horror* carefully. In fact, she chooses all her words carefully, pausing every now and then to think. "Even after my great-granddad died — which was way before I was born, so it's not like I remember him — Salt Winds was this . . . this *thing* that you sometimes heard whispered, and never asked questions about.

I didn't even know it was the name of a house until Granddad Theo told me he used to go there as a boy."

Virginia walks toward the window, and her reflection comes to meet her. The watery light is coming from the other side of the house now. Midday has passed; the seesaw is tipping toward night.

"Granddad Theo," she laughs, too quietly for Sophie to hear, before raising her voice to ask, "What else did he tell you? He must have said something else?"

"Well, no. Not really." Sophie comes to stand next to her and their arms touch. The girl is still shivering, and no wonder when you consider how she's dressed. What on earth was she thinking, on a December day like this? Silly child. Not that it matters. It's no business of Virginia's if a Deering chooses to die of exposure.

"It was like he'd inherited this superstition about the place. All he said — eventually — was that he'd grown up in a village called Tollbury Point, and he used to visit a house called Salt Winds with his father, during the war. And then suddenly, when he was twelve, the visits stopped and they moved to Putney, and he wasn't allowed to ask any questions about it, or mention it at all. The one time he tried, his father thrashed him so hard he broke his arm."

"Hmm," Virginia replies, pursing her lips. The girl is expecting a better reaction than that — *He broke his own son's arm? How horrible!* — but Virginia is unmoved. Instead, she's been concentrating on Sophie's voice rather than her words; straining to catch the Deering timbre. Sometimes she thinks she hears the faintest whisper of Max a split second behind, repeating everything his great-granddaughter says. Sophie's tone is childishly earnest, but the echo is contemptuous, as if to say, *I'm still here, Miss Wrathmell. You might have known I'd still be here.*

Virginia decides to match her voice to the echo, and fight mockery with mockery.

"So," she says, folding her arms across her chest and swallowing a cough. "You fancy yourself as a bit of an amateur sleuth, do you? Dragging skeletons out of cupboards for the fun of it?"

Their eyes meet in the window. Virginia's gaze is steadfast, but Sophie's is anxious.

"I didn't mean to cause any . . . It *was* partly curiosity. But it was mainly because I knew they wouldn't look for me here."

"Your family sounds surprisingly superstitious, given they're all so highly educated?"

"Yes." Sophie is on firmer ground. "When it comes to Salt Winds they are supersti-

199

tious. Well, Dad and Granddad Theo, anyway. That's exactly the right word."

Virginia bats the air impatiently and moves back into the room. It's not for her to scoff at other people's demons. God knows she's plenty of her own. Besides, the girl's private reasons for coming are unimportant. The question — the urgent question — is what to do with her now she's here.

Virginia sighs. She has to take the weight off her feet before her legs give way, so she lowers herself onto the edge of the bed. It's a bit soft and low for sitting on, but it's better than nothing. She can look straight into the curlew's left eye socket from this vantage point, and she searches it for an answer, but it stares back without giving anything away. Virginia frowns and strokes the frayed bedspread, seeing it in her mind's eye when it was rose pink and new. It's a sort of fawn color now, or at least it is on top where the sun has bleached it. The wallpaper's in much the same state.

"You're thinking I ought to ring them, aren't you?" Sophie asks. She's followed Virginia across the room and now she's standing by the bed, running a nervous finger around the phone in her pocket.

"No!" Virginia's eyes snap open. She may

not know what to do, but she knows what *not* to do. Somehow or other, the Deering girl belongs to the mysteries of this day, and there's no question of her leaving now. Not any longer. Everything has changed.

"Anyway, I thought you said the battery was dead?" Virginia is trying hard to sound indifferent — too hard, perhaps, because her voice is trembling.

"That's true," Sophie agrees. "But I think . . . Did you say it'd be OK if I used your phone? Not that I necessarily want to ring them, yet. It's just . . ."

The girl's shivers become more pronounced and her eyes start swimming again.

Virginia gathers herself. "Before you do anything, let's go down to the kitchen and make a pot of tea." Her tremors subside as her confidence grows, and she thinks she sees a gleam at the back of the curlew's eye. "What do you think? We both need a hot drink and a bite to eat. And then we can see."

She staggers to her feet to show she means it, and Sophie nods obediently. "Actually, that would be nice."

They hobble onto the landing arm in arm, but when they reach the top of the stairs, Virginia halts.

"I've forgotten something," she says.

"Oh, do you want me to —"

"No. You carry on downstairs and fill the kettle. I'll be half a minute."

Virginia wasn't intending to use violence. All she meant to do was fetch her nail scissors from the dressing table and snip through one of the wires to make the telephone impotent. And then, since she was passing the wretched thing on her way to the bedroom, it seemed simpler — less destructive, in fact — to unhook it from the wall and hide it.

The trouble is, it won't unhook. She'll need a screwdriver, and even then she'll have a job, because the screws are fiddly small and rusty and difficult to get at. She tries to unplug the cord but it won't budge, so she yanks at it, first with one hand and then, instinctively, with two, growling through her teeth as her walking stick falls to the floor.

The cord rips apart, leaving bits behind in the socket, and now Virginia begins to grapple with the rest of the machine, tearing at the casing, the dial, the wires. She snags several of her nails, but she doesn't care. The telephone creaks and pings and rattles; bits of plastic crack under her hands and skitter across the floor; wires spray from broken fibers; plaster tumbles off the wall. The phone is unrecognizable by the time she's finished: a mutilated corpse still screwed to the wall, with its spilling entrails frozen in midair.

Virginia stumbles backward and leans against the opposite wall to see what she's done. There's the sound of the kitchen tap gushing: thank God the girl didn't witness this. Virginia covers her eyes with her crooked hands. A moment ago she wanted to laugh with elation, but now she wants to cry quietly, with someone's arms around her.

January 1941

"But we *can't* send him outside again!" Virginia whispered fiercely. "He'll freeze to death out there. Mr. Deering might be here for ages."

As she spoke, the Austin 12 curved out of the lane and braked in front of the house with a gentle squeak.

"Where then? Where?" Lorna was twisting her fingers in her hair, on the brink of tears. "Oh Lord . . ."

There was a shuffling noise behind them, and they turned to see the stranger standing at the kitchen door, wrapped like a pilgrim in Bracken's rug. He swayed slightly and his lips started to move, but no sound came out.

"Don't you dare collapse on my kitchen floor." Lorna grabbed him by both elbows and hauled him away from the lighted doorway.

"All right," she said, turning back to Virginia. "You can take him upstairs, but for goodness' sake be quiet. I'll keep Max outside for as long as I can."

Mr. Deering's voice sounded horribly close, and he hadn't even come inside yet. He was peeling his driving gloves off — Virginia could hear the leathery flourish — and locking the car, and saying how disappointed Theo was that the snow wasn't going to stick. He didn't even ask for news of Clem.

"I think it is sticking, a little," Lorna rejoined brightly. "Look there, on top of the wall. And you never know, there may be more tonight."

Virginia gripped the man's hand. He was leaning on the wall at the top of the stairs with his eyes closed, listening carefully to something inside himself. He scarcely seemed to register Mr. Deering's arrival on the scene, let alone show special alarm. Only when the wind blew the front door open with a bang did he jump, and his teeth started chattering.

"*Shh!*" Virginia whispered, squeezing harder on his hand. His teeth were absurdly loud, like a handful of dice rattling in a cup, but he looked at her helplessly and shook his head, unable to stop.

"Let's get out of this blasted wind," Mr. Deering was saying. "I could do with a shot of scotch, if there's any left."

Virginia dragged the man away from the staircase and propelled him along the landing. He moved willingly but clumsily, and the floorboards shrieked beneath his stockinged feet. She glanced at every door they passed but none was safe. If she took him in there, they'd be right over the kitchen; in there they'd be over the sitting room, or the dining room, or the library — and who knew where Max Deering would decide to settle with his glass of scotch?

Footsteps crunched over snowy gravel toward the front door.

"Bother, I've lost my headscarf," Lorna called, half laughing and faraway. "The wind just whirled it off . . ."

Well, we're not looking for it now." Mr. Deering stopped to wait for her, but he was beginning to sound testy. "Drat it, Lorna . . ."

There was no more time to think.

The attic. Of course, the attic.

They sat down on the mattress, side by side. Mr. Deering's voice had vanished now, and there was nothing to hear but the wind in the eaves. The man held his bent legs against his chest and laid his head on his knees. There were a few twisted blankets on the mattress, decidedly moth-eaten and damp to the touch, but Virginia gathered them up and bundled them over his rounded back.

"Danke," he murmured, without moving.

Virginia smiled, even though they were invisible to one another in the dark. Somehow Mr. Rosenthal's presence was a good sign; a message from Clem that all would be well, if she kept faith. It was the first time she'd managed a smile in hours, and the muscles in her cheeks felt stiff and strange.

"Mr. Deering is always getting in the way," she explained, after a while, anxious to signify her dislike of Mr. Rosenthal's enemy. "Lorna finds it difficult to get rid of him. I don't know why. I don't think she likes him, really, it's just . . ."

She trailed off. The man made no response, and she thought perhaps he'd gone to sleep. He should have a proper wash and something to eat. There was something unsettling about the state he was in now; he seemed to be exuding cold from the very core of his body and chilling the entire attic. He smelled unhealthy too: like mud and stagnant water and rotten vegetation. For half a moment, before she could dismiss the idea as stupid, Virginia thought he smelled of drowning.

Virginia shivered and fidgeted with the bits and bobs inside her cardigan pocket: a handkerchief, a pencil stub, a box of matches. She spent hours on her bed with a book — stillness was her usual preference — but this particular evening, stillness hurt. All her muscles ached to walk about and chatter, and do somersaults across the mattress.

"You're good at keeping quiet," she observed wistfully, when she could bear it no longer. The man stirred, which encouraged her to go on. "I suppose you're pretty exhausted though, from your escape. You must have had to walk a long way."

She had a feeling that he'd turned to face her, and that his eyes were searching for her through the darkness, but she couldn't be sure. He didn't say anything. Maybe she was wrong. Maybe he was still asleep.

Her fingers clutched the little matchbox in her pocket, and with a guilty start she remembered the candles she'd lit last night, all over the house, for Clem. Carefully, and pausing with every creak, she slid off the mattress and went to the window, where she felt about for the jam jar. Here it was — and there was still a lump of wax at the bottom, with something of a wick, but it was difficult to reach, and she wasted four matches and burnt two fingers in lighting it.

"What are you doing?" The man's whisper was more alert than she expected.

"It's for Clem," she replied. "He went out on the marsh yesterday; that's why you've not seen him."

His eyes were definitely on her now: she could feel them.

"Clem," he repeated warily.

"Yes. You see, an airplane came down on Tollbury Marsh, and Clem went to try and rescue the airman. I didn't want him to, because it was a German plane — I mean a proper enemy German, a Nazi, not like you — but he went anyway. And now he's having trouble getting back. I mean, he'll be all right, because nobody knows the marsh like Clem . . ." She stopped for breath, conscious that she was babbling

The man was watching her intently, and in the jagged candlelight his face seemed to gape like a tragedy mask.

"Clem?" he asked, hoarsely. "This . . . Clem . . . this is your father?"

"He's — yes, sort of. My actual parents died when I was two weeks old, so I grew up at Sinclair House, but then Clem and Lorna . . ." The explanation petered out. "I suppose you wouldn't necessarily know about me. I've not been here very long."

The man stared at her, and then at his feet. Slowly, he began to nod.

"I am very sorry to hear it," he whispered. "He was a good, good man."

"*Is* a good, good man," she retorted, forgetting to keep her voice down. "He's not *dead*, Mr. Rosenthal."

"*Is* good," he repeated, raising his hands in the same gesture of surrender he'd used when they found him in the shed. "I'm sorry."

His apology was so heartfelt that Virginia felt bad for having snapped. She sat down beside him again and patted his sleeve, and in return he tried — not quite successfully — to smile.

"Please, I want you to call me Jozef," he whispered, holding out his right hand as if intending her to shake it. She did so, though it was rather awkward because they were sitting side by side. "And your name . . . ?"

"Virginia."

Another burst of wind rattled the slates, but this time there was a noise hiding beneath it: a short, fierce note; a cry of protest; a "No!" They both lifted their heads and looked toward the attic door, but Virginia grabbed Jozef's sleeve.

"It's all right," she said. "It was something from outside."

Quickly, in her head, she ran through all the things it might have been. There were enough possibilities. It might have been a fox, or a stoat, or a bird. It might have been the wind, singing at a strange pitch. Revelers drinking on the wall. A ship's whistle.

"It came from inside the house," Jozef insisted, staggering to his feet.

"No, no." Virginia held on to the raggedy hem of his blanket and tried to remember some of the bird facts Clem had taught her. They'd been so firmly fixed in her brain before, but now they felt shaky. "It was a bird. Maybe . . . maybe a curlew. I'm not sure. Clem will tell us when he gets back. Please sit down. *Please.* If Mr. Deering sees you here, that'll be bad for all of us. Me and you and Lorna . . ."

Jozef didn't sit down at once, but he didn't break away either. Virginia hung on to the corner of the blanket and tried to ignore the images that kept flashing through her mind: Mr. Deering's teeth shiny with spit; his lips moist with drink; his fingers strong and hungry, snaking through Lorna's hair, and down her neck, and inside her clothes. Virginia clenched her teeth and shut her eyes tight, but all she saw in her mind's eye was Mr. Deering's face moving over hers, like a big yellow moon. It was horrible, the way he seemed to look down on her, with his lips hanging open in a smile. She couldn't push the image away, even after she opened her eyes.

The cry came again, with no gust of wind to disguise it. Virginia remembered the shotgun in the kitchen and tried to stand up, but her legs were empty and they wouldn't bear her weight. She sank back down again and pressed her knees with the flats of her hands to try to stop them from shaking. Her breathing had gone ragged, but she forced it to settle and declared, firmly, "That was a curlew."

"A bird?" Jozef wasn't convinced.

"Yes. I know it. I've heard it before."

He tore his eyes from the door and sat down slowly. Virginia slumped against him, as unceremonious in her exhaustion as if he were a wall or a post, and he put a tentative arm around her shoulders. She shivered, pulling her cardigan tight, and promptly went to sleep.

It was strange, waking underneath the rafters in the ghost light before dawn. The candle had burned out by then and all the darting shapes and shadows of the night were gone, leaving the attic gray and calm.

Virginia sat up squinting and massaged her stiff neck. Lorna must have been here during the night because there were fresh blankets and pillows, and Jozef was sprawled, facedown, in a pair of Clem's pajamas. His left ear — which was as much of him as she could make out beneath the jumble of blankets — was pink with warmth, and he smelled all soapy and healthful. His hair had dried into soft tufts, like a teddy bear's fur, and she couldn't resist touching it, which made him twitch.

Virginia found she'd been asleep at the foot of the mattress, curled up in a ball, like a cat. It took a few limping circuits of the attic to get rid of the cramp in her legs, and she finished up by the window, rubbing the crust from her eyes. Her head felt empty, as if all her thoughts had drained away overnight, slipping like spilled water through the bare floorboards. Everything — Clem's disappearance, and the cries in the night, and Mr. Deering's monstrous car — seemed like fragments from an absurd dream that would break apart any moment now, dispersing in the morning light the way dream fragments do.

She cleared a bit of the moisture from the window and looked out. Gray snow lay along the flint wall and on the shed roof and in long, uneven patches across the marsh, while black smoke twisted upward, passing close to her face. She watched it dispassionately for a while as it whirled in the thin wind and dispersed in the sky, but then the stench of petrol hit, and it occurred to her to wonder — and then to worry about — what exactly was burning.

Lorna was in the corner of the garden with her back to the house, leaning on the garden fork. The bonfire roared a few feet away, and currents of heat competed with the wind to lift threads of hair from her face. Virginia stopped in the kitchen doorway, her chest thumping, and allowed herself to breathe again. It was all right. The house wasn't in flames and Lorna wasn't dead. There hadn't been a bomb.

Lorna looked unexpectedly gaunt from this angle. Despite her winter coat and proximity to the fire she was rubbing her arms, and there was something about the way she stood that made her seem alien. Virginia decided to shut the kitchen door quietly and retreat, but before she had a chance Lorna turned and saw her. They stared at one another for a moment, like two trespassers, but then Lorna raised her hand in greeting and Virginia had no choice but to cross the grass and join her.

"I'm burning his clothes," Lorna explained dully, thrusting the fork into the fire and giving it a stir. She didn't say "Jozef's clothes," or "Mr. Rosenthal's" — just "his" — and, at first, Virginia wondered whose clothes she meant. She thought, stupidly, of Mr. Deering's expensive pinstripes, and her stomach lurched.

"You're burning them?"

"It's all they were good for. He'll have to borrow some of Clem's."

"Oh . . . Yes."

Virginia narrowed her eyes against the smoke and stared into the depths of the bonfire. That flash of gray might have been the coat that looked so much like Clem's — Jozef's coat — but the holly-green knit was surely Lorna's sweater, much darned at the elbows — the one she'd been wearing yesterday — and wasn't that a scrap of yesterday's blouse, and a flash of pattern from yesterday's skirt? And there, wasn't that a length of stocking, twisted up with something else in oyster-pink silk? Virginia blushed like the accidental intruder she was, and tried to look away.

"Why —" she began, but she couldn't finish the question out loud. *Why are you burn-*

ing your own clothes? Lorna would have to come up with a lie in order to hide the answer. It seemed silly to trouble her.

"Mr. Deering's gone to London for the week," said Lorna, and Virginia nodded. She almost said, "Thank goodness!" but that felt risky too, so she said nothing. Lorna usually snapped when Virginia was being unresponsive, but she didn't seem to mind this time.

The smoke was stinging Virginia's eyes and making them water, so she turned to face the marsh. She stared at the luminous horizon, willing herself to see a tiny, moving speck, growing and thickening and assuming human features the closer it came to the house, until there could be no doubt it was Clem. She stared until her eyes were dry, and promised the fates she wouldn't shout out until she was sure. There were several specks in her line of sight, and she followed them all avidly, but they turned out to be birds or particles from the fire.

"Is he still asleep?" Lorna interrupted, jabbing at the heap with her garden fork. Big black flakes and motes of ash flew in her face, but she didn't stop or turn aside. The scrap of oyster-pink underwear flickered into flame and fragmented in the black heart of the fire.

"What? Oh, yes."

"That's good."

Virginia licked her dry lips and glanced at Lorna sidelong.

"We don't really have to hand him in, do we?" she asked.

"Mmm?"

"Can't we keep him?"

"You make him sound like a stray cat." Lorna stuck the fork into the ground again and leaned, with both arms, on the handle. It was good that she could still smile.

"No, but really," Virginia persisted. "Can't we?"

Lorna plucked the fork from the ground and stabbed it in again, hard. "No, of course we can't."

There was a long, nervy silence. Lorna sighed and looked away, wiping her sooty sleeve across her forehead.

"We'll make him a nice breakfast," she conceded, as if that would make all the difference. "But that's as much as we can do. As soon as he's eaten, I'm going to telephone the police."

Virginia nodded, because she had no choice, and they remained there, side by side, watching the fire burn itself out. Strange, she thought, that a bonfire could be such a depressing thing; she wouldn't have believed it if she hadn't found herself standing over this one. She'd loved Clem's autumn bonfires, when he burned dead leaves and hedge clippings: she'd loved the hiss of boiling sap and the snap of sticks and the sweet, pervasive fragrance of the blue smoke.

"Well." Lorna dragged her gaze from the dying reds and blacks. "I suppose we must get on."

It *was* a nice breakfast — almost pre-war in its niceness — with bacon and eggs, tea and toast, and the last of Mrs. Hill's marmalade. They carried it up to the attic on two trays, and Virginia led the way.

The sun was rising as they entered the attic, and for a minute or two the light was lovely — not glorious or bright, but lovely; the palest of pale yellows. Jozef was sitting up in Clem's stripy pajamas, with one arm in a bandage and a heap of papers on his lap, and he started talking the moment they came in. None of this struck Virginia as strange, even while part of her acknowledged that it was. Perhaps it was because she was still tired that everything felt so oddly familiar, as if she and Lorna had been bringing breakfast trays up to the attic for years.

"Look!" Jozef cried, waving a handful of

papers in the air. "Look at these drawings. They're extraordinary. They were lying just here, under the mattress. Have you seen them?"

"Hmm." Lorna set her tray on the floor with exaggerated care. She glanced very briefly at the papers before turning to the window with a shrug and sticking her hands in her pockets.

Jozef was undeterred. "Look!" he insisted, holding them out to Virginia. She plumped herself down on the mattress, near his feet, and began to skim through the pile. Lorna — who was still at the window — said something curt about the scrambled eggs going cold, and Jozef began to eat, but he kept his eyes on Virginia's face, as if he couldn't wait for her reaction.

"Aren't they good?" he said. "Maybe it's wrong, but when I look at these drawings I am happier than I've been for months. For *years.*"

Virginia wouldn't go that far, but she was impressed. They were such self-assured creations — each pencil line so perfectly balanced between precision and energy — that she'd have been less surprised to find them published in an art book, or framed on a gallery wall, than lying in a crumpled heap on the attic floor. She moved carefully from page to page, from portraits of people to careful studies of birds' heads and flowers, to pictures of goblins, fairies, castles, crooked trees, witches, and strange animals. There was something familiar about the style, but she couldn't think what it was until she turned a page and saw a stout guinea pig in a gingham housecoat, and remembered a drawing she'd found on Clem's desk last winter. What had it been, again? A bird of some sort. A duck. Yes, that was it. A duck in a businessman's suit. She'd wanted to keep it, but Clem had bundled it into a drawer as if he found it embarrassing.

"Did Clem do these?" she asked, looking up.

"Clem?" Lorna had kept her back to them, feigning an interest in the view, but at this she turned. "No, he did not. They're mine."

She faced them with a kind of defiant glee, her hands fidgeting inside her pockets, the corners of her mouth unsteady. She had the uncomfortable look of someone who hasn't the right to be happy — not even briefly — but can't quite prevent a smile from flowering. When Jozef looked at her and said, "I take my hat off to you; I think they're truly wonderful," she bobbed her head and turned back to the window.

"Where did you learn to draw like this?" Virginia asked out loud. *And why didn't you tell me about it?* she added internally, surprised by the strength of her own resentment. The pictures amazed her. It was as if she'd discovered the house had a secret wing full of treasures that no one had bothered to mention before. Jozef offered her a triangle of toast and she accepted it, absent-mindedly.

"London," Lorna replied. "The Slade."

Virginia must have looked blank.

"The Slade School of Fine Art."

Lorna took the pages out of Virginia's hands and returned to the window, where she began to leaf through them slowly.

"These aren't from my student days. I did all these up here, in the attic, when —"

She stopped herself abruptly but continued to turn the pages, one by one. Virginia watched the fluid motion of her fingers as they plucked the top corner of each sheet, and realized there was a sureness about them that she'd never noticed before.

"I used to come up here at odd times to draw," Lorna explained rapidly, as if anxious to forestall questions. "Clem didn't really —" She hesitated. "Art never seemed to mix very well with married life."

Virginia picked uneasily at a strip of loose

skin on her thumb. Whatever that was meant to imply, she couldn't worry about it now. She filed it away at the back of her mind, for consideration at a later date, and smoothed her thumb against her skirt. Jozef passed her his teacup, and after she'd taken a sip and handed it back, he offered it up to Lorna.

"Have some," he said.

Lorna glanced from the teacup to his face, as if she suspected foul play.

"Go on," he urged.

Lorna placed the pictures on the floor and took the cup from his hands with a small *thank you.* After she'd sipped once or twice she became less prickly and sat down, not on Jozef's mattress, but on a dusty packing case, with her back against the wall.

"Please finish it off," he said — and she did. He watched as she drank, tilting his head to one side, as if he was trying to work something out.

"You know what they remind me of?" he said, as Lorna set the empty cup on the floor by her feet.

"You mean the drawings? No. What?"

Jozef leaned back against the pillow with his sound hand behind his head. He, too, wore a shamefaced smile — like a man at a funeral who finds himself suddenly, helplessly awash with high spirits.

"Well you see, I used to write stories in the evenings, after work." He hesitated, suddenly unsure of himself. "This was before the Nazis — before their evil war — when I was still living at home with my parents. They were children's stories, you know. Fairy stories, for my little nephew."

Lorna stared, sightlessly, at the patch of wall above his head, and it was impossible to tell whether she was listening or not. Virginia frowned as she readjusted — again — all her ideas about Mr. Rosenthal, knife grinder. She felt embarrassed by her own lack of judgment. She'd had him down as someone else; someone old and weather-beaten and unschooled.

"A few of them got published," he went on, glancing shyly at his audience. "It was all on a small scale, you understand, in magazines and so on, but I used to fantasize about a beautiful book with all my stories collected together inside. Just *my* stories, no one else's, and my name in big letters down the spine and across the front. I can see it now in my head: it has a bright red cover — hardback, of course — and creamy pages and illustrations. Lots of illustrations. One for every chapter."

He sat up again and reached for Lorna's

drawings, shuffling through the pile until he found the one he wanted. Virginia could see it upside down from where she sat, but it looked like an illustration for "Rapunzel" — at any rate, there was a tall, ivy-clad tower and a woman sitting behind a window, reading a book. Privately, Virginia thought it a bit muscular for a fairy-tale illustration. The lines of the woman's face were strong and hard, and not as pretty as you might expect.

"This one I like very much," Jozef enthused. "I wrote a story just like this, called 'Die Hexe-Prinzessin.' "

Lorna's eyes came into focus and she stared at him, if not quite kindly, then at least observantly. " 'The Witch-Princess'?"

Jozef nodded and passed the paper over.

Lorna studied her work critically, narrowing her eyes. "I didn't see it as a pencil drawing, when it was in my head," she said. "I was planning a whole series of woodcut prints, but obviously I couldn't really . . . Printing's just so big and messy, and I didn't have the materials. Or the time."

Jozef picked more pictures out of the pile, and they passed them back and forth as the sun appeared in the window, edging everything with a fragile light and making Lorna's hair glow like a halo. It ought to have been a drab scene with all that grubbiness and dust, and everyone's eyes hooded with exhaustion, but somehow it was anything but. The sun didn't reach Virginia's end of the mattress, and she felt like a shadowy observer on the edge of a charmed circle. She'd been wearing the same clothes ever since Clem disappeared, and it hadn't bothered her up until now, but the sudden brightness made her skin feel prickly and sour smelling.

"Will you tell us the story?" she asked, in case they'd forgotten she was there. She didn't expect a yes because she thought she knew adults and their prosaic ways of looking at the world. There would be lots of weary sighs and they'd say, *What? You mean, now?* and Lorna would stand up, all businesslike, and announce that she needed to *get on.*

But Jozef smiled as if Virginia had handed him a gift. "You want me to tell you the story of the Witch-Princess?"

Virginia nodded and Jozef glanced across at Lorna, who didn't make any objection. In fact, she shrugged and folded her arms, like somebody settling down to listen.

"All right." Jozef lay back again, his bandaged arm across his chest, and fixed his gaze on the cobwebbed ceiling as if he were stargazing. He thought for a long while, but his audience was patient.

"Once upon a time," he began, "there was a forest where the beech trees grew so tall and green that they hid the sky. In the daytime the light fell through the leaves like a shower of emeralds, but at nighttime the darkness fell like pitch, and that was when the witches came down from their tree houses and stalked the forest floor in search of prey.

"Now, late one afternoon as the sun was starting to set, a young traveler entered the forest and lost his way among the many winding paths . . ."

Jozef flopped back on his pillow, laughing at Virginia's applause. He kept one eye on Lorna too, as she got to her feet and began gathering up the breakfast things. She made no comment at all — she didn't even look at him — but there was a faint smile on her lips, which was, perhaps, enough.

He rolled onto his side and closed his eyes, and they lingered by the door with their trays, waiting for him to drop off. It was strange to watch the pleasure draining from his face the deeper he fell, and Virginia wondered what he was seeing in his sleep. He looked scary, with his mouth plunging at the corners and a frown flickering across his forehead. She was half inclined to wake him up again, but Lorna whispered, "No," and jerked her head in the direction of the stairs.

The house got darker and colder the farther down they went, and by the time they reached the landing it seemed as though the sun had never risen. The air down here was thick with the stink of lilies, and Virginia wondered whether the flowers were still lying broken on the bedroom floor, or whether Lorna had put them in a vase to please Mr. Deering. She didn't dare mention his name.

"I suppose we ought to have some breakfast too," said Lorna, shutting the attic door behind them with her elbow.

"Can I have a bath first?"

"Yes, if there's enough hot water."

Virginia righted the teacup on her tray before it tipped. They both seemed stuck, too tired to move on.

"I suppose there'll be lots to do today," said Lorna. "About Clem, I mean. People to talk to, and things to sort out . . . goodness knows what, exactly. Everything's so strange."

Virginia nodded. Lorna spoke like one grown-up talking to another — as if she'd finally shrugged off her ill-fitting role as *mother* — and Virginia replied in the same spirit.

"Jozef should stay then, don't you think?" she said cautiously, as if she didn't much mind, except for convenience's sake. "I mean, when there's so much else to think about. And he's not in anyone's way, up in the attic."

Lorna didn't answer. She seemed transfixed by the egg stains on his empty plate.

"Please?" Virginia hated the childish resonance of that. Real adults never said *please* in such a wheedling way, but she wasn't sure how else to put it. "You won't send him away, will you?"

Lorna sighed and took Virginia's tray, balancing it precariously on top of her own.

Virginia sat upright in three inches of bathwater and sloshed her legs to create waves. She'd washed her hair with soap and squeezed it dry, and although she was very cold she felt cleaner and better. If Clem were to come home this minute — and he might — he would surely be pleased with her behavior over the last twenty-four hours.

A spider dropped off the ceiling into the bath, and she scooped it up in her hands. Above all, she thought, she'd done the right thing by Mr. Rosenthal. Lorna had been altogether too eager to summon the police, and Clem would not have approved of that.

The water seeped out between her fingers, but it was too late for the spider — its legs were all awry, its body crushed and saturated. Virginia poked at it with her finger, but it just floated in her palm, as repulsive as a smear of dirt now that it was dead. She clambered out of the bath and ran onto the landing, slipping and dripping as she adjusted the towel around her body.

"What now?" Lorna was measuring porridge oats into a saucepan, but she paused when Virginia burst into the kitchen. "Well?"

Virginia shivered and pulled the towel tight around her shoulders. Bracken was gobbling his breakfast in the corner by the door, his collar clanging against the metal bowl. She felt like an idiot.

"It's just . . . I was just thinking about Jozef."

"What about him?"

Virginia lowered her eyes and watched the drips that tumbled off the ends of her hair and flattened themselves on the tiles by her feet.

"He is . . . I mean, he *is* Mr. Rosenthal, isn't he?"

Lorna took the saucepan to the sink and stood with her back to Virginia. She turned the tap on and ran water over the oats.

"Who else could he be?" Lorna asked, after the water had stopped.

Virginia moved from one foot to the other and shivered.

"I don't know," she replied. The colder she got, the more stupid she felt. "Nobody."

New Year's Eve 2015

Virginia has to kneel on the floor to reach the bottom drawer of the dressing table. It's a painful process, bending her body against its grain, and if she were on her own in the house she might shout a bit to help things along, but she mustn't do that now. She doesn't want to alert the Deering girl.

There. Success. She's down, without so much as a squeak.

Virginia rests her arms and head on top of the dressing table and closes her eyes. When she opens them again she finds her face is on a level with the curlew's skull. It looks different from this perspective — larger, of course, but also more sure of itself — and she studies it. Now she understands why its stare is so blank. It's urging her to be blank too; to be cold-eyed and clear; to see beyond Sophie's charm to her inherited essence. *Justice.* That's what it's telling her.

"Justice." Virginia repeats the word in a whisper to show she's understood, and then she stoops to open the bottom drawer.

There's a spiral-bound photo album on top, and a bundle of orange Kodak envelopes, and a few photos that are curled and bent because she's stored them loose.

Lorna used to roll her eyes at Virginia's hoarding habits. "Things with sentimental value I can understand," she used to say. "But why hang on to everything?" Virginia had just shrugged.

Most of the photographs are benign records of her adult life: the trips abroad, the family Christmases, Joe's fortieth birthday party. If today had turned out as she'd imagined, she would be lingering over these, but Sophie is waiting downstairs and there isn't time. Virginia knows which one she wants.

It's right at the bottom, of course, upside down and damaged at the corners. She stares at it for a long time, although her knees are starting to feel like bruises. It's much smaller and crisper than those bright, soft snaps from the 1970s and '80s, and the people in it are not so free and easy. They make her feel scrutinized. She realizes she hasn't looked at it once since the day Mr. Deering gave it to her all those years ago, and she's suddenly unnerved by the sureness with which she's laid hands on it.

Sophie has put a cozy on the teapot and set two matching mugs beside it. Silver is arching his back and wreathing himself around her legs, but she's not paying him any attention; she's too busy frowning and sniffing at the milk. She jumps when she notices Virginia, as if she's been caught stealing.

"Sorry," she says. "I just thought it smelled a bit funny."

Virginia winces — not because of the milk, but because her knees hurt. She gestures to Sophie to sit, but the girl can't seem to relax. She continues to stand with her back to the fridge, and although she forces her lips into a smile, she forgets to remove the frown. It's possible she overheard something when the phone came off the wall. It must have made some noise — all that jingling and cracking, and the plaster coming off in gobbets.

"Do you want me to do anything else?" Sophie wonders. "I could get you something to eat?"

It strikes Virginia that Sophie is a nice girl, judged by any ordinary standards. Nicer than she was at the same age. Virginia can see the girl's school report as clearly as if it were lying open on the table. *Sophie is a pleasure to teach,* it reads. *Sophie is conscientious and thoughtful. Sophie is an asset to the school.* Oh yes, Max Deering has disguised himself well over three generations — but that doesn't mean he isn't there. Ordinary standards are all very well, but they don't apply at Salt Winds. Not today.

Justice, she thinks, to bolster her resolve.

Sophie looks nervous. "Sorry?"

"What?"

Virginia is startled. She wonders whether she often says things out loud without meaning to. How would she know? She used to worry all the time about going mad, especially after Joe started talking, with casual frequency, about care homes. Right up until ten o'clock last night she worried about it; picturing herself lining an armchair in the TV lounge with no teeth, no space, no sense of herself. Now, thanks to the curlew, she's free to think, *So what? So what if I'm mad?*

"Look at this," Virginia says. "I've found something that'll interest you." She huffs and puffs, doing battle with stick and legs and hands, until she's managed to sit herself down. Sophie brings the mugs across and puts them on the table before sliding into the opposite chair. There are white spots floating on the surface of the tea.

Virginia pushes the photo across the table and something seems to loosen inside the girl, the way it did in the attic when she first caught sight of the view. She picks the photo up, careful not to mar it with fingerprints. Silver jumps up and starts treading circles on Sophie's lap, and she pushes his tail out of her face.

"Your Granddad Theo took that picture," says Virginia. "May 1941. The little girl is me."

"Oh!" Sophie stares hard at the girl with skinny plaits and a Peter Pan collar. She doesn't say, *Weren't you pretty,* just to be polite; instead she says, "You look very intense." Virginia tries to resent it but she can't.

"OK," says Sophie. "So that's you on the left. And of course I recognize Great-Granddad Max in the middle, and then, on the right . . . that's the woman in the wedding photo, isn't it? Your adoptive mother?"

"Lorna. Yes."

Sophie keeps looking at the photo.

"Is that a picnic hamper in the bottom corner?"

"Yes."

"It looks cold for a picnic somehow; maybe it's just the way you've got your hands scrunched up inside your sleeves. Are you at a beach?"

"Warren Sands. It's a few miles down the road from here. Your great-granddad took us in his car."

"That's nice. I love old photos. Everything looks so . . . like something out of a film. All the old-fashioned clothes and hairdos."

Virginia knows where Sophie's eye is drawn, and she's tempted to say it for her, but she waits. A hush falls over the table as the child keeps on staring. They ought to have the light on, really. The daylight is failing and it's making them both monochrome, like the figures in the photo.

"Great-Granddad Max has his arm around your mother's waist," Sophie remarks, bashfully. She turns the picture in her hands, and Virginia leans forward to inspect it, as if this is news to her. The sunlight is making Lorna squint, giving her smile a mischievous slant. She is leaning into Max, and his hand is sliding, like the head of a snake, across her back and over the belt of her jacket.

"Hmm." Virginia nods. She watches closely as Sophie takes the photo back for another long look.

"So they had an affair?" she asks, in the end, scandal-hungry. "I kind of guessed it would be something like that. What happened?"

"An *affair*?" Virginia bridles at that. "No, it wasn't an affair. Quite apart from anything else, they were both widowed by then. Or at least . . ."

No, *widowed* will do. She doesn't like it, because Clem was never exactly dead, but it serves a purpose. It discourages awkward questions.

"Oh." Sophie is disappointed for a moment. Her face softens and she grows wistful. "They look so quaint."

"Quaint," Virginia echoes. She takes the photo out of Sophie's hands and studies Deering's face properly for the first time in seventy-odd years. She's struck by the fact that he doesn't have any whites to his eyes. Presumably it's a trick of the shadows, but it's as though his eyeballs were black through and through, without so much as a pinprick of light to give them life.

Virginia looks at herself across the years, and the eleven-year-old looks right back. She isn't smiling — then or now — but there's something complicit about the child's gaze that makes the old woman nod. Lorna, she notes, is smiling — but tightly, with her lips closed. Max is baring his teeth at the camera.

". . . and so in love," Sophie adds.

Old Virginia locks eyes with young Vi and smiles slightly. *Quaint and in love.* Oh, this is going to be easy after all. No need for qualms. The person sitting at the kitchen table is nothing but a Deering — a Deering with a smile and a soft voice, clever but not-so-clever-as-she-thinks, charming and well-bred and hateful — and it's such a relief. Such a relief, not just to have this long-awaited revenge, but to want it. Oh, this is more like it. This is how it's meant to feel. Justice doesn't have a flavor, but revenge bubbles up like blood from Virginia's lungs and floods her mouth with a coppery tang. She's careful, this time, not to say the word out loud.

"In love?" Her voice has gone gravelly, but she doesn't clear her throat.

"Oh, but there must have been more to it, to make him leave the village and everything," Sophie protests. The quaint love story is starting to pall; she's after something more gutsy. "What happened? They can't just have fallen out. He didn't murder her, did he?"

Silver has settled on the girl's lap now; Virginia can see the tips of his ears above the table's edge, and hear his purr. She takes a sip of tea while she thinks, but she has to spit it straight back into the mug. It tastes sour. The milk must be off.

"He *didn't,* did he?" Sophie's voice has gone all whispery and she's stopped stroking the cat. This time she's not going to flit straight to her next question. You can tell. This time she's going to wait for an answer.

Virginia takes her time. She pulls herself up and wheezes over to the sink, where she pours her tea away. There's no view through the kitchen window, with its grimy curtain of sweat, so she doesn't look up. She doesn't have to see the marsh to know it's there. It's present in the creeping darkness and the failing colors and the droning wind.

"You're right," she agrees. "There was more to it than that."

She can feel Sophie's gaze on her back, like an itch she can't reach, and her shoulders shift uncomfortably. She runs some water into the kettle, just for something to do, and empties it again. She sets the kettle down on the sideboard.

"The thing is," she says, "it's not really something I can tell you."

"Oh, *please!*"

Silver objects to the plaintive rise of Sophie's voice. He jumps off her lap and starts making up to Virginia instead, rubbing her knotty ankles with his forehead.

When she pushes him away with her stick, he nudges that instead and purrs.

"What I mean is, it's not something I can *tell* you. It's something I have to show you."

"Oh. OK." That's stumped the girl. She doesn't know what to ask next. *Where? Why? What?* In the end she goes for the latter.

"What do you have to show me? Sorry, I don't understand."

Virginia glances up at the window — not for the view, but for the blur of her guest's reflection. She wishes she hadn't asked her name when they first met this morning. It confuses things. She keeps thinking of her as Sophie now, whereas she would like to be able to think of her as simply *the girl* or, even better, *the Deering girl.*

"You can manage a walk this evening, can't you?" she asks. "You feel well enough now?"

"Oh yes, I'm fine. But . . . a walk? Where to? I don't really know —"

Silver jumps onto the sideboard and starts dabbing with his paw at the Go-Cat bag. He chirrups as Virginia reaches for his bowl.

"I can't tell you anything else." Virginia's hands fall still as she concentrates on what she's saying; on trying to make her voice sound roguish and enticing. Silver yowls

240

and butts his head against the empty bowl. "It's a short walk. Perhaps a couple of miles? It'll be better if I show you. Clearer."

That's an outright lie, of course. Virginia pictures the weave and whirl of tide and sand, foam and wind, solidity and void. She pictures the points of the compass falling in on themselves and disappearing under the snow-flecked mud. Clarity is one thing Sophie Deering will not find two miles out on Tollbury Marsh.

"It'll be dark soon," the girl objects, "and you were wanting to eat."

The cat biscuits chink into the metal bowl. Silver thrusts his head under Virginia's arm and starts to gobble before she's finished pouring.

"Oh, we can walk there in the dark." She tries to sound offhand. "I've got a flashlight, and I can lend you a coat and some boots."

Of course the child will refuse. She'll say she's not *that* curious, not *that* stupid, and then she'll walk away intact. Nothing can stop her. Virginia looks down at her own twisted hands. The skin is so thin, the veins so blue, the bones so light. They could be the hands of a ghost. How can she make anyone to do anything? Virginia grips the edge of the sink with both hands. She's going to faint. She's going to be sick. She's going to die on her own kitchen floor, watched over by a Deering.

She leans against the cupboard and listens to the fluttering of her own pulse. She draws a careful breath, and then another, and then another. The blurry girl in the window is uncrossing her denim legs and rubbing her palms uneasily over her knees.

"OK then," she's saying. Her voice sounds remote, as if she's speaking through a telephone. "Why not? I'm up for it."

May 1941

During January and February Virginia had made steady progress — a few more yards each time — but it had ended in mid-March, the day she lost her shoe. The mud had pulled on her foot, really pulled, like something willful and alive, and although she'd freed herself without much difficulty she still remembered the slow, sucking relish with which it had swallowed her left shoe. In retrospect, she supposed she ought to have knelt down and tried to fish it out again, but she was glad she hadn't. There was a dark pleasure to be had from imagining her familiar brown sandal, with its fraying strap and buckle, as it sank, mile by fathomless mile, through the ooze. Maybe that's what Tollbury Marsh wanted in return for Clem — sacrifice. She gave up the other sandal on the same day for good measure, tossing it into the water with an overarm throw, and a week later she left a hair ribbon fluttering under a stone. But there were only so many things she could offer up. Lorna hadn't been cross about the lost shoes — hadn't paid much attention, in fact, to Virginia's carefully contrived explanation — but it had still meant a trip to town, and expense.

Today Virginia wore her winter coat on top, as usual, in case Lorna spotted her leaving the house. She didn't remove it until she reached the old harbor steps, and even then she unbuttoned reluctantly, with furtive glances to left and right. This was the worst part of the whole process — worse than losing her shoe — but it had to be done.

Virginia folded the coat and laid it on top of the wall. She looked down at her dress and gave the hem a tug. It had looked all right when she was ten; she hadn't minded wearing it to the school concert last Easter. Even in December — on the fateful day of Theo's party, when it had remained safe and snug inside the wardrobe — it was still halfway decent. But she'd had a growth spurt since then, and the red dress wasn't meant to have breasts inside it — not even small ones. It wasn't that sort of dress. Wearing it was anguish: worse than any physical pain she could imagine. But that was the point.

She gave the dress a final tug and started down the steps. The marsh was playing all innocent this morning, making out it had no secrets. There were still a few veils of mist drifting over the ground, but wherever they parted she glimpsed streaks of gold, which must have been water but looked like pure light. A skylark was hovering and singing, too high up to see, and the wind — such as it was — came and went, touching Virginia's skin and toying with her hair. In some ways she preferred the marsh in a drearier mood, when the wind cut across her bare legs and the waters were as dull as lead. At least then she felt as though she was doing something dangerous; something that deserved a return.

She walked quickly to begin with, because the first quarter mile was familiar and no longer frightening. If Virginia had still been given to laughing, she could have laughed at the memory of her first forays, back in January: how she'd paused to test the ground between every step, and raced back to the wall with her heart in her mouth after half a dozen paces. These days she strode through the periphery, pushing through the stiff, knee-high grass, impatient to reach the danger zone.

When the turf became thinner and spring-
ier Virginia began to slow and look back
toward the wall, and feel how far she was
from safety. She would stop, force herself
on, stop again — frightened by the gushing
of waters she couldn't see and conscious
that her soles were starting to leak. *One
more step,* she'd dare herself. *One more. Till
that post comes level with the church tower.
Till you can dip your hand in that channel of
water. Till you've stood with both feet on that
strip of sand.*

The wreck of the Messerschmitt had disappeared long ago, sucked into the sands a
day or two after the crash. Some of the girls
at school swore that the German airman's
ghost stalked the marsh at night — blond
and brutishly handsome — and Virginia was
inclined to believe it. There were whispers,
too, about the ghost of Clement Wrathmell,
but she blocked her ears against them.

She got as far as the dead seagull before
her nerve ran out. It was exactly the same
distance as she'd made four days ago — no
more, no less. The seagull had been plump
and white on Tuesday morning, and now it
was stinking and crawling with flies.

Virginia crouched down as close as she
dared, careful not to breathe through her

nose. The gull was lying on the edge of a stagnant pool with its neck awry and its left wing splayed like a broken fan. Virginia thought about the Romans — they'd been doing the Romans at school this term — and the priests who studied birds as a way of interpreting the will of the gods. *Augurs,* they were called. She picked up a stick and gave the carcass a tentative poke. The flies rose, briefly. One of the gull's wings flopped open at a wider angle and its body sank a little farther into the mud.

Virginia walked back with her head down. By the time she'd noticed Mr. Deering it was too late to pretend otherwise: he'd caught and held the sharp glance that she reserved, ever since Clem's disappearance, for any man in a trilby hat. She toyed with the idea of avoiding him, but it was pointless. He was sitting on the wall by the steps, and that was the only way off the marsh between Salt Winds and Tollbury Point. Besides, she needed to fetch her coat.

He was sitting on it, though; using it as a cushion while he smoked his cigarette and squinted at the view. When he waved, her first instinct was to cover her chest with her arms; her second to pull the red dress as low over her knees as it would go. Her third instinct was to stop fidgeting and get the encounter over with.

"You're up early," he shouted when she was in earshot, but he wasn't looking at her face in a conversational way. He was contemplating the dress. He stared at it very seriously, like an artist trying to get to grips with his subject matter, and as he stared he pulled fiercely on his cigarette. Virginia glanced left toward Salt Winds, knowing full well that they weren't visible from the attic at this angle. Perhaps she should have brought Bracken with her. She might have done, if his waggings and snufflings had been compatible with her ritual.

Virginia fixed her gaze slightly to the left of Mr. Deering's face, on the slick curve of the car's black hood.

"Can I have my coat please?" she asked, holding out her hand as she climbed the steps. It came out like one, rapid, breathy word — *canivmycoatpls* — and she expected him to laugh at her, but he didn't even smile.

"My coat," she repeated. "Can I . . . ?" Mr. Deering moved, but slowly, as if it was a gross inconvenience. He stubbed his cigarette on the wall with a long sigh, uncrossed his legs, and — eventually — shuffled sideways. He hadn't teased her yet;

there'd been no lingering handshake or *How do you do, Miss Wrathmell.* She risked a quick glance at his face as she unfolded the coat. Maybe it was just the early morning light, but she felt as if the usual shine was lacking. His moustache looked as though it was made of hair rather than lacquer.

"I'll drive you home," he announced, sliding down from the wall as she pushed her arms into the sleeves. He didn't ask what she'd been doing out on the marsh, or say how long he'd been watching.

"Oh no, that's all right," she mumbled. "Thanks all the same." Even he must realize it was a silly offer, given that the front door was a two-minute walk away.

"Just get in."

He made it sound as if she'd been trying his patience for hours on end and he'd reached the end of his tether. The bones seemed to melt inside Virginia's fingers, and she gave up trying to fasten her buttons. She couldn't have opened the car door if she'd tried, so perhaps it was just as well he did it for her. She perched on the edge of the front seat and adjusted her coat so that she wouldn't have to feel the leather against her bare calves.

Mr. Deering threw himself into the driver's side with a groan and felt inside his breast pocket for a fresh cigarette. After it was lit he let the match burn all the way down to his fingertips before tossing it out of the window. Virginia thought he was bound to switch the engine on after that, but he just leaned back in his seat and shut his eyes, the cigarette drooping from his lips. She looked down the lane toward Salt Winds, with its peeling walls and high windows. She could have been there by now, if she'd walked. She could have been there two or three times over.

Mr. Deering was breathing so evenly he might have been asleep. Virginia glanced at the door handle. She knew the clunk it would make when she opened it and wasn't sure she had the nerve. She swallowed noisily and made the calculations in her head. Two seconds to open it, another two to push herself forward and leap into the lane —

Something landed on her leg, just above the knee. She looked down. Mr. Deering's fingers were moving up the softest part of her thigh as lightly as a spider's legs, keeping time to a tune that only he could hear. Her eyes darted to his face. He was still leaning back in his seat, and his eyes were closed, except for a razor-thin glint. The cigarette was burning up in his mouth and crumbling over his shirtfront. She didn't look down again, but she could picture his hand very clearly in her mind, and the signet ring he was wearing on his little finger. Every now and then she felt the metal brush against her warm skin.

"It's Lorna's birthday next week," he remarked. She looked straight ahead and said nothing.

"Do you know how old she'll be?"

Virginia shook her head, imperceptibly.

"Thirty." Mr. Deering spat a shred of tobacco onto his thumb and flicked it out of the window. He stopped drumming his fingers and let them rest on her inner thigh, quite casually, as if his thoughts were elsewhere.

"I don't know what she thinks she's playing at, at her age. I presume she's aware that any man with taste . . ." He laughed sharply and his thumb traced a circle on Virginia's skin. "Perhaps she thinks she's immune to the ravages of time? I wonder. But don't tell me she's saving herself for Clem. Not after five months."

Virginia shivered and managed to inch away, pulling her coat tight across her chest and legs. Mr. Deering let go of her abruptly and discarded his half-smoked cigarette.

"Tell her we're going for a picnic today at Warren Sands," he said. "All four of us.

Theo's home for the long weekend, and he deserves a treat. Tell her I don't care if she's got a headache or a bellyache or whatever else it is; I'm coming with the car at ten."

"Virginia? That you?"

"Yes."

Lorna was leaning over the landing rail, on her way upstairs with the breakfast tray. Her hair was knotted inside a scruffy scarf and she was wearing Clem's gardening shirt over her slacks — the shirt that still smelled of pipe tobacco and bonfires. It had been frayed but clean when Clem wore it last autumn, but now there were splashes of color all over the sleeves and down the front.

Lorna leaned sideways and peered past Virginia's head. "*Just* you?"

"Yes."

A quick heat washed over her, but Lorna couldn't have seen Mr. Deering, let alone the goings-on in his car. She wouldn't have sounded so blithe if she'd had him in mind. She was just being cautious.

"Could you bring the teapot up? I've got my hands full with this tray."

Lorna carried on along the landing, and there was a rattle of plates and cups as she hooked the attic door open with her foot.

"Virginia?" She had to shout now to be

heard. "Bring a plate and cup for yourself as well."

The brown teapot was on the kitchen table, sunlit steam coiling from its spout. Virginia frowned at it while she buttoned up her coat. Then she grabbed it by the handle and followed Lorna upstairs.

Jozef was winding a new sheet of paper into the Underwood as Virginia entered the attic, but he paused to look up at her and smile. Back in January, he'd asked if she'd mind him using Clem's typewriter, and she'd said it was fine. After all, he might as well; it wasn't sacred or anything. Clem used to call the Underwood *an infernal machine* and preferred to write all his notes and first drafts by hand with a fountain pen. Virginia could see him now, hunched grumpily over his desk, jabbing at the keys with his index fingers. Jozef typed like a concert pianist, with his eyes on his hand-written notes, and when Virginia was in the right mood she enjoyed watching him at work. So there was no good reason to start minding now.

Lorna had set up two trestle tables in the attic — the kind that decorators use for wallpapering — and arranged them in an L shape so that she and Jozef could confer while keeping their work spaces separate. Jozef sat on a kitchen chair with a stack of paper, an ashtray, a pencil, and the typewriter to hand. Lorna didn't have a chair; she roamed the floor while she worked, or perched on the edge of the trestle amid a chaos of rollers, rags, gouges, woodblocks, and ink bottles. She'd slung a clothesline across the room, from eave to eave, where she pegged out her finished and half-finished prints — the mermaids with seaweed hair, the walking trees, the flying ships, the canny-looking birds and animals.

The attic was a studio from dawn till dusk. Jozef's living quarters — the old mattress, a rickety settee, and a rocking chair — got pushed back against the wall while he and Lorna worked. The jam jar was still standing in the round window where Virginia had put it on New Year's Eve, but she was forbidden to light the candle anymore. A dead bluebottle lay on top of the hardened wax with its folded legs in the air.

Virginia put the teapot down on Jozef's table, since there was no room on Lorna's, and sat on the edge of the rocking chair with her feet flat on the ground. She hunched her back and shivered, despite the sunshine, and tried to pull her coat closer, especially where it parted at the collar and the knee.

The grown-ups ate hungrily but distractedly, absorbed by their work. Jozef poured the tea because Lorna's hands were covered in printer's ink; even her wedding ring was black. Virginia stared at them as if they were characters in a film whose lives she could watch and wonder about, but never enter into. At one point Jozef said, out of the blue, "You are sure, then, about the story of the talking fish?" and Lorna replied, "Hmm," and he said, "Perhaps we have to think about this again?"

Lorna never seemed to know when Virginia was watching her, but Jozef did. When he'd finished his breakfast he came and sat on the mattress so that they were face-to-face: her staring down from the rocking chair and him smiling up.

"It's good you have come upstairs," he said. "We've just finished another story, so —"

"*Nearly* finished," Lorna interrupted. She was peering at an inky woodblock and picking a splinter from one of the grooves with her fingernail. "Hang on. I just have to do this, and then I've one more layer, and then I'm done."

"All right, *ja,*" Jozef corrected himself. "We have *nearly* finished. So we are needing the expert eye of our chief critic. Isn't that so?"

"Mmm?" Lorna looked up blankly and caught Jozef's eye. "Oh yes," she agreed, in a show of enthusiasm. "Indeed we do! In fact, Virginia, why don't you read it now? And I'll show you the illustrations afterward, just as soon as I get this . . . sorted out." She broke off for a gulp of tea, leaving black fingerprints on the mug handle. There were smudges on her forehead as well, where she'd pushed the hair away from her eyes and tried to tuck it under the scarf.

Jozef stood up to fetch the papers. Virginia said, "I met Mr. Deering in the lane just now."

When the light drained from Lorna's face, Virginia experienced a split-second of pleasure. She looked away toward the marsh, although the sun was dazzling and she couldn't see a thing.

"He wants to drive us out to Warren Sands for a picnic. He said to be ready by ten."

She felt as though she'd dragged Lorna back from make-believe; back onto the real-life side of the cinema screen where the audience sat. Jozef was left alone behind the glass, reciting lines from a script.

"Why don't you tell him no?" he kept saying. "Why do you have to go if you don't want to? He can't force you."

Lorna didn't reply, except by shaking her head slowly and wiping her hands on a rag, finger by inky finger.

Theodore had brought his camera. He sat next to Virginia in the back seat of the Austin 12 and clicked the lens cap off and on with an expert frown. When she failed to show any interest he started yakking on about shutter speeds and daylight-loading cassettes. Virginia closed her eyes and leaned her forehead against the bumping window. She felt sick.

The conversation in the front of the car was similarly one-sided.

"Do you miss me when I'm in London? Lorna?"

"Of course I do."

"What about these headaches you keep having, every time I happen to call round?"

"Mmm?"

"All right now?"

"Oh yes."

Lorna was wearing a gray skirt and jacket, with pearls and gloves and a hat, but she seemed fidgety, as if those smart clothes no longer fitted as well as they used to. She kept twisting her skirt at the waist and scratching her wrists. Virginia wondered how clean her fingers were now. She'd scrubbed at them for ages, standing over the basin in her slip with one eye on the clock, but printing ink was difficult to remove.

Theodore put the camera back in its case and hung it around his neck.

"So what did you bring for the picnic?" he demanded.

"What?" Virginia couldn't pretend an interest in the view because there wasn't one, but she didn't bother to turn and face him.

"I thought your mother might have put something toward the picnic, that's all. My father got Cook to pack shrimps and boiled eggs and things like that; the hamper's in the boot. There's champagne for them, as well. You and me have got ginger beer."

Champagne? Virginia frowned, but she made herself stay put, lolling indifferently, with the glass cold against the tip of her nose.

"He didn't say to bring anything."

Theo huffed derisively and folded his arms across his chest. She watched his reflection flicker through a blur of leaves and cow parsley.

"The Women's Institute met at Thorney Grange the other night," Mr. Deering was saying. "The village hall was double booked, so I offered them the use of my drawing room."

"Oh?" Lorna plucked at the creases in her sleeves. That jacket had been stuck at the back of the wardrobe for months on end and there hadn't been time to iron it. All Lorna's smartest clothes seemed to be in need of washing or mending; as of this morning they formed a panicky heap on the floor of her bedroom. The gray outfit had been the best of a bad lot.

"I got chatting to some of the ladies after they'd finished." Max laughed lightly and glanced at his moustache in the rearview mirror. He'd done something to it since Virginia saw him on the lane; it was all slick and straight again. "I gather you've said no to taking on an evacuee?"

Lorna crossed her arms with a shrug, but Mr. Deering was content to wait for an answer, and he had a way of making silences ache. After a while she said, quietly, "I've got Virginia to think of. Just because Salt Winds is large, that's not everything. Clem didn't exactly leave us well off."

Max read — or pretended to read — intimacy in her soft tone. He took his left hand (tanned and polished now, in a driving glove) off the steering wheel and squeezed her fingers hard. If she flinched at all, she recalled herself quickly, and when he carried her hand to his lips she didn't resist.

"Well, you know what the answer to that is," he whispered. He didn't exactly kiss Lorna's cotton gloves; rather he ran them over his lips and gently nibbled them, and when he caught Virginia's eye in the mirror he smiled.

He parked the car in a sheltered spot beside the road and they straggled over the dunes to the beach, laden with rugs and baskets. The easterly wind was picking up, and when they emerged in sight of the sea it flew at them, throwing sand and sunlight in their eyes. The tide was way out, and acres of hard, wet shore glinted between them and the first line of breakers. The only person in sight was a dog walker, who marched briskly with her hands in her pockets and her collar turned up, and threw stones for her collie. Bracken would have been in his element, but Mr. Deering wouldn't allow animals in his car.

Virginia's shoes were packed tight with sand by now, but she intended to keep them on. Thank goodness it wasn't picnic weather and she didn't look out of place in her woolen stockings and calf-length skirt. Theo was wearing shorts and his legs were already pimpling with cold.

They spread a tartan rug among the dunes and weighed it down with stones and Theo's cricket stumps. Virginia couldn't catch a ball and wasn't sure how to hold a cricket bat, and she foresaw an interminable afternoon. The grown-ups would tell them to run off and play, and Mr. Deering would watch from the picnic rug, laughing into his champagne while Virginia sweated and swiped at thin air. She couldn't even look forward to lunch, and how often did she get the chance to eat potted shrimps and ginger beer? Especially nowadays, with Mrs. Hill gone and Lorna no ace with the rations.

"You children keep an eye on things," Mr. Deering said, pulling Lorna's arm through his. She was shivering inside her thin jacket and trying to pretend she wasn't. "We're going for a walk. No pilfering the sandwiches while we're gone." Lorna shot a quick glance back over her shoulder, and then she was led away through the soft foothills, her arm squashed into his side.

Virginia huddled on the edge of the rug and watched the collie chasing through the distant waves and pouncing on another stone. What was the meaning of Lorna's glance just now? Supplication? Apology?

Collusion? Virginia wasn't sure, but she felt she ought to know. She laid her cheek on her knees and looked left to see if the pair were still visible, but they'd disappeared, their shapeless footprints indistinguishable from all the other dips and dimples in the sand. Virginia kept staring at the emptiness, wanting Lorna to be all right.

Theo was trying to make a heap of sand, but it was too soft for castle-building and the sides kept collapsing in thin streams. He stamped his efforts out and stood in the ruins with his hands in his pockets, squinting out to sea.

"We're going to be brother and sister," he remarked, his mouth puckering as if the words tasted bad. "What do you make of that?" When she didn't answer straightaway, he turned to look at her, his right foot kicking at the loose sand. He had the advantage over her — standing so tall with the sun behind his head.

"I don't know what you're on about."

"They're going to get married, aren't they." Theo nodded toward the dunes. It wasn't a question.

Virginia dug her fingers down in search of warmth, but it was dank and cold beneath the sand.

"They are not!" she snorted. "Anyway,

Lorna couldn't, even if she wanted to. She's still married to Clem."

Theo jingled the coins in his pocket and smiled at the horizon, like a man of the world.

"She'll marry him all right," he said definitely. "My father says she needs him more than he needs her. He says she can't support herself — let alone the two of you — on the pittance Wrathmell left behind."

My father says. Virginia clutched fistfuls of sand and glared straight ahead. Theo began pacing up and down the length of the rug and his legs kept flashing past her eyes: his white, skinny, goose-bumped little boy's legs.

"I don't care what your father says." The tremor in Virginia's voice was an effect of the easterly wind; she hoped Theo realized that. "Lorna will never say yes to him. She'll never say yes to anyone. Ever. How can she?"

They watched the collie gallop out of the sea and shake itself, shedding water like sparks of light. Its owner called and it streaked to her side, a flash of black and white. Theo continued to smile his private smile.

"She will, you know," he said. "She owes him."

"*Owes* him? How —"

"And anyway. You can tell she'll say yes by the way she acts around him."

Virginia raised her eyebrows as if this was too, too funny. "You think my mother is spoony about your father? *Really?*"

Theo shook his head with a humorless laugh. Despite his shorts and skinny legs and his being four months her junior, he had an unmistakable authority about him, as if he knew things she couldn't hope to understand.

"Not that she is *actually* your mother," he said. "And anyway, that wasn't what I meant."

All along the dunes, the marram grass bent and rustled in the wind. It sounded like someone screwing up bits of paper, and put her in mind of Jozef and the typewriter.

"Darling? Show the children."

That was the first thing Mr. Deering said when he brought Lorna back to the rug. She'd lost her hat and several pins, and her hair was gritty with sand.

"Darling?" Mr. Deering didn't like having to repeat himself.

Lorna opened her fist and the children peered, obligingly, into her black glove. It was a ring; a gold band crusty with emeralds and diamonds. Theo said, "Why aren't you wearing it?"

"Oh, well I haven't —" Lorna began. "At any rate, not till Clem's been gone a year. At least a year . . ." Max caught her eye and she stopped.

"It's a bit small," he explained to the children, closing Lorna's fingers over the ring. "But we can have it altered."

Theo tugged the camera from its case, on a sudden impulse, and squinted at them through the viewfinder. He lowered it again to uncap the lens and twiddle a dial.

"Good idea, Theo," said his father. "Come on, girls."

He drew them to his side and put his arms around their waists: a game hunter posing with his trophies. His grip was so tight that they lost their balance and fell against him as if fond, or giddy, or both. Virginia fought for a foothold in the slack sand.

"Come on, Virginia!" Theo shouted. "Smile!"

"Yes," Mr. Deering urged through his teeth. "Smile." His nails jabbed at her sweater, pressing into her flesh, grating against her rib cage. She tightened her jaw and stared at the thin clouds above Theo's head. They could do as they liked, but they weren't going to squeeze a smile from her.

She wanted Mr. Deering to look at the developed photograph and feel uneasy. She wanted him to wonder what had been going through her mind as the shutter clicked.

It was half past eleven. Theodore said he was hungry, but his father told him it was too early for lunch and he'd have to make do with a taste of Moët et Chandon instead.

"What's that?" Theo asked suspiciously.

"Champagne, of course," said his father. "It's not every day a man gets himself engaged."

There may have been champagne and photographs, but it didn't feel like a celebration. Nobody said anything nice; there was no laughter or congratulations. Even when the cork popped and Mr. Deering said "Jolly good show!" he said it satirically, to himself. Virginia swirled the sand with her toe, and when he distributed the glasses she accepted her juvenile portion without a thrill. Mr. Deering didn't announce a toast, but he touched Virginia's glass with his own when the others weren't looking, and winked.

"Pity it's gone a bit warm," he said aloud after his first sip. "It was nicely chilled when I packed it."

It tasted cold to Virginia. Cold as the wind off the sea, and sour.

■ ■ ■ ■

It was four o'clock by the time they got home. Mr. Deering drove all the way down the lane to Salt Winds, but wouldn't come in for tea. He said he was sorry to part from them so early, but he had to take a telephone call at half past. He'd come up tomorrow morning and drive them into town. Wouldn't it be nice to go to the cathedral together for Communion?

Virginia and Lorna stood side by side on the doorstep and watched the car glide away toward Tollbury Point. Once it had disappeared from view and the engine noise had faded, they remained a few minutes more, listening to the wary silence. When Lorna finally turned to unlock the front door, it felt as though she were doing something risky; as though she were unlocking a secret.

Lorna tossed her gloves onto the hall table. She'd succeeded in scrubbing the ink off earlier, but all the same Mr. Deering must have wondered about her skin when he was trying to jam that engagement ring onto her finger. It looked so tough and red these days, and she kept the nails so short and square. They were no longer the hands of the lovely Mrs. Wrathmell; they were a working woman's hands.

"I know what you're thinking," Lorna murmured, with her back to Virginia. She rubbed her eyes wearily and half turned her head. "You want to know why I didn't refuse him? Don't you?"

Virginia shook her head slowly. If she didn't say anything it was because she could hardly admit she was remembering the feel of Mr. Deering's fingers on the inside of her thigh, and how she'd sat so still, and how afraid she'd been at the time of saying, or doing, the wrong thing.

The minute she'd changed out of her gray clothes, Lorna ran up to the attic. Virginia followed as far as the first-floor landing before changing her mind. She stood at the closed door for a minute, listening to the floorboards creaking beneath their feet and their conversation coming muffled through the ceiling, and felt a sort of pity for the rest of the house, which used to be so full of firelight and tobacco smoke and BBC voices.

Through the long summer twilight she loitered in the downstairs rooms, poking about in drawers and cupboards where she had no business, and munching on a wrinkled apple that had kept its sweetness through the winter on the wooden fruit rack under the stairs. The photographs on the dining-room mantelpiece held her attention for a while. She nibbled through the core as she stood tiptoe on the hearth and studied the pictures of Lorna: Lorna in the garden, Lorna on a windy pier, Lorna as a wan bride. It was funny how you could hate and love the same person according to whom they were with, and what they were doing, and even where they were. Virginia tossed the remains for Bracken and he settled down with his paws outstretched, leaning on the skinny core with the side of his mouth as he chewed. There was something about Lorna-in-the-attic that made her angry, though she couldn't say why.

She went upstairs with Bracken and joined them, all the same. It felt like failure, but she needed the company: once night had fallen, life tended to flicker out altogether in the downstairs rooms. Salt Winds was an abandoned house, not a home, and Virginia couldn't redeem it all by herself. She'd had enough of the dust on the table where they used to eat their meals, and the dirty plates gathering in the kitchen sink, and the mail (some of it still addressed to *C. G. J. Wrathmell Esq.*) lying unopened in the hall. At least there'd be light in the attic, and someone to say hello to, even if she could only belong with them fleetingly: an émigré from below.

There was no electric wiring in the attic, but when Jozef and Lorna were working on their fairy-tale book at night (which they did without fail, unless Mr. Deering was expected) the place dazzled, with lanterns hanging from the rafters and candle wax drooling down the sides of bottles. The two of them had flattened out a cardboard box, which they tacked over the window frame in lieu of a blackout curtain. Virginia's defunct candle-in-a-jam-jar made the cardboard bulge outward, very slightly, and she wondered why no one had bothered to throw it away.

There was just a single candle burning tonight. Jozef sat in front of the typewriter, but his arms were hanging down by his sides and he was looking across at the mattress. The candle had been placed in such a way that Lorna's sleeping face shone brightly, leaving the rest of the attic a dusky jumble of blankets, table legs, and discarded papers. She'd obviously been crying; there was a telltale puffiness near her nose and eyelids, and a sticky sheen on her cheek. Jozef's attention didn't shift in Virginia's direction until he heard her whispered greeting, and even then his eyes were slow to refocus.

"I hoped you would come!" he said belatedly, scratching the dog between its ears. Bracken closed his eyes with pleasure, although he didn't lean into Jozef's legs or sit on his feet as he would have done with Clem. "We missed you this evening. We always do, you know."

Virginia made no answer but picked her way across the cluttered floor and sat on the end of the mattress. Bracken slumped down beside her with a grunt. Jozef spoke so gently, as if he owed her a thousand unspecified apologies, and sometimes — in her darker moods — she felt inclined to fulfill his expectation. It was true, she *was* bitter. Not against him, of course — but he was the only person to allow the possibility, and even to expect it.

"How's your book?" she asked, with a patent lack of interest. His white shirtsleeves were rolled up to the elbow, as usual, and baggy near his upper arms. All Clem's clothes were too big for Jozef — even the braces had to be twisted up and knotted — and it ought to have made him ridiculous, but he was one of those people who'd look fine in sackcloth and ashes. It was a pity

Lorna had burned his own things in the beginning, instead of washing and mending them. Somehow, Virginia didn't like to picture Clem coming home and seeing his old clothes put to such elegant use.

"The book is very well, thank you." Jozef had enough enthusiasm for two. "Very well indeed. We're trying to think of a title for it; I think perhaps *The Witch-Princess, and Other Stories,* but maybe this is too simple? I don't know. What do you think?"

He pushed the hair from his eyes and Virginia saw glints of gold where, in flat daylight, there were only browns. When he picked up a sheaf of typed sheets and shuffled them against the tabletop she sat very still and glared at the floor, a picture of indifference. He hesitated before laying the papers down again.

"As for Lorna's prints," he went on, nodding at the squares of paper pegged out beneath the rafters, "they are perfect." He pronounced the word *perfect* as if it barely came close to his meaning, and Virginia looked up, but Lorna's pictures were almost invisible in the dark: abstract whirls of line and shadow curling in the draft.

"But what will you do with it all when you're finished?" She hated herself for pricking and prodding, but she couldn't seem to stop. "I mean, you can't exactly march off to a publisher and say, 'I'm Herr Rosenthal and this is my book,' can you? And if Lorna does it — well. Her *fiancé* might have something to say."

She intended to shock, but Jozef just sighed and leaned back in his chair. Lorna stirred in her sleep and hunched deeper beneath the blankets.

"Who knows?" Jozef said. "Who knows. Maybe it will never be finished."

Virginia rubbed her eyes against her knees. She was surprised by how much she wanted to cry, because she felt angry and not at all soppy. Anyway, she couldn't give way to tears, so that was that. Lorna had got in first. One hysterical female flinging herself facedown on Jozef's mattress was bad enough; two would be verging on comedy. She looked up with a sniff and made her expression hard.

Jozef sat back in his chair with his hands behind his head and contemplated her for a long time. The candle guttered, and waves of gold and black rippled across his face and arms and the front of his shirt.

"One day soon I will write a story just for you," he said. " 'Virginia's Tale.' I think about it a lot, actually."

She wiped her nose against her woolly

knee. Jozef was staring right through her now, right through the attic wall, right into space, his eyes darting and narrowing, as if he glimpsed things there that troubled him.

"I'd like that," she murmured.

Jozef nodded abstractedly to show he'd heard, and pressed his lips together.

New Year's Eve 2015

The baked beans are sweet on her tongue, and hot all the way down to her stomach. Virginia started eating because she needed the strength, but now she's enjoying herself. Even the look of them — vivid orange on blue china — is good, verging on poignant. It's a long time since she's noticed color. It's a long time since she's taken pleasure in food.

Virginia leans in for another forkful and eyes her visitor. Sophie is arranging her beans in a zigzag pattern across the plate and stroking the cat, but she's not doing much eating. It's funny how the Deeringness of the child doesn't leap at you straightaway, even when you know it's there. Sometimes you have to look for it. Those strong bones in her cheeks and nose, for instance, come via a different ancestral strand; Max's nose was much less patrician. Virginia smiles meagerly. How he would have hated that.

"Eat up," Virginia urges. "I thought you said you were hungry?"

Silver is sneaking his front paws onto the table; he'll be licking the plate next, if the girl doesn't push him off. Poor little thing; she needs building up. Don't they feed their children in Putney? Not that Virginia cares — at least not in *that* way. She's just worried that the child will come over all faint with nothing inside her, and give up on the walk before they've even left the lane. They'll have to go a fair way out before she can feel sure of victory. How long will it be, she wonders, before Sophie senses danger? How long before she demands to turn back?

"Shoo! Greedy animal!" Virginia flaps her sleeve at Silver and he retreats with poise. Sophie eats a single bean and glances at her watch.

It's started snowing again. It's too dark to see anything through the indigo window — and anyway their reflections are in the way — but Virginia senses it all the same. There's a prickly silence that comes with snowfall, and it's more than just absence of sound. It's heavy. If you put that silence on the kitchen scales, they'd tilt with a loud clang.

Virginia tries to scrape up the last of the sauce with the edge of her fork. She'd run her tongue over the plate if she could, but she has her dignity, even today when worldly perspectives are meant to be falling away. The grimy saucepan is on the table between them, so she scours it with the wooden spoon and licks that instead. She thinks of all the meals she's eaten alone in this kitchen over the years, but the memories merge into one gray lump. It never seemed to matter much, when or what she ate. Her senses were racing ahead to the future: to this moment; to the last day of her life. She's never had time or patience for the present.

Sophie's gaze keeps straying to the window, and she looks as if she wants to say something. Virginia sits up straighter and drops the wooden spoon into the empty saucepan. She needs to get in first, before the girl starts demurring about the walk, or asking to use the telephone, but her mind's a blank. She buries her hands in her lap, taken aback by the tremors in her fingers. What on earth is she going to say about the phone? That it *fell* off the wall?

"I was just wondering . . ." Sophie's fork pauses in midair. "Were you ever married?"

Virginia frowns and blots her lips on a tissue.

"I was married to my work," she answers primly, and immediately wishes that she'd just said *no.* Apart from anything else, it isn't true. She was faithful to her work — for better, for worse, for richer, for poorer: all that and more — but romance never came into it.

"Oh." Sophie nods slowly. Now that she's got something to ponder she begins to eat, albeit slowly, forking up the gloopy beans and pushing the toast to the edge of her plate. Virginia wonders whether to bother qualifying her answer, and decides against. If they must talk about the past, she'd rather talk about work than anything else.

"But weren't you just a secretary or something?" Sophie has the grace to go pink about the ears as soon as the words are out, and Virginia can't bring herself to mind. It's childish plain-speak, not cruelty.

"I traveled the world," she retorts, dabbing at the corners of her mouth. "I was useful to the people who needed me . . ." It's meant to be a long list of justifications, but she struggles to think of anything else.

"Oh, but . . ." The pinkness spreads across Sophie's cheeks. "But you can't just go around being *useful* all the time, and doing what other people want! I mean, what about *you*? Didn't you want to — I don't know —

278

like, make your own mark on life?"

The more excited Sophie gets, the faster she eats. In a few moments her plate is empty, except for the soggy squares of toast she's pushed to one side.

Virginia stares coldly. "My life has been quite satisfactory, thank you very much." *Typical Deering.* Virginia tries to whip herself up into a rage, because it is typical Deering behavior, this elbowing in on other people's lives. This judging and censuring and reorganizing. It is right, right, *right* that Sophie should suffer for the sins of her fathers. Virginia pictures her in the beam of a failing flashlight — wet, muddied, and weeping — and refuses to flinch.

Sophie glances up. "What? Oh no, no, I didn't mean —" She trails off. The fact is, she'd been addressing herself. The old woman on the other side of the table is of marginal interest; she has her own career in mind. Sophie is full of the future — full to overflowing — and it makes her eyes gleam and the rings on her fingers flash. Virginia lays her fists on the table and uncurls them with a sigh.

"You sound like Lorna," she mutters, without expecting to be heard or understood. "She was always telling me to spread my wings."

"Yes, exactly!" Sophie is suddenly gleeful, and she reaches out to press the old woman's hand. "That's it! We have to spread our wings!"

Virginia glances through the window at the tumbling darkness, and wonders whether to explain that up until now her life has been all about waiting; about filling in the time as best she can. She decides not to. Sophie won't understand. She'll just say, *How do you mean? Waiting for what?* And anyway, they shouldn't be sitting about chatting. They should be getting ready to go.

The cat yowls as Sophie slides him off her lap and stands up. Virginia tenses, wondering what she's after now, worrying about the mangled telephone — but it's all right. She's just gathering up the plates. Good.

"Pass me that notepad on top of the microwave, would you? And a pen. There should be a couple of pens lying about. Thank you."

Sophie does as she's told and Virginia begins to write on the first page: *Flashlight, stones, manuscript.* This is better. This is more like action. Sophie drops the dirty cutlery into the sink and opens cupboards in search of washing-up liquid. She doesn't ask for directions; she just acts. When she finds there's no hot water in the tap, she boils up the kettle.

Virginia finishes her list and smooths a shaky hand over a fresh page. She's known she'll have to leave a note for Joe. You can't close a life — not even a life like hers — without tying up the odd loose end.

Salt Winds
31.12.15
Dearest Joe,

It's a confident start, but that's because it's been years in the planning. This is her one chance to tell him, in so many words, that she loves him, and if he's embarrassed . . . well. Too bad. At least she won't be there to see his face. What comes next, after *Dearest Joe*? So many nights she's written and rewritten this note in her head, and now she can't remember how it goes.

When she looks up the sink is brimming with suds and Sophie is taking off her jacket. Virginia can see the pinkish glow of the girl's back through the white gauze shirt. She shivers inside her dressing gown as Sophie rolls up her sleeves.

Dearest Joe, my own little brother,

The saucepan slips out of Sophie's hands,

281

into the sink, with a slosh. Virginia looks up again. Perhaps she should tell Joe that she's not gone on her own. She doesn't want to tell him because he won't understand, but it feels wrong to make no mention at all. It reduces her own farewell to half a story.

Virginia forces her eyes back to the paper. Sometimes, when she's writing this note in her mind, she moves herself to tears. She's not moved now.

> Dearest Joe, my own darling little brother,
> I have decided to leave this world for good,
> but before I do I wish
> I wish to assure you
> I wish to tell you how much
> I want you to know

Of course, the girl's disappearance will be all over the news. Virginia rests her chin on her thumb and resists the temptation to look up again. How long will it take them — the police, the press, the Deering family — to link Sophie with Tollbury Marsh? Perhaps they never will. Why should they? Virginia nibbles her thumbnail and reads what she's put so far. She screws it up, stuffs it in her pocket, and starts again.

Joe — the cat will need feeding now I'm gone. Take him home with you, if it's easier. There's a new bag of Go-Cat by the front door and a box of pouches. He prefers the fish-flavor ones, as you know, though I like to shake things up occasionally! Very best wishes, Virginia

She folds it hastily, not bothering to line the edges up, and scrawls *JOE* across the top. She places it in the middle of the table, where he'll spot it straightaway, and weighs it down with one of the stones she pocketed last night. Good. That's one job done. What next? She glances at her list.

"Sophie?" It's the first time she's addressed the girl by name, and she falters self-consciously so that the syllables fail to link as fluently as they should. "When you've finished, would you go to the cupboard under the stairs and find yourself a coat? There should be some boots there too." They'll never make any progress if the child isn't properly dressed to begin with.

The plug gurgles as Sophie squeezes the dishcloth and spreads it over the side of the sink. She crosses the room, light in her ballet slippers, skipping over the stick that's leaning at an awkward angle against the table.

"Yes, sure." She stops at the door, and there's something conciliatory about the way she holds up her hands. "I will. But first I'm going to give my mum and dad a quick ring." She doesn't add *if that's OK,* or *if you don't mind.*

Just wait a moment — that's all Virginia intends to say, but she can't seem to get further than "J . . . Jus . . . Just . . ." When she tries to get up, her stick clatters to the floor. The chair is too far under the table and her frantic feet can't get any purchase on the floor.

"Oh no, don't get up!" Sophie makes that gesture with her palms again, as if gently commanding a dog to sit. "I know where the phone is; I saw it on the landing. I'll be two seconds."

There's nothing for it. Virginia has to sit back and listen as Sophie shuts the kitchen door and fumbles for the light switch in the hall.

August 1941

Virginia was curled up beside the attic window with her book, so she caught the faint crackle and bang from the lane, though she didn't pay it any attention. It couldn't be — for instance — the sound of rolling tires and the slamming of a car door, because who drove down to Salt Winds these days? Mr. Deering did, but rarely at this hour of the morning, and besides, he was supposed to be in London till Friday.

Bracken was asleep on his side, basking in a slice of hot sunlight, and he didn't seem worried either. He twitched in response to the bang, as if a fly had landed on his ear, but he didn't open his eyes. Neither Lorna nor Jozef heard a thing; they were too busy whispering and smoking.

Virginia turned the page, though she wasn't really reading. Clem had given her this book a year ago today; his hands had touched these covers and riffled its very pages. Clem and Lorna had given it, she should say, though the idea was surely his. There'd been a whole set of hardbacks with sprightly pictures on their dust jackets: *Little Women* — the one she was reading now — *Black Beauty, Treasure Island, Five Children and It,* and *The Jungle Book.* And after she'd unwrapped them they'd had tea, as grand a birthday tea as Mrs. Hill could muster, with shortbread and Welsh cakes, and the periwinkle crockery.

If there was a sound from inside the house a couple of minutes later, Lorna's laugh masked it pretty well, though Bracken raised his head. Virginia saw the hairs bristling on his neck and remembered that the front and back doors had been propped open to create a breeze.

And then that silky voice, right at the foot of the attic stairs, calling upward and silencing their chatter.

"Hello?"

Everybody froze, lips parted in midspeech.

"Anybody home?"

Lorna turned her back on Jozef and spread her arms, as if to hide him from view. Then she cleared her throat, tried on a smile, and shouted, "Max! I'm coming! One moment!" Nobody moved, and there was no reply from downstairs. Lorna locked eyes with Virginia and motioned her toward the door.

Yellow spots drifted across Virginia's vision as she felt her way down the stairs and onto the dark landing. She couldn't make Mr. Deering out until he moved across her open bedroom door and became a silhouette against an oblong of pink. She could see her unmade bed over his shoulder, with the pillows plump against the headboard and the sheets all tangled.

"Ah-ha!" She couldn't see his smile, but she could hear it. "The birthday girl!" His hot face touched hers, so that his breath was on her neck, and she thought she'd suffocate in the oily perfume of his hair. Later on, she wondered how he'd managed with two hands, because she distinctly remembered a pressure on the small of her back, and a tight grip on her upper arms, and at the same time her fingers being molded around a square envelope.

"Open it," he murmured, and she began to fumble — all thumbs — with the seal.

There was a card with a picture of an old-fashioned lady standing by a garden gate. Virginia's eyes must have been getting used to the light, because Max had dainty hand-writing and she managed to read the greeting inside. *Dear Virginia,* he'd written. *Happy 12th Birthday to our favorite girl, from Max and Theo.* And then, slipping out of the card, was the photograph — a few square inches of black-and-white gloss — with Max grinning and Lorna squinting and she herself scowling into the sand-blown sunshine. *Warren Sands,* it said on the back. *May 1941.*

"Thank you."

"My pleasure." His lips were wet on the rim of her ear. "Many happy returns." But then there was a clatter of feet on the attic stairs and he drew back, and Lorna's voice came bright and breathless through the gloom.

"Max? Is it you? But I thought you were in London?"

"And yet here I am in Tollbury Point," he retorted, stepping forward to meet her. He picked up her ink-stained hand, as if to kiss it, but dropped it before it reached his lips.

"Virginia and I were having a big clean up in the attic," Lorna babbled, dusting down the front of her shirt. "I know I look a fright! I spilled a pot of paint — she probably told you — and now look at me! Not to worry. I'll go and get changed and we'll take some tea into the garden."

Mr. Deering picked up Lorna's hand again, and opened her palm. The colors of the inks — the greens and blues she'd been using lately — were gray in that half-light. With his forefinger he traced the outline of each spot and spatter, and they waited for him to say something, but he seemed lost in thought.

The ceiling creaked, as though someone in the attic was shifting, ever so carefully, from one foot to another.

"What was that?" Mr. Deering frowned and let go of Lorna's hand. He set his foot on the bottom stair and peered up through the winding shadows.

Lorna and Virginia exchanged a furtive glance. Mr. Deering narrowed his eyes and took another step, and suddenly the staircase was a racket of scrabbling claws and thudding paws as Bracken came bowling down to join them.

"That dog," muttered Mr. Deering. He returned to Virginia's side and Lorna closed the attic door with a flick of her foot.

"Well?" she smiled. "Why don't we go and sit outdoors, since it's such a lovely day? It won't take me a moment to make myself decent."

"Don't trouble yourself." Max's fingers

ran like cold water down Virginia's spine, and she shuddered. "I can't stay. I simply came to wish this one a happy birthday."

"Virginia! Your birthday! Why on earth didn't you remind me?"

All morning the house had rung with Lorna's guilt, and Virginia was sick of it. She'd made the mistake of snapping back at one point, which had made things ten times worse.

"I didn't remind you," she'd said, "because I wanted you to remember by yourself." *Like Clem would have done,* she'd managed not to add.

"Well, we'll have to mark the day somehow," Lorna declared testily, wiping her hands down her shirt. "What do you want to do? You can ask a school friend over for tea, if you like."

"No thanks." Virginia twisted the toe of her shoe against the attic floor and tried to scowl her blushes away. She could feel Jozef's scrutiny, even though he was just a blur in the corner of her eye. He would understand, by the way she said *No,* that she hadn't got any friends — whereas Lorna would think she was just being difficult.

"All right." Lorna had just unscrewed the lids from four ink bottles, but now she replaced them, one by one, with a slam and a twist. "Fine. We'll get the bus into town and you can choose a present. How about that? And I'll take you for afternoon tea at Delafield's, just for good measure. Yes?"

"Yes. Thank you." Virginia tried to sound grateful in the same way that Lorna tried to sound benevolent, and with about as much success.

Lorna ran a lingering hand over her sketches. "Good," she said. "In that case, I'm going to go and have a quick bath and tidy myself up. I'm sorry you can't come too," she added, presumably addressing Jozef, though she was still studying her papers.

Jozef touched her lightly on the wrist. "I'm sorry too. But you'll both have a wonderful time, and you'll tell me all about it later. Yes?"

There wasn't much point in Virginia getting changed, since she didn't own anything smarter than the skirt and blouse she was already wearing. Her hair was tidy but she brushed it anyway, because she had to do something — even if it was just a gesture — toward Getting Ready to Go Out. Once she'd finished she sat on the edge of her bed with the Warren Sands photo in her hands, and listened to the water thundering from the bath taps.

Someone knocked, and she stuffed the photo into her open drawer.

"What is it?" she called, but it was Jozef — not Lorna — who poked his head through the door. Virginia started to her feet. If there was one unwritten rule — one law — in their disorderly realm, it was that Jozef stayed in the attic during daylight hours and didn't venture down until night, once the doors and windows were locked and the blackout curtains drawn.

"I wanted to give you this," he whispered, before she had time to object, and he held out a scroll of papers, tied together with a neat green bow. "Happy birthday!"

She took the scroll with a nervous smile and a glance over his shoulder onto the landing.

"You shouldn't be here," she whispered back. "Does Lorna know?"

Jozef shook his head. "This is a secret for you and me. I finished it last week, and I was wondering when to give it, so your birthday is well-timed."

He waited, eager-eyed, while she undid the bow. The first page read, simply:

"Call of the Curlew"
For Virginia
With all good wishes on her twelfth birth-
day
J.

Virginia looked up. "You wrote a story for me!"

"I said I would."

She sat down again and flicked, damp-fingered, through the pages of type. She couldn't think of what to say. She was over-whelmed.

"Is it really for me? I mean, *just* for me? Nobody else?"

"Nobody else."

Virginia had never known anything like it. At the orphanage they used to hand out useful gifts on birthdays — needle cases or pincushions or notebooks for writing recipes in — and you knew what you were going to get in any particular year, because all the girls received the same thing at the same age. Last year had been different, when Clem bought her all those books, but even *Little Women* and *Treasure Island* — as wonderful as they were — couldn't compare to a story that had been written for her, and her alone.

She looked up at Jozef's expectant face,

293

and down at the bundle of papers. It was like being at the fair and waiting in a line at the fortune teller's stall. She wanted to read straight away and she wanted to procrastinate. She wanted to believe it meant everything; she wanted to believe it meant nothing at all.

"Is it *about* me?"

"Maybe." Jozef smiled. "You'll have to see."

She sifted the pages, and individual words caught her eye like flashes of light from a jewel: *marsh, father, sand, ship, bird.*

By the time she looked up again, Jozef had gone.

"Thank you," she said to the empty air, and then she took a deep breath and began.

Once upon a time, a king lived with his daughter in a castle on the edge of a marsh. It was a windy and desolate spot, but it was home and they loved it. Every morning they would take a telescope to the window in the highest tower and sit for hours, studying the shifting lights on the waters and listening to the cries of the birds, until they understood the marsh as well as they understood their own thoughts . . .

■ ■ ■ ■

"You seem very preoccupied," Lorna remarked, while they were waiting at the bus stop by the church. "What's the matter?"

"I'm fine."

Virginia was thinking about Clem. How many times had she tried to imagine taking hold of his hand, only to be left feeling empty and sad? Today — by some miracle — it had worked, and when she closed her eyes she could feel the rough leather of his palm against hers.

"So this king," *she whispered, stroking the tendons on the back of his hand.* "This king goes out walking one New Year's Eve, and he finds a beautifully carved wooden curlew on the path beside the marsh — in fact he steps on it by mistake and cracks its wing a tiny bit — and he brings it home and gives it to his daughter. But it turns out that this is no ordinary gift."

"No?"

"No! Because the curlew is magic, and it can talk."

"Virginia, what are you *doing*?" Lorna snapped her handbag shut with a loud click. "Are you talking to yourself?"

"No."

"Well, I do wish you'd stand still."

Lorna herself seemed downright nervous, pacing about in front of the bus stop and poking at her hairpins the way she used to do in the old days. Every time a car came puttering along the road from the direction of the Deerings' house she'd seize Virginia by the arm and pull her backward into the shadow of the lych-gate. It was like being in a spy film, Virginia thought distractedly, though she didn't dare say so, even as a joke.

She plucked Clem's sleeve and he smiled down at her.

"What does the magic curlew say?" *he prompted.*

"It tells them that it belongs to an enchanted ship, which is moored on the other side of the marsh. It's desperate to get back there, but it can't fly anymore because of the damage to its wing, and in the end the king agrees to carry it home through the mudflats and treacherous sands. His daughter wants to come too, but he won't let her." *Virginia laid particular stress on the last sentence, and Clem squeezed her hand to show he understood.*

"Virginia? The bus is here."

296

They stood aside for the people getting off. Mrs. Hill was among them, and she met Virginia's eye as she elbowed past, which felt almost — though not quite — like a greeting. Lorna nodded cautiously and murmured, "Afternoon," but Mrs. Hill pretended not to hear.

The sliding window was open over the seat in front, and a lush breeze blew through the bus. Flowering gardens passed them by, and after that — as they left the village behind — hedgerows and ripe fields and overhanging trees. Even when she closed her eyes, Virginia could smell the greens and yellows, and the splashes of sunshine. She was surprised. She associated August, and her birthday, with dust and tiredness; the ugly end of summer.

"The trouble is," *she said, nestling against Clem's side,* "the king and his daughter and the curlew are not the only characters in this story."

"No?"

"No. There's also an evil baron."

"An evil baron? Oh! I should like to hear about him."

Clem bent his head to listen.

"Well, you see, this baron pretends to be

a friend to the king and his daughter, but deep down he's eaten up with envy of them and wants their castle, their lands, and all their possessions for himself. When the king disappears into the marsh with the curlew, and a whole year passes without sight of him, the baron thinks his dreams have come true. There's nobody left to defend the kingdom, except the king's lonely daughter — and there isn't much she can do, all by herself, is there?"

"No, indeed."

Virginia became aware that Lorna was looking at her.

"Are you all right?" she said, in a kindlier tone than before, and Virginia nodded.

Lorna raised her face to the open window and her hair began escaping from its pins, fluttering like ribbons from under the brim of her hat. Virginia thought Lorna would get rattled when she noticed what was happening, but she didn't. In fact, the farther they got from Tollbury Point, the more tranquil she seemed.

"So what happens?" *Clem was nudging her elbow.* "Does the baron get his way?"

Virginia shook her head with a slight smile.

Somebody farther down the bus was sucking on a peppermint; she could smell it on the breeze. It seemed a lifetime ago, although it was only a year and a half, since she'd worried about being sick over her navy coat and Clem had given her a mint from his pocket.

"He nearly does," *she said.* "You feel sure he's going to, but just as he's marching with all his forces to the castle, the girl spies the enchanted ship through her spyglass."

"Oh, so the ship returns?"

"Yes, it comes back right at the end, just when you think it's disappeared forever. As soon as she sees it on the horizon, the girl sets off across the marsh, but the baron chases after her. Dozens of times she falls and sinks and nearly drowns, but at last she reaches the sea — and there's the ship, and the magic curlew calling out her name, and — best of all — her father, leaning over the side to help her on board. The baron is hard on her heels and he reaches out a hand to seize her, but the tides seize him instead, and pull him under the mud."

"Ah-ha! So the evil baron gets his comeuppance?"

"Yes."

"And the king and the curlew have not been drowned, after all?"

"No."

"And the three of them live happily ever after, on board the magic ship?"

"They do."

Clem's hand was warm on her shoulder, like a patch of sunshine through glass.

"Well, I call that a good ending, Vi," *he said.* "A very good ending."

It was nice to doze against the window and think about him for a while — which was odd, because ever since his disappearance, thinking about Clem had been a brutal compulsion, and there'd been nothing nice about it at all. The thought of him was endlessly sad, but today the sadness was tinged with something sweet, like sharp mint tinged with sugar.

They got off the bus before most of the other passengers, because Lorna wanted to walk through the park. Even in the middle of town it felt like a fine day, and the green scent of summer still surrounded them, but now it was mixed up with other smells, like car exhaust, dogs, chip shops, cigarette ends, and hot tarmac. Virginia seemed to see things more vividly than she usually did — she noticed the ducks fighting for tidbits on the pond, and the cornflower sky, and the way Lorna was walking with her shoulders back and her hair blowing, like someone perfectly familiar with happiness. As they turned off into the main street, the park keeper tipped his hat at them and Lorna nodded back with a sort of brimming amusement.

"What a lovely day to have a birthday," she said, taking Virginia's arm as they stopped outside the stationer's shop and studied the window display. "I'm glad we came out, after all."

Virginia suppressed a smile. Lorna didn't usually say things like that; she wasn't one for pleasantries and chitchat — or for taking people by the arm. Virginia felt suddenly proud of her birthday, as if the loveliness of the day were a measure of her own wisdom in choosing to be born in August.

Their eyes roved over notebooks, packets of pencils, labels, paint boxes, bottles of ink, balls of string.

"It's a shame Jozef couldn't come with us," Virginia murmured.

Lorna cupped her hands around her face and pressed them against the window, so as to see more easily through the jostling lights and shadows.

"Maybe we could buy him a present?" Virginia went on. "Just something small, I mean, to make up for not coming." She had a horrible feeling she was saying all the wrong things, without knowing how, but when Lorna turned from the window she was still smiling.

"Good idea. I wish I'd thought of that."

They linked arms again and walked on down the street. The cathedral clock boomed over the medieval rooftops: three o'clock.

"You like him, then?" It seemed such a trivial question, but the way Lorna said it you'd think she was dredging it up from the dark depths of her soul. Virginia wriggled uneasily.

"Yes, of course I do."

"Good. I was only asking."

The bookshop was a few doors down, across the street, and this time they went inside. Virginia hovered uncertainly near the children's section, wondering where to begin, but Lorna took the first volume that came to hand, opened it at random, and read for a couple of seconds before putting it back and taking another. Virginia wished she could keep up with Lorna's excitement; wished she could be sure it was just about blue August skies and sunshine.

"What about this for a birthday present?" Lorna held out a copy of *Black Beauty.* "I used to love this; I was a big fan of horse books at your age."

Virginia hesitated. "You got me *Black Beauty* last year."

"Oh." Lorna grimaced ruefully and put it back. "Sorry."

"I haven't read it yet," Virginia confided, taking another book from the children's shelf and turning it over in her hands. "The horse on the cover puts me off. His eyes are sort of . . . rolling in his bony head, and he's baring his teeth. He looks more like something from the book of Revelation."

Virginia expected to be laughed at, but Lorna gave a sympathetic shiver and said, "You'll have to show me when we get home."

In the end Virginia chose a copy of *The Snow Goose,* and the shopkeeper wrapped it in a paper bag while Lorna rooted in her purse. They returned to the stationer's after that, where they bought a box of editing pencils for Jozef, and then they went to Delafield's for tea.

"It was lovely in here before the war," Lorna whispered, leaning across the table. "Really, it was. Quite posh."

Virginia tried to imagine what Delafield's had been like in the days before rationing and make-do-and-mend. The ghost of the old days was there, right enough; you didn't have to look too hard. The lace curtains were greasy and yellow now, but you knew they'd been frothy white once upon a time; and if the fine bone china was chipped, you could still picture it in its perfection. The old ladies, sipping tea with their hats on, would have sipped just the same before the war, but Virginia couldn't help thinking they'd have looked less tired in those days, and their hats would have sat more plumply on their heads.

She prodded her Victoria sponge experimentally with a fork.

"What do you think of the cake?" Lorna's whisper lowered even further. "It's not too awful, is it? Though it's a shame they didn't manage to mix the egg powder in properly. It sort of . . . clags on the tongue, doesn't it?"

It was true, and Virginia got the giggles. One of the ladies shot her a horn-rimmed glare, but Lorna didn't seem to mind; she was on the brink of laughter too.

They ate another forkful and Lorna said, "Isn't it nice to be away from Tollbury Point for a bit? I love towns. I love the bustle and noise and . . . just the *life* of them."

She paused, waiting for some casual assent, but Virginia busied herself over the last few mouthfuls of cake. She didn't love the town. She loved Salt Winds and the marsh.

"Lorna?" she asked, as she finished. "What's going to happen to you and me? I don't mean today, I mean . . . you know, in the future."

Lorna sat back with a sigh and opened her handbag.

"What's going to happen?" she repeated, rummaging for her cigarette case. "Well, let's see. What's going to happen is that I'm going to become a world-famous illustrator, and everyone's going to want my pictures in their books, and as a result I'll make pots of money and buy a fancy flat in London. Or . . . no, not London. Manhattan." She slung an arm over the back of her chair and smiled through a cloud of smoke. "What about it?"

Virginia moved the cake crumbs about with the tip of her little finger, until they formed a thin line across the plate.

"Manhattan," she echoed, without smiling back.

"Mmm. Or San Francisco. Or both.

What's the matter? I'm being silly; you don't have to look quite so scandalized."

Virginia tried to excise the passion from her face and her voice. "I just . . . I don't ever want to leave Salt Winds."

Lorna narrowed her eyes. "Why not?" Through the smoke she could have passed as a film star — one of the ones who manage to look sharp as a tack and half asleep, both at the same time.

Virginia pressed her teeth together hard and stared at her plate. Lorna reached for the ashtray and tapped her cigarette on the rim.

"Because of Clem?" she said, softening.

Virginia nodded stiffly, but under the table she was knotting her fingers. The bell tinkled over the door as people went in and out. The till rang, voices buzzed, and crockery chinked. One of the waitresses came over with a jug to top up their teapot, and Virginia waited until she was done.

"Why didn't Clem like you being an artist?"

Lorna frowned, but she didn't go mad, or silent. In fact, she placed her elbows on the table and leaned forward, twisting the half-smoked cigarette between her fingers. Ash floated, like tiny flakes of black snow, onto the cloth.

"I think . . ." She leaned forward even farther, until her face was hovering over Virginia's half of the table. "I think Clem thought he'd rescued me from this dreadful bohemian lifestyle, and that I ought to be grateful. Perhaps I thought the same, at first. Well, I did think that. He was my white knight, snatching me from the jaws of failure and loneliness."

Virginia looked up from the plate. "And from the jaws of Mr. Deering."

Lorna began to deny it, but then she sighed and nodded. Neither of them spoke for a while.

"I was horribly young when I got engaged to Max," she said eventually, keeping her voice low. "Far, far too young. He seemed so awfully glamorous to me at that age — a lonely widower, with masses of charm and wealth. I think I thought I was Jane Eyre or something; I don't know." She laughed tonelessly and the cigarette trembled in her hand. "In fact —"

Lorna looked at the walls, as if searching for words.

"In fact, as it turned out, he wasn't very nice at all."

She pulled on her cigarette and laughed again — the same bleak and inadequate laugh.

"I wanted to break it off," she went on, without meeting Virginia's eye, "but I was too scared. The best I could do was drag the engagement out. I was halfway through my second year at the Slade by then, and I begged Max to let me finish my studies before we married. He didn't like it one bit, but he agreed. He visited — oh — all the time, every weekend, sometimes more, and occasionally he'd bring along his oldest pal; his fuddy-duddy bachelor friend from Tollbury Point."

Lorna laughed, as if she was still incredulous after all these years.

"Sometimes I wonder whether Clem really meant to propose at all. Perhaps it was just a gallant jest that I took far too seriously."

Virginia stared. Her throat felt tight and she couldn't have interrupted, even if she'd wanted to.

"Anyway." Lorna shook her head. "I didn't question the wisdom of it; I was too relieved. Max couldn't touch me if I was someone else's wife — that was my first thought. Whether or not I loved Clem — whether Clem loved me — seemed secondary. He was decent and well-meaning, and I believed that was enough."

She leaned her chin on one hand and blew

a feather of smoke from the corner of her mouth.

"Wasn't it enough?" Virginia knew it was a gauche question the moment she said it.

"No," said Lorna, quietly. "No, it wasn't really enough. But there we were, anyway. *Stuck.*" As she said the word *stuck,* she crushed her stub in the ashtray. It smoldered there for ages.

"Of course, Clem thought having a child would be the answer to everything . . ."

Virginia rearranged the cake crumbs to form a neat ring.

"Which isn't to say I didn't want you . . ." Lorna realized what she'd said, and laid a pleading hand across the table. "Virginia?"

People came and went from the tea shop. From the kitchen at the back they could hear a whistle rising in pitch and someone shouting, "Eileen! The kettle!"

"If you weren't burdened with me, you'd be free," Virginia observed, as coolly as she could. "You could do anything; you could go back to London and be a proper artist again. I bet you think that sometimes, don't you? You must do. I would, if I were you."

"Virginia!" Lorna was still reaching across the table, but Virginia kept her hands in her lap.

"Will you send me away?"

"No!" Lorna cried, and heads turned all over the tea shop. "No!" she repeated more moderately. "Of course I won't!"

They stared at one another helplessly.

"But then, what will happen? Really?" Virginia asked. "I mean, assuming you don't get rich and buy a flat in Manhattan."

"Will I marry Max, you mean?" Lorna rubbed her temple, the way she did when she was starting a headache. "I don't know why you should mind so much. He likes you."

Virginia shifted uncomfortably in her chair. "But you wouldn't do it, would you?"

Lorna poured the last of the tea into their cups

"I don't know," she whispered, as if she was talking to herself. "I just . . . I don't know how to . . ."

Virginia glanced at Lorna's left hand. It occurred to her that the emerald engagement ring had not reappeared since that afternoon on Warren Sands. It had been too small — or too big, she couldn't remember which — and Mr. Deering had promised to have it altered.

"If you do marry him," Virginia observed, "then Jozef will have to go away."

Lorna stirred her tea, making slow circles with the spoon.

"Yes," she said, eventually. "Yes, I know. That had crossed my mind."

Unless you knew her well, you'd assume she didn't care very much, or that her thoughts were elsewhere.

New Year's Eve 2015

Virginia salvages her stick with a few breathy curses and frees herself from the chair. She hobbles to the kitchen, setting things straight.

The plaster's always been crumbly round the telephone. It's because of the damp. I knew it was a bit wobbly, but I didn't know it was THAT bad! She tries a throwaway laugh, but it sounds like a canine snarl and she makes a mental note not to use it in front of Sophie.

It's not a convincing show. Even in rehearsal, she feels embarrassed, but she hasn't any better ideas. She's on edge, waiting for the big outcry; for the thunder of feet on the stairs; for Sophie's voice shouting that the phone's been disemboweled. She's taking a long time about it. Virginia stands still with her fingers around the whisky bottle and listens, but there's nothing. Not a peep. She decides she won't tidy the whisky away, after all; she'll leave it out and have a final swig before they go. Other than that, the kitchen is done. Kettle emptied. Heater off. Table wiped. The place looks stark and flat, as if nothing has ever gone on here; as if nothing much has ever been felt, or thought, or done inside these clammy walls.

Joe's note is lying on the table. Virginia turns it and adjusts the placement of the stone, so as to be sure he'll notice his name straightaway. Her fingertips linger on the corner of the page. Perhaps it's not too late to soften her words? To deepen them a little? Even if she just crosses out *Very best wishes* and puts *Love* instead? She picks it up, but something passes over her face, like a shiver of wind across water, and she puts it down again. It'll have to do as it is.

Virginia paces the floor and begins to fancy that this silence is more than strange. It's alarming. What if the child has taken it into her head to creep away? What if she's slipped out of the front door while Virginia is pottering and muttering in the kitchen? She could be at Tollbury Point by now.

Virginia shuffles into the hall, where the light is thick and yellow and clings like paste to the edges of things. It's been like that ever since the seventies, when she took it into her head to fit a hessian shade. But Sophie is here. She's here, standing on the bottom stair, peering through the window. There's something unreal about her continued presence in the house, for which Virginia is inclined to blame her own nerves. Just at the moment Sophie looks less like a solid person and more like a loose assortment of shadows and lights. A ghost, in fact.

"Sophie? Did you find the telephone?" Virginia's voice is as reedy as a child's and she imagines, for a second, that the years have fallen away. She has to look upward, since Sophie is above her on the stairs, and that reminds her of childhood too: always having to look up because you're small; always being a little bit amusing, no matter the strength of your feelings. She pictures herself with a boyish body and brown hair and a red party dress, but at that point her imagination fails. The decay inside her bones and lungs is too insistent, and anyway she can see the white hairs hanging like cobwebs over her eyes.

"The telephone?" Sophie is pressing her face against the glass and staring into the night. "Oh no, not yet, I got sidetracked. Look — there's a car parking up in your lane. I saw it bumping along as I was going upstairs, and now it's stopped and there are people getting out. I think there are, anyway; it's quite hard to tell with the lights on full beam."

"People?" That's the word that bothers Virginia and brings her, muttering and huffing, to the window. *Person* would almost certainly mean Joe, but *people*? People don't call at Salt Winds.

The first thing Virginia sees, reflected in the glass, is a heart-shaped face with black hair and eyes, and she can't help thinking how perfectly Sophie's face would fit inside her own cupped hands. Then the child catches her eye and says, "Look!" and she's forced to refocus on the scene beyond the window.

The headlights shine like a dragon's eyes, bright and unblinking, and she cannot stare them out. They don't belong to Joe's old heap of metal, that's for sure. The car — or it might be a van — has stopped halfway along the lane, where its lights pick out bumpy bits of wall and falling freckles of snow, and the cold, black gap where the old harbor steps start down to the marsh. There are people, just as Sophie said, wandering about in the gloom, never straying far from the car. Virginia thinks there are two of them, though it's hard to be sure: all she

315

can really see is movement in the darkness and the occasional flash of a fur trim, or a leather boot, when they pass in front of the headlights.

If someone had placed a rock inside Virginia's stomach, she could not feel more sick and heavy.

"They've just taken a wrong turn," she says, with an airy flutter of her fingers. "They'll have got lost on their way to a New Year's party. It's always happening."

Only it isn't. It never happens. Nobody takes that turn by mistake because the entrance is concealed by brambles, the surface is more pothole than mud, and there's grass running all the way down the middle, tall enough to tickle the belly of Joe's ancient Renault. He's often moaning about it. He prefers to park at the top and walk, unless he's loaded down with shopping.

Virginia pulls on Sophie's sleeve, but Sophie won't be distracted. Her face and hands are pressing against the glass, as if to push the whole pane outward, and a patch of condensation flowers and furls with her every breath.

"What if it's them?" she says. "What if it's my mum and dad?"

"Wait! Don't go outside! I want to show you something!" Virginia thinks she's never been so aware of her body's dilapidation — of the papery husks that used to be bones, and the flaking rust that used to be fluid muscle — as she is now, when she tries to hurry. Up the stairs she goes, past the telephone's hanging corpse, into her bedroom, a fumble in a drawer for the book, then off again. She pounds the floorboards firmly enough with her stick, but she has to wait for her slippered feet to catch up, and that's what slows the process down. *BANG, flap, flap* . . . *BANG, flap, flap,* all the way along the landing and down the stairs.

"Look!" She waves the book in Sophie's face and its pages flutter like wings. "Never mind the car; I want to show you this."

Even now, when everything is rushing toward the end, the book has the power to make her pause. She holds it in both hands, half-forgetful of her own urgency, and turns it over for the hundred-thousandth time. It's been around the world with her, but she's looked after it well, and you'd never guess it was published so many years ago. The cover has faded from red to coral pink, but apart from that it looks new: the pages are creamy, the woodcut prints sharp, and there are no rips or creases or stains. You'd think it had never been read.

"*The Witch-Princess, and Other Stories,* by J. Friedmann," she reads aloud. "Illustrated by F. L. Leonard."

"It can't be them, though, can it?" Sophie asks urgently, still transfixed by the headlights. "How could they possibly know I'd be here?"

"Look at it. Isn't it beautifully made?"

Sophie glances absently in the direction of the book and glues her eyes to the window again. Virginia turns to the frontispiece — the picture of the witch-princess arriving at the end of the world — and traces her thumb over the wavy lines of the sea. The blocks of ink are strong and yet they're delicate, echoing the warp and grain of the wood from which they were pressed. Virginia holds the volume out, pushing it into Sophie's hands, obliging her to take it.

"I think it should say 'by J. Friedmann and F. L. Leonard,' but Lorna wanted it like this, especially after he'd gone. She reckoned her illustrations were secondary; that it was Jozef's book first and foremost." Virginia knows she's gabbling, but she can't help it. Somehow it matters that Sophie should hear all these things before the car starts moving toward the house. "The publishers were all for changing his surname to 'Freeman' to make it sound less German, but of course Lorna wouldn't have it. The whole thing almost fell through over that, but she stuck to her guns."

Something has got through to Sophie. She's still watching the car, but she keeps darting glances at the book in her hands.

"Lorna? Lorna, as in your mother? As in the woman in the photograph?"

"Yes."

Sophie leafs through to the next picture. She studies it properly this time, inch by inch, like someone hunting for clues.

"So, you mean Lorna is the same person as F. L. Leonard? The artist who illustrated this book?"

"Yes."

"The artist you worked for?"

"Yes, yes. I told you that earlier; I'm sure I did. Leonard was her maiden name. Frances Lorna Leonard."

It's Virginia's turn to take a furtive look at the car. If it reverses down the lane and disappears into the night now, while the girl is distracted, then Virginia will be able to breathe again. *Go,* she wills it. *Go.* Why are those people lingering by the old harbor steps? What are they hoping for?

"I don't think you *did* tell me that." Sophie is as mild as ever as she hands the book back, but there's a kind of mutiny in her side-long glance. *Silly old bat,* she's probably thinking, and Virginia begins to doubt herself; to doubt what the girl does and doesn't know. She knows she's a Deering, doesn't she? Yes, she does, because it was she who first mentioned it, up in the attic. But does she know what *Deering* means in this house?

"You're crying," Virginia observes. It isn't as if Sophie is trying to hide it, either: she's sniffing and wiping her cheeks with her cuffs, and can't seem to decide whether to turn the corners of her mouth up or down. Why should the child weep over this? Has something touched the Deering conscience after all this time? Three generations on? But Sophie isn't thinking about the book. She stopped thinking about it the moment she handed it back and returned to the window.

"It *is* them," she stutters. "It's my mum and dad. I never thought they'd guess, and then drive all this way to find me."

It's obvious that Sophie's going to break for the door, and Virginia is about to seize her by the arm, but her sleeve is so mucky with tears and snot that she wavers. A moment later the girl has her hand on the latch and Virginia is grasping at thin air. It strikes her as a sad sight: her own veiny claws reaching with such eagerness and catching at nothing.

"Don't go!" Virginia pleads, and by the tone of her voice you'd think she felt nothing but affection for the child. "You know what they're like; they'll invent a life for you. Law degrees and Oxford and all the rest of it. There'll be no art school if you go!" *Nor if you come with me,* she might have added, but she pushes that observation aside for now.

"They're my mum and dad," Sophie argues weakly, one hand still on the door. With her other hand she rubs her eyes, like a toddler who's just about had enough for one day.

"They're Deerings."

"I know they're *Deerings.*" Sophie shakes her head. "What do you mean?"

Virginia glances into the night. The headlights are jolting about and getting bigger; the people must have got back in the car, and now they're driving toward the house. Perhaps they *are* just strangers who've lost their way and want to turn the car around.

"Do you know what your Great-Granddad

321

Max did?"

"No." Sophie's voice is small and her fingers are sliding off the latch. This is better; she's paying attention at last.

"He . . ." The brutal truth — the specifics — are on the tip of her tongue, but Virginia catches Sophie's eye and stops.

"I'll tell you what he did," she continues, haltingly. "He tried to break Lorna into tiny bits and fashion her into something new; something better suited to his tastes. He very nearly got his way."

Sophie doesn't move, but she's taking it all in.

"What stopped him?"

There's a question. Virginia waves the fairy-tale book, as if they were in court and this were her evidence.

"Lorna did. Eventually."

Sophie seems to think Virginia is offering her the book, and she comes forward to take it. She looks at it properly this time: at the names on the cover and the contents page and the picture of the witch-princess.

"Keep it," says Virginia, unsure quite what she intends by such a gift. The girl doesn't seem to understand either. She falls still and casts her eyes down, and there's no *Really?* or *Thank you!* or *Wow!* None of that guff.

The car pulls up outside the front door

and a woman gets out. Even in the dark you can tell she's moneyed, and it's not just because of the purring car at her back. It's the way she holds her shoulders, and the way her hair falls when she pushes it off her face. It's the way she walks and looks up at the house.

The woman knocks on the door and turns her back immediately, as if she's already decided there's nothing to wait for.

The man stays in the car, staring straight ahead in the direction of the marsh. Virginia can't see much of him: just a heap of darkness, and the glint of an eye, and knuckles tight around a steering wheel.

New Year's Eve 1941

> Master Theodore Deering requests the
> pleasure of your company on the occasion
> of his twelfth birthday.
> Wednesday, 31st December, 1 o'clock till 4.
> Thorney Grange, Tollbury Point.
> RSVP

The wording was almost identical to last
year's, except for the jaunty note at the bottom, which read: *Lorna — Don't bother walking up, I'll pop down in the car at a quarter to
one to collect her. No mishaps en route this
time!*

Mishaps. Virginia had been repeating that
word to herself ever since the invitation arrived last weekend, and it had lost its force
through overthinking. It had become a
jumble of letters, and she could hardly
remember what it meant or why it had hurt

so much to begin with.

For a while, she'd hoped that the invitation might be allowed to sink under the pile of mail on the hall table, never to be seen again, but Lorna had fished it out and propped it up against a vase. Apparently there was no getting out of Theo's birthday party this time — the expectation that she'd attend was so absolute, she didn't know how to resist, let alone dare try — but at least she was determined not to have another ride in Mr. Deering's car. She would walk by herself, mishap or no mishap.

At a quarter past twelve on the afternoon of the thirty-first, Virginia snatched the invitation off the hall table and stuffed it in her coat pocket. She tried to fit Theo's sweets and birthday card in her other pocket, but they wouldn't go, so she carried them loose.

"Bye?" she called, with a querying rise, to the empty downstairs rooms. There was no reply; they couldn't hear her in the attic. She slammed the front door shut, and as she walked along the lane she crumpled the invitation up as small as it would go and shredded the edges with her nails.

The wind was galloping off the sea today: breakneck, black, and scented with rain. Virginia clambered onto the wall and stood to face it, Lorna's green dress rippling at her shins. Of course the dress was too big, but there'd been nothing else for her to wear — or nothing smart enough, anyway. She was like Alice in Wonderland, veering from one proportion to another and never quite finding her proper self. In the red dress she'd been lumpen and fleshy, but this green one swamped her and turned her back into a stick-limbed child, foolish in plaits and scuffed shoes.

The cold was making her eyes stream. She ought to get on, before Mr. Deering came gliding down the lane in his car to pick her up. *"The evil baron,"* she whispered to herself with a secret smile. The evil baron in Jozef's story had yellow eyes and a fork at the end of his tongue, but in every other particular she was sure he looked exactly like Mr. Deering.

"Dark rumors swirled about him," she declaimed into the wind, quoting Jozef's story word for word. *"It was said that the rooms of his palace were painted black, and that he dined every night on raw gulls' eggs. It was said that he'd had a wife, many years ago, and that he'd kept her in a cage."*

It was hard to tear her gaze from the horizon. It wasn't that she believed in Jozef's "Curlew" — she was twelve years old and knew a made-up story when she read one — but a part of her wanted to, and over the last four months she'd begun to keep a lookout, just for fun. Just because it was hard to tell what might be lurking in that strip of haze where marsh and sky met and mingled. Nothing, of course — or at any rate, not the enchanted ship that Jozef's story kept leading her to believe. She knew that. But there was no harm in standing still from time to time and making sure.

It was the church clock that roused her. As the chimes struck the half hour Virginia jumped down from the wall and broke into a run; after a minute, and a few stumbles, she slowed to a resolute march.

She thought of Lorna and Jozef, cozy in the attic with the blackout cardboard tacked up and a gas fire hissing. Their book was pretty well finished, and they were going to spend the afternoon drafting letters to publishers.

Lorna had been so pleased yesterday when Virginia announced she was going to walk to the party. "Good idea!" she'd said, looking up from her latest print with a frank smile. It meant she wouldn't have to spruce herself up for Max and come downstairs to say hello.

Hours later, when she was scrubbing her

hands at the kitchen sink, she'd remembered to add, "You'll be all right, will you? Walking to Thorney Grange on your own?"

"I'll be fine."

"I suppose one of us ought to give him a ring and let him know?"

Virginia had crossed her fingers behind her back. "All right," she'd lied. "I'll do it." She'd tried not to imagine the novelty of speaking to Mr. Deering on the telephone; of voluntarily pressing his voice to her face and allowing it to caress the delicate folds of her ear.

Virginia trudged to the end of the lane and turned, one last time, to look back across the marsh. *The great silence,* as she'd thought of it on her very first evening, when Clem was bringing her home from Sinclair House. The great, secret silence.

It was tempting to do something else with this Wednesday afternoon. Hide inside St. Dunstan's and take a proper look at the nativity scene. Catch the bus into town and see what they were playing at the cinema. Walk across the marsh, polishing off Theo's birthday toffees as she went; walk all the way to the brink where magic might — or might not — be; where sky, sand, and water dissolved into nothing and nowhere.

In the end she turned onto the main road and made her way to the village, and Thorney Grange. Not today. But if the worst came to the worst — if Lorna and the evil baron really did get married — she knew where her refuge lay.

Every time Virginia came face-to-face with Thorney Grange she wondered whether Mr. Deering employed someone to scrub the walls. It was a genuine question — though doubtless he'd think it was cheek — otherwise, how did those red bricks stay so clean? There were no weeds poking out of the mortar, no mossy stains, no mottling, not even the ghost of a creeper. Every single brick was shiny and smooth, as if he wrapped them overnight in tissue paper. It was the same with the roof tiles and the windows and the white gravel in the drive. Even the lawn looked dusted and polished. There were horse chestnut trees in the churchyard next door, but Virginia had never seen a horse chestnut or a rusty leaf on Mr. Deering's grass. Maybe one of the servants kept watch and rushed outdoors with dustpan and brush if anything untoward drifted over the wall.

She dithered again on the edge of the drive, standing between the stone lions, pretending to check her pockets. She'd been here a few times for afternoon tea, and once for dinner, but always with Lorna — never alone. Just as well it was a party. However dire the prospect of an afternoon spent passing the parcel with Theo and friends, at least there'd be safety in numbers.

"Virginia?" Mr. Deering was scrunching across the gravel driveway with his hands in tight fists.

"Virginia? What are you doing here so early?" An elderly couple emerged, arm in arm, from a cottage across the way, and Max hid his fists inside his jacket pockets. "I was just about to get the car out. I told Lorna I'd fetch you; that was the plan." He was doing his best to sound amused, but his pockets kept twitching.

"We didn't like to trouble you."

She followed him up the drive and he ushered her inside, murmuring something in her ear as she brushed past.

"You know, you could be more gracious when a fellow offers you a compliment," he said more loudly, as the door closed behind them and the sound of the wind was replaced by plush silence. Apparently his humor had improved.

"What?"

He laughed as he came up behind her and

peeled the coat from her shoulders, like the good host he was. The housekeeper — pale-faced Mrs. Bellamy — bustled by with a tray of jellies, her lips tight with concentration. Mr. Deering waited till she'd gone before he ran a finger around the nape of Virginia's neck, snagging his nail on the little hairs that didn't fit into her plaits.

"I was complimenting you on your dress, you little goose."

You'd think he'd have jumped or faltered when his son came thundering down the stairs, but he merely straightened and smiled, and kept his hand on Virginia's shoulder.

"Theodore! Your first guest!"

Theo scowled. "I thought it was Robert. He said he'd come early."

Max pushed her forward and Theo kicked the banister. The silence that followed was awkward for the children but not, apparently, for Mr. Deering, who stood at ease with his arms folded, watching and waiting.

Virginia held out the birthday card and the squashed box of sweets, and Theo took them begrudgingly. Not a word was exchanged.

"Isn't that kind?" Mr. Deering murmured. "Hmm?"

The children weren't free to breathe until

the doorbell rang and Theo ran to admit his friends. Virginia loitered by the stairs, unsure what to do with her hands now that she had no pockets and no present to hold.

"Robert's here!" shouted Theo. "And he's brought Charles!"

"Good, good," said Max under his breath, and she could feel his gaze fixed on her neck, and on the little pulse that throbbed under her jawbone.

The boys didn't invite Virginia to come upstairs but she followed them anyway, breaking into a run to keep up. There was a little sign on the first door they came to — a flimsy thing made of wood and decorated with bumblebees — that said *Juliet and Theodore's Playroom*. Theodore scowled at Virginia before opening the door and elbowing his friends inside. She hated to trail them, but she could hear Max's velvety tread coming up the stairs, and there was nowhere else to go.

The playroom was long and light, with diamond-bright windows and a table groaning with party food. Balloons had been tied to every available mooring — chairbacks, table legs, the fire screen — and they couldn't have been the normal kind you blow up yourself, because they were floating upward on their strings, the way they do in picture books. Mrs. Bellamy was fussing over the table, arranging plates of sandwiches and jugs of lemonade, and she regarded the four of them sharply as they trooped in. Theodore shrank a little under her gaze and stuck his hands in his pockets.

"My father had a proper cake delivered from Fortnum's," he told his friends, and they all looked with interest at the creamy creation in the center of the table.

"You could layer bricks with that icing," Mrs. Bellamy sniffed. It was hard to know whether or not she was trying to be funny. One of the boys chuckled appreciatively, but Theo just scuffed the floor with his heel.

Virginia sidled to the nearest window. The playroom was at the side of the house, with a view over the main street so she could see the post office and the pub, and if she stood on tiptoe she could just make out the weathervane on the school roof. There were two old men chatting in the doorway of the Black Horse, and a woman was pushing a pram along the opposite pavement.

More guests edged into the playroom. Boys — all of them boys — scrubbed up and slicked down. They handed over their gifts as quickly as possible, or slid them onto the table, as if there was something shameful about colored paper and ribbons; as if to say *I wouldn't have bothered, you know, but my mother insisted.* It seemed to her that they were still individual people for the moment, with their own ways of seeing — but she knew it wouldn't last. Any second now they'd shed their singularities and meld together as a gang. You could see them searching for a way in: jostling one another; trying out grimaces and lame jokes; looking for Theo's approval.

Mrs. Bellamy surveyed the table — and them — with her arms folded across her chest. She seemed unhappy, especially when her eyes fell on Virginia, as if she'd have liked an explanation for this odd one out. Virginia pulled discreetly at her unfilled dress, and wondered whether she should have resisted shredding the invitation inside her coat pocket. She would have liked to produce it now, to prove her right to be here.

"Are you going to play something nice?" demanded the housekeeper. "Come on now, Theodore, you're the host. You should organize a game while you're waiting for everyone to arrive."

The boys gathered into a whispering huddle and a bark of laughter rose from their midst — then another, and another. One or two turned to stare at Virginia, but their eyes carried the gaze of the whole pack. She ran a finger inside her collar and turned back to the window. The wind was speckling it with rain.

"Theodore?" Mrs. Bellamy's voice had developed a warning tone.

"We're going to play hide-and-seek," Theo replied, daring the housekeeper to object. He and his friends were waiting openly for her departure now, insolent in their unity, and she gave in.

"Don't you go leaving anyone out."

The pack quivered with amusement, but Theo kept a straight face. "We won't."

"And you're not to eat a crumb of that food until teatime. Understood?"

"Yes, Mrs. Bellamy."

The boys rustled with excitement as she creaked away down the stairs. When she'd definitely gone, Theo took a jam sandwich from the table and pulled it apart. The others watched him with a kind of admiration as he swallowed it in two mouthfuls and wiped the back of his hand across his mouth.

"You're 'It.'" Theo tossed his order across the room, and the others followed its trajectory with their eyes. Virginia shrugged; she'd expected worse. At least if she was "It" she'd be alone for a minute or two while she was supposed to be counting.

"Well? Go on then."

Virginia covered her eyes and began slowly. "One . . . two . . . three . . . four . . ." When she was sure they'd all left, she lowered her hands from her face and looked out of the window again.

Mrs. Hill came into view, walking down the main street with her back to Thorney Grange. Mrs. Hill with her claret headscarf and herringbone coat and a shopping basket over one arm. The sight of her was so redolent of times past — of a warm, gossipy kitchen, and rabbit pies and marmalade making; of God in his heaven and Clem in his study, and all well with the world — that Virginia almost banged on the window, with the unformed idea that she might beg some of these things back if she asked nicely enough.

"Ten . . . eleven . . . twelve . . ." Virginia murmured, as Mrs. Hill carried on. But what was she doing now? Pausing to wave; trying to attract the attention of someone farther down the street. Whoever it was must have seen her, because she stopped waving and stood waiting, her hands folded under the handle of her basket and her headscarf fluttering near her ears. Virginia shivered. Someone was walking over her grave, as Mrs. Hill herself would have said.

"Fifteen . . . sixteen . . . seventeen . . ."

The man Mrs. Hill had hailed came pushing his clunky tricycle along the middle of the street, stopping to lean on the handlebars while the two of them exchanged a few words. Virginia stopped counting. Slowly — very slowly, and hardly daring to breathe, as if the slightest movement might be fatal — she rested her fingertips on the glass. *Rosenthal Knife-Grinding and Repairs.* She closed her eyes and opened them again, but the words were still there, emblazoned in white letters across the trunk at the back of the trike. The door of the playroom opened behind her and shut again softly, but she paid no attention.

That man in the street was Mr. Rosenthal; the real Mr. Rosenthal who'd come to Salt Winds all those months ago in order to sharpen the kitchen knives and mend Clem's shears. Virginia tried to convince herself he wasn't, but he was. There was no helping it. This was Mr. Rosenthal, and Mr. Rosenthal was not Jozef. He was an old man with gray hair and leathery skin and wrinkles near his eyes and a big greasy coat.

Virginia stared and stared as Mrs. Hill chattered and the knife grinder listened. Every now and then he bowed slightly, and once he scratched his ear, but he didn't have much to say.

The floorboards creaked right behind her, and a damp darkness pressed itself against her eyes. She recognized Mr. Deering by the soapy scent of his hands and the metallic bite of his signet ring.

"Guess who?" The question licked at her ear.

If it hadn't been for Mr. Rosenthal she'd have frozen with fear, but above all else Virginia wanted to keep looking; to keep gauging the reality of the man outside, with his ancient face and tradesman's tricycle. She batted Mr. Deering's hands away with more impatience than fear, and as she did so the pair in the street began to draw away from one another, nodding their good wishes and farewells. Virginia stood on tiptoe to see which way the knife grinder would go, but Mr. Deering's hands came over her eyes again. He wasn't so gentle this time, and he began pressing against her from behind as well, squashing her body against the windowsill.

"Stop it!" There was no space in which to turn or hit out; all she could do was shout. "Stop it! I need to see!"

Virginia twisted and bit, but her teeth found only the thick weave of his jacket, and all the time he was laughing at her and making soothing noises. At one point her nose got pressed up against his shirtfront, and she was surprised by the flabby softness of his chest. She'd thought he'd feel more solid than that; an edifice of stone.

"Shush now!" he cooed, as if she were a fractious baby, though his hands were tight around her wrists and his face was buried in the curve of her neck. He seemed to be everywhere, like a noxious vapor that swirls and spreads and fills every last space, until she felt as though she were breathing him in. She became dizzy for lack of air, and when she closed her eyes she saw tiny lights popping on and off inside her head.

With one almighty effort, she placed her palms flat against his chest and shoved. Mr. Deering looked so surprised as he staggered backward that Virginia might have laughed, if she hadn't felt so desperate. His arms flailed and he fell, dragging a dining chair with him, and a great bunch of balloons burst, one after another, in quick succession, like a volley of gunfire. She saw the whites of his eyes and the black circle of his mouth as it searched in vain for words — or even sounds. When she began to run he rolled onto his front and clutched at her ankles with both hands, but she was too far away and too fast.

"You bloody . . ." Mr. Deering's words chased Virginia down the stairs, and she crossed the fingers of both hands, her eyes fixed on the front door. By the time she noticed Theo's arm snaking through the banisters it was too late to avoid him, and in the effort to do so she tripped and fell down the last three stairs. As she tumbled she bumped her nose on something, and a stringy trail of blood spewed over the wall and floor.

She scrambled to her feet and clamped her hand over her nose. The front door appeared to be bobbing about from side to side, and there was a sound like rushing water in her ears. She sat down, perching on the bottom stair with her head between her knees, and listened to her own ragged breathing. It sounded as if she was crying, but she knew she wasn't — at least not in the way Theo would call *girlish*. When Theo came and stood in front of her, and the others began crawling out from underneath tables and hatstands, she glared at them. Blood was still dripping through her fingers and onto the floor, but she made no attempt to stanch it. There was a kind of satisfaction in letting it come.

"You idiot!" Theo whispered, ashen-faced.

"You prize idiot! You've got blood all over the place!"

He spat on a handkerchief and began to dab — then scrub — at the long red streak on the wall, but that just made it spread, and took the shine off the wallpaper. The other boys stood about exchanging sheepish glances and biting their lips. Mrs. Bellamy started up the stairs from the basement kitchen, crying, "What's going on? What's happened?" The playroom door crashed open and heavy footsteps thundered along the landing. Virginia got up and pushed her body across the hall.

"What on *earth* . . .?" she heard as she tumbled outside, but then the door shut, and all the shouts and murmurs stopped as though a switch had been thrown. She found her feet and careered out of the driveway, stopping to lean against the churchyard wall and close her eyes for a moment. The wind rested on her forehead like a cool hand, and she wished she could stay with it forever and never have to think again.

"Virginia Wrathmell?"

Her eyes snapped open with thoughts of Mr. Deering, even though it wasn't his voice. It was Mrs. Hill, emerging from the main street. The knife grinder had gone. She stood in front of Virginia, her expression more curious than sympathetic, and addressed her for the very first time since their rift. Trust Mrs. Hill to be brought around by a bloodied nose.

"What in heaven's name has happened to you, child?"

Virginia accepted Mrs. Hill's hanky without answering the question.

"That man you were talking to —"

"You'll need to moisten it a bit first. Here, let me do it. What man?"

"The man with the tricycle. The knife grinder . . ."

Mrs. Hill spat into the handkerchief and began polishing Virginia's chin and lips.

"Ira Rosenthal? What's he got to do with the price of eggs?"

The handkerchief was black with blood, but Mrs. Hill spat on it again and began working around Virginia's nostrils. "You remember Mr. Rosenthal, don't you?" she went on. "He was interned on the Isle of Man a year or so back, on account of his being a German — do you really not remember? They let him out again a few months later." She stopped to inspect the hanky, in search of a clean patch. "Anyway. Poor old Mr. Rosenthal is neither here nor there. What *I* would very much like to know —"

But Virginia broke away and began her stumbling run toward the lane. Something hideous began pushing up through her insides — a noise of some kind, an obscenity — that frightened her, and she pressed it down again as hard as she could. She tried crying instead, but that was no good, and her sobs emerged dry and inauthentic. The pounding of her head started to keep time with the pounding of her feet — and what with that and the exaggerated rasping of her own breath, she couldn't hear a thing outside herself. Mrs. Hill's indignation blew away, unheeded, like a feather on the wind.

Virginia didn't know what she wanted, other than to go home. Or perhaps it was just that everything she wanted was a paradox. She wanted Jozef to tell her the whole truth, and she wanted him to say everything was fine. That he'd lied without being a liar, that he was an enemy airman but not a villain, that he'd emerged from the marsh wearing Clem's coat but hadn't left Clem behind.

Virginia stopped for breath once, when she was halfway home, turning her face toward the marsh and the strong, wet wind. She didn't look back, so she didn't see the black car that stopped when she stopped, and edged forward into the lane as soon as she began to run again.

New Year's Eve 2015

Sophie lets her mother walk to the car and slide back into the passenger seat before emerging from the house. Even then there's no hysterical rushing into the night; she just stands in the doorway with the grubby hall light behind her and drums her fingers on the cover of the book.

The Deerings might easily drive off without observing their daughter, but they don't. It's the father who spots her as he's reaching sideways to release the hand brake. Virginia sees the reflection of his eyes in the rearview mirror and, after a few moments of absolute stillness, the motion of his jaw as he speaks a few cryptic words to his wife.

Mrs. Deering gets out of the car again and returns to the house. She's long and lean, and Virginia retreats toward the stairs, her shoulders rising. She thinks about switching the light off, but it's too late now; she'll draw attention to herself. She wishes she were Silver, sitting by the hall table inside the tidy circle of his own tail, cleaning his paws, watching without being watched.

Something explosive is bound to happen now. It's inevitable. There'll be wails and recriminations; bone-crushing hugs; laughter and tears; declarations of love and remorse. The mother will shake her daughter by the shoulders like a rag doll and thank God she's alive. That's what it's like when you find something you feared you'd lost forever. Virginia has meditated on reunions a lot, in her time, and thinks she's something of an expert on the subject. She knows the thoughts that have been spinning around Mrs. Deering's head ever since this morning, when she discovered Sophie's bed empty and the sheets all smooth and cold. She knows the darkness behind those thoughts; the patient horror that promises to be there still, when there are no more thoughts to think.

"So," says Mrs. Deering, stopping in front of her daughter with her arms calmly folded. They share the same facial structure — the same strong nose and cheekbones — but the ins and outs are more exaggerated in the older woman. Her face is like a totem chiseled from wood.

Sophie stares back without a word and hugs the fairy-tale book to her chest, almost her mother's equal when it comes to self-possession. Her rings catch the taillights of the car and make her fingers flash like red stars.

"Well," Mrs. Deering continues. "Your father was right. He said we'd find you here." She speaks in a husky accent, which clashes with her sangfroid. What is it? Spanish? Something like that. Something full of vigor and heat and flavor. She zips her coat right up to her chin, and when it's as high as it will go she pulls the fur collar up around her ears, as if to demonstrate how much she objects to this weather — and to being out in it.

"How?" Sophie wonders. "How did he guess?"

"Oh, by knowing you so much better than I do." On the last couple of words something cracks inside Mrs. Deering's voice, and in the same instant she notices Virginia. She's startled but manages a smile.

"Oh my goodness, I'm so sorry." Mrs. Deering approaches Virginia with her left hand placed lightly over her heart. "I don't know how to apologize enough for all this; I don't know where to start." She holds her right hand out, for shaking. "I'm Adriana.

I'm Sophie's mother."

Whatever it was — that tiny warning crack — has been filled in, sanded, and smoothed away. Virginia takes Adriana's hand, and the feel of it makes her think of wood that's been polished till it shines like silk. After all, she reassures herself, things could be worse: wood is not a bad substance; not entirely without warmth or give. She'd rather Sophie's mother were made of wood than, say, stone or metal. She stares at the woman's hand and realizes she's letting her thoughts spiral when she ought to be saying something. She runs her dry tongue over her lips, but the fact is, she's forgotten how to make conversation.

"Has Sophie been with you all day?"

Virginia stiffens, still feeling for the woman's tone. Is this a straight question or an accusation? The car engine cuts out and the ensuing silence is heavy. Blue police lights start spinning through her mind and she imagines New Year's Eve in a cell, with a Styrofoam cup of tea and no view of the marsh.

"I kept telling her to contact you," Virginia insists. It's true, up to a point. "I couldn't get hold of anyone myself; my phone isn't working."

Mrs. Deering encloses Virginia's featherweight hand in both her own. "Bless you," she whispers. What with all that padded goose-down and fur edging, it's warm inside her hands. Virginia allows herself to rest a moment in the simple pleasure of it before her conscience gets the better of her and she pulls away.

"Why would you want to do that?"

"What?"

"Bless me."

Adriana beams with compassion — the type of compassion that people reserve for querulous babies and crazy old ladies. Virginia could say almost anything — *for much of the day I've imagined myself capable of sinking your daughter in the marsh* — and Mrs. Deering's expression would stay much the same.

"Bless you for letting Sophie shelter in your home, on such a day. Just to think . . ." A shudder runs the length of Adriana's body, and her glance flickers to the open doorway behind Virginia. "I don't know what possessed her. She didn't even take a proper coat."

"Dad?" Sophie is moving off into the darkness, step by careful step. The driver's door is hanging open and Mr. Deering is no longer inside the car. It's a while before Virginia spots him, standing by the harbor wall with his back to the house, and even then she's not entirely sure. She can make out the very vaguest shape of a man, but if she didn't know the landscape so well she could believe it was a boulder or a stumpy tree or a fluctuation of the light.

Adriana sighs. "I honestly don't know how to begin thanking you, Miss . . . Mrs. . . . ?"

Perhaps civility is not Mr. Deering's thing; perhaps he thinks it's a feminine virtue. His wife is certainly good at it, though Virginia rather wishes she'd stop now. She foresees flowers arriving in a few days' time: a seasonal poinsettia, perhaps, or some blood-red amaryllises, with a little card purporting to be "from Sophie." She pictures the delivery-man walking around the house, knocking and peering through windows. He'll have to leave it on the doorstep, eventually, where the wind will pick it to bits.

"I'm worried you'll catch cold, standing about in this weather," Adriana persists. She doesn't seem remotely worried by Virginia's reluctance to speak — thank goodness.

Sophie stops a few feet away from her father, as if she's afraid to go any closer. Virginia's eyes follow, adjusting slowly to the dark. Now she can see that Mr. Deering's head is bowed, and that he's leaning on the wall with both hands, as if he were trying to topple the entire age-old structure.

"He's not throwing up?" Adriana mutters, under her breath. "Oh, please God. Whenever I so much as put the heating on in that car . . ."

Mr. Deering's shoulders are, in fact, heaving, but not because he's being sick. When Adriana realizes he's weeping she says, "Oh," and turns away. She taps out a quick rhythm on the ground with the toe of her boot, and frowns.

"Dad?" Sophie's plea is tentative. "Daddy?"

He doesn't respond, but then he probably hasn't heard, because the wind snatches the words straight from her mouth and carries them off in the opposite direction. Sophie closes in on him slowly, step by tiny step, holding out her hand as if he were a dog with an uncertain temper. She's left her denim jacket in the kitchen and her white shirt flutters, wraithlike, in the wind.

When she touches him, his arms seem to melt so that he can't lean on them anymore. It's not just his arms either, it's his neck and legs and spine. He's losing his solidity — dwindling to an invisible core — and the thing that's holding him together is Sophie herself. The wind rattles the upstairs windows, like a ghost dragging a chain, and whatever they say to one another — if they say anything at all — is lost in the din. Sophie wraps her father in her arms, and he wraps her in his, and the darkness seems to tumble around them like water.

"Sophie is very close to her father," says Adriana, apologetically.

I was very close to mine. Virginia tries to utter it aloud, conversationally, but her voice gurgles in her throat and comes out as a cough.

"He's good at this whole parenting thing," Adriana goes on. She probably thinks she's talking to herself by now. "A bit bossy at times, but good. I mean, the two of them argue — God, do they argue — but in the end . . ."

Her voice peters out and the two women stand in silence, united by their own private defeats. They watch from the doorstep as Sophie and her father hold tight to one another and sway from side to side in desperate exhaustion.

Virginia would know him anywhere. Adriana tells her his name is Phil, or Fred, or something like that, but as he approaches the house all she can think is *Max.* He must be a good ten years older than his grandfather was in 1941, and he's almost completely bald, but there's hair on his face, and it's been carefully trimmed to form two broad stripes — one across his upper lip, the other down his chin. He's the same height and build as Max, with the same pale hands, and the same glint of a signet ring on his little finger. Virginia tightens her grip on the walking stick and plunges her right hand deep in her dressing-gown pocket, in case he offers to shake it. (He doesn't.)

They nod at one another watchfully. "Virginia Wrathmell," he states, and she feels wrong-footed by the baldness of his tone. What does he mean? Is he asking her if that's her name? Or telling her he already knows?

Even his swollen eyelids remind her of Max, and the evening after Juliet was killed when he drank himself stupid on Clem's whisky. This Mr. Deering has had a bad day too, and it shows. He's transparent in a way his wife could never be: to look at him, you'd think Sophie had been gone a week, or a month. His eyes and nose are red. His shirt is patched with sweat, and the buttons aren't done correctly. Even the sculpted beard, when you study it more closely, risks losing itself in a rash of black stubble.

"I knew your grandfather," says Virginia carefully. "And your father."

When Mr. Deering licks his lips you can tell, by the tacky sound, that his mouth is dry.

"Yes," he replies. "Yes. I know."

The silence swells with unspoken — unspeakable — knowledge. Virginia ponders the darkness beyond the wall and shivers.

"Well," she concludes. "I'm glad you found your daughter safe and well." They're just words; they fill a gap. As to whether she really means them, she can worry about that later.

"Thank you." Mr. Deering holds Virginia's gaze a moment or two longer than before and nods once.

Virginia remembers the denim jacket and goes back indoors to fetch it. Mr. Deering keeps jangling his keys and saying, "Well . . ." as if he's keen to get going, so she doesn't feel obliged to invite them inside. Adriana looks like she could do with a drop of whisky, and it might not do him any harm either — but best not. The kitchen is well and truly closed for business now. All the mugs and glasses are clean and neat, and so they shall stay until Joe wraps them up in newspaper and takes them down to the charity shop.

Virginia unhooks the blue jacket from the

back of the chair and brushes it down, as if it'd had time to gather dust. Sophie has followed her into the kitchen, and she takes it from Virginia's hands with a smile before shrugging it on over her arms. That done, there's nothing to keep her, but she lingers for a minute over Silver, crouching down to rub his chin every which way, and making little sing-song farewells.

"I'm sorry you never got to show me your walk," Sophie says, glancing up at Virginia. Silver is on his back now with his eyes half-closed — shameless creature — while she strokes his downy stomach. "Maybe I could come back and see you in February, at half-term break? Would that be all right? We could do it properly then, in the daylight, and you could tell me more about Lorna, and your life and everything."

Virginia makes a mumbling sound, which may or may not imply assent.

"Look after that book," she says, to change the subject. She likes the careful way Sophie holds the volume, as if she's frightened of dropping it.

"Oh, I absolutely will. And I won't forget what you told me."

"What?"

"About my great-grandfather being a bit . . . you know . . . *control-freaky.*"

Virginia smiles slightly at the choice of words, which prompts Sophie to hug her. Sophie probably flings her arms around everyone she meets — people have a tendency to do that these days — so it's silly to be moved by the gesture. Virginia returns the embrace robotically, as if she's not quite sure how to go about it. The child feels so fine and delicate — so crushable — inside the circle of her arms that she's afraid of squeezing too hard. She's reminded of the curlew's skull as it sat on the palm of her hand last night, quivering in the air, as light as an empty eggshell.

Virginia decides not to wave the Deerings off. It's not as though anybody's expecting it: Adriana keeps telling her to get indoors out of the wind, and he (Phil? Fred? Frank?) hasn't made eye contact since the one halting exchange.

She hobbles upstairs, thinking she'll sit for a minute with the curlew's skull; give them time to get going before she locks up the house and leaves. They're so noisy, though — even from her bedroom she can hear them slamming the trunk, calling at one another through the wind, bleeping about with their phones — and they prevent her thoughts from sinking below the surface.

In the end, she picks up the curlew's skull and crosses the landing to the spare bedroom.

The black car is almost invisible in the darkness, but just as she reaches the window and looks down someone opens one of its doors, and a golden light floods the interior. Virginia is startled by the charm of it: the car looks like a magical box filled to the brim and spilling over with sorcerous warmth. Sophie climbs wearily into the back seat; Virginia hopes they'll let her sleep on the way home and leave their questions till morning. Adriana pockets her phone, catches the keys from her husband, and climbs into the driver's seat. Mr. Deering takes one last, furtive look at the house, but he doesn't linger.

The kindly light disappears when he shuts his door, and the occupants are lost from view. Sophie is safe, and the sheer relief of it seems to have hollowed the old woman out. She watches the car move off and disappear down the lane, and when it's quite gone she brings the curlew's skull level with her face. She hardly dares look it in the eye.

"Bereft," she observes. "Bereft of our revenge."

In this light, with the spare room in darkness and the landing muted, the skull has adopted yet another expression. Just the twist of an edge here, and the wrinkle of a shadow there, and Virginia could swear the bird has a sense of humor.

New Year's Eve 1941

Even though she'd raced till her lungs were raw, stopping once to catch her breath, Virginia didn't rush to the attic the moment she got home. All the way along the lane she'd been firing imaginary questions at Jozef, but her anger seemed to dissipate as the front door swung to behind her — or at least it started to lose its fire and turn into something colder and harder.

She stood panting in the quiet hallway, her eyes streaming and the blood crusting on her nose. Her shoes were hurting — they'd been on the small side for a while now — so she kicked them off without bothering to undo the buckles. Perhaps this was what it felt like to come home and discover you'd been bombed? All the solid pieces of your life turned to charcoal; your treasures blasted to rubble; the hidden parts of your house ripped open and bared.

Virginia turned on the spot, and her breath hung in the air like smoke. To think she'd been stumbling around this place for a whole year, without seeing it for what it was.

Of course Lorna knew everything, she realized, as she went through to the kitchen and splashed her face at the sink. That hadn't occurred to her until now, but as soon as it had, it was obvious. Lorna knew what Jozef was; she'd known all along, and encouraged Virginia's idiotic belief in Mr. Rosenthal.

She cupped her hands under the cold tap and sucked water into her mouth, remembering how she'd felt in January and the things she'd said: *Oh, please can we keep him? . . . We don't have to send him away, do we? . . . Clem likes Mr. Rosenthal.* The tap water tasted metallic, and when she spat it out, the sides of the sink got spattered with red droplets.

Bracken whined in his sleep and Virginia turned to look at him, pink water dripping from her chin. When she felt sad, she often knelt beside his basket and fondled his ears — not because he'd ever come around to liking her much, but because he was warm and alive and his loyalties would lie with Clem. This afternoon she could hardly bear the sight of him. He looked more like a gargoyle than a dog, lying on his back like that, with his top lip hanging open and all his teeth exposed.

Virginia rubbed her upper arms, but there was no getting warm today. She glanced at the clock and thought back to the same time last year, when Lorna was helping out at the Women's Institute and Clem had been gone a few minutes, and Salt Winds was still its old, wholesome self. The range had been hot; the pantry stocked; the sitting-room fire laid. They'd been on the brink of atrophy, and they hadn't had a clue. How had they not known? She ran her fingers through her hair and screwed her eyes shut as she wandered back into the hall. How had she not known? Why hadn't she stopped it all from happening?

It wasn't even two o'clock, but the hall had grown darker since she arrived. When she ran her thumb along the underside of the banister, she felt the fluff gather like cotton candy on the soft pad of her skin. Her hand flopped to her side again, and she didn't bother to look at it or wipe it clean. Sightless, she stood at the bottom of the stairs. There seemed no point in going up. In going anywhere. In doing anything.

It was the sound of the wireless that roused her — at least, she thought it was the wireless, though it wasn't coming from the dining room. It was a zinging, crackling beat — barely audible — which wound through the moaning of the wind and the silence of the house, and refused to let her attention dissolve.

The more she listened, the more it seemed to Virginia to resemble band music, with swooping trombones and dancing drums: the sort of stuff that used to make Clem mutter, with a trace of self-mockery, about how old he felt. They — Lorna and the German — must have taken the wireless up to the attic so that they could have it on while they worked. That's what must have happened; that's where it was coming from.

Virginia followed the music up the stairs, like a thread through a maze, and up again to the attic. The music was distinct now, but not loud: she could hear their voices beneath it, and their stifled laughter. Despite her resentment, all of a sudden she felt shy, and she hesitated for a long time before nudging open the door and peering in through the gap.

The gas fire was on high, its hisses and sputters undercutting the rise and fall of the big band music, but the heat wasn't radiating from there. Or not just from there, anyway. It seemed to pour out of everything:

the walls and floorboards; the ochre trestle tables; the flattened Tate & Lyle box across the window; the velvety shadows in the rafters; the prints that hung over the room and fluttered in midair. Even their naked bodies seemed luminous with warmth, as if Jozef and Lorna were gods from Mount Olympus, and not ordinary people who suffered from chapped skin, and didn't get enough vitamins, and spent all day wrapped in itchy woolens.

When Virginia saw them lying like that on the mattress, their bare arms and legs woven in a loose braid, her first instinct was to run, or at least to look away, but she didn't. Her second instinct — the instinct to freeze — was stronger. Was this it, then? Was this Sex? Or the prelude, or the aftermath? Whatever it was, it was unbearable; it made her insides lurch — and at the same time she wanted, desperately, to watch.

Lorna was lying across Jozef's chest, and he was sitting with his head propped up on a pillow, tracing dreamy shapes down her side and over her bare breast. They'd just finished laughing about something, and the humor lingered in the shape of their lips and the lines at their eyes.

It wasn't just their nakedness that shocked Virginia; it was the ease with which they shared it, as if their bodies were every bit as nice as clothes — nicer, even; more comfortable to move about in; pleasanter to the touch. There were plenty of blankets, but they were all messed up at the foot of the mattress and concealed very little from view. Jozef was bending his head and kissing Lorna on the lips. He did it with a strange thoroughness, as if there was a message in it, or an answer to something Lorna had said — though she hadn't said anything — and not only did she let him do it, she twisted around and propped herself up on her elbows, so as to take the pressure of his mouth more fully, and return it with greater force.

They were — what was it they were? Virginia rummaged through the shadowy borderlands of her vocabulary, searching for a word to describe Lorna and Jozef, and what they were doing. The best she could come up with was *perverted,* but she wasn't convinced it was right.

It was very cold at the top of the stairs, and just as the attic's warmth seemed to pour out of the music and the furniture and the lovers themselves, so the landing's chill seemed to emanate from Virginia's own body, as though her blood had turned to seawater and her flesh to ice. She felt like one of those evil queens from fairy tales who walk in winter, and bring the cold with them everywhere they go. If she burst into the attic now, the gas fire would fizzle out and the lovely, rosy light would fade to gray. They'd stop laughing, too. Oh, they'd stop laughing all right, when they clapped eyes on her.

Virginia squeezed her eyes shut, bowed her head, and thought how much she hated them both. Yes, she did, she hated them. How could she not? Jozef was a German and an adulterer and a liar and a pervert, and for all she knew he'd murdered Clem. Held him facedown in the lapping waters and stripped him of his coat, his house, and his wife. No doubt he'd told Lorna all about it. Maybe — probably — that's why they were both laughing as Virginia came up the stairs. She curled her hands in on themselves and dug her nails into her palms. She did hate them; she could feel it now, like a creeping flame beneath her skin.

"Let's take a trip in a trailer," sang the impish voices on the wireless. "No need to come back at all . . ."

"We never used to listen to this kind of music," Lorna remarked, sliding a cigarette between her lips. The attic was already grainy with smoke, and there were a handful of stubs in the ashtray. They must have been saving up their week's supply for today, when they knew Virginia would be out of the way. No wonder she'd been forced, against her wishes, to go to Theo's party. They'd had their own party planned.

"Clem wasn't keen," Lorna added, by way of explanation. Jozef rolled onto his front and leaned over her, so that they were touching all the way along their bodies, from their feet to their chests. You couldn't have got a cigarette paper between them, as Mrs. Hill might have said if she'd been there — assuming the spectacle hadn't rendered her utterly speechless.

Lorna stroked his head, winding her fingers in and out of his curly hair. "Yes, we're leavin'," she sang along with the band. "Oh we're hittin' the road, oh, we're gettin' away from it all." Her voice was soft and not quite in tune, and she managed to make the song sound sad, which it obviously wasn't meant to be.

Jozef touched her collarbone with his lips. "When we're rich and famous . . ." he began, moving his head down her breastbone and pausing every few words to deposit a kiss, ". . . and the war is over . . . and we're far away from Tollbury Point . . . I shall buy you a gramophone . . . and we'll fill our house with Tommy Dorsey records."

Lorna tried to smile. "Don't talk like that," she murmured. "I thought we'd agreed . . ."

Jozef lifted the blanket aside and kissed her on the navel. Lorna's stomach looked rounder than it used to, and it rose rather oddly from the rest of her body, like a hillock from a plain.

"Please don't," she repeated, as if Jozef was doing something unkind. He kissed her belly again, and she dug her fingers into his hair and stirred it restlessly, as if she couldn't decide whether to push him off or force him to stay put.

The song finished with a brassy clash, and in the moment between its ending and the BBC man speaking there was a loud bang from downstairs. Lorna and Jozef sat up and Virginia leapt backward, before they could spot her.

"What was that?"

"I don't know. It sounded like the front door."

They flicked the wireless off, and for a few seconds there was nothing but the hiss of the gas fire, and the noise of everyone's breathing.

"Maybe it was just Bracken knocking something over . . ." Lorna whispered.

"Or Virginia?"

"But she's not due back for ages."

There was a flurry, as of clothes being reached for and disentangled, and a sudden hush as Mr. Deering's voice shouted up from the hall.

"Lorna? Are you home?"

One of them turned the gas off, and after that the stillness was complete. Even the wind seemed subdued, as though it had decided to stop fighting the silence and become a part of it instead. Virginia pressed her back against the wall and held her breath.

Mr. Deering waited for a long time, as if he was listening to the house. He opened a few doors before climbing up the main stairs and pausing on the first-floor landing.

"Virginia?"

Once he'd decided Lorna was out, he stopped shouting and his voice began to drip honey.

"Virginia?"

When there was no response he began to plead, in a carrying whisper: "Vi? Where are you? We're still friends, aren't we?"

He was coming very close to the foot of the attic stairs now. She could tell precisely where he was by the telltale whining of the floorboards under his shoes: he was passing along the landing and stopping outside her bedroom door. She could hear his breezy knock, and the creak of his knees as he got down to look under her bed, and the clang of hangers as he opened her wardrobe and pushed her clothes aside.

There was a ruffling noise — ever so slight — from the mattress. Virginia's blood went hot and her thoughts lost all sense of order.

Mr. Deering might have come up to the attic of his own accord. Who knows? It might just have occurred to him. In the decades that followed, Virginia tried to believe it, but the fact remained that she had shut the door behind her when she came up, and even if Mr. Deering had thought to open it, a single glance up the poky stairwell would probably have persuaded him that there was nothing there but damp and darkness, and enough cobwebs to ruin his Savile Row suit. Why on earth — he'd have thought — would anyone be lurking about up there?

In other words, if Virginia's feet hadn't taken it upon themselves to break the suspense, clomping down the stairs and kicking the attic door wide open so that it bounced twice against the wall, then Mr. Deering might have given up his search and gone home. But Virginia's feet did exactly that. She landed rather weakly off the last step, and waited for him to see her.

He was still in her bedroom, with her pajama jacket in his hands, but he poked his head through the door to see what the noise was.

"Vi!" He tossed the jacket onto the bed and came to meet her with his arms out.

"What's the matter?" he smiled, when she backed away. "You know I'm not cross with you?"

Virginia shook her head. He didn't seem able to see past her, to the gaping black doorway and the upward-pointing stairs.

"There," she said, wriggling free of his hands and pointing at the open door. "Lorna's up there . . . Go and see!"

The words were out, and immediately she wanted them back. She made a tiny grasping motion with her fingers, but it was no use. They'd floated out of reach. They were gone.

Max screwed his eyes and peered up the stairwell. He was probably imagining a practical joke: the little devil was going to try to lock him in the attic or scare him with a pretend rat, and he was damned if he'd be fool enough to fall for it. Thank God he wasn't going to fall for it. Virginia clapped her hands over her mouth, but not in time to suppress the relief that came bubbling up out of her throat. What was it — a sob? Or a laugh? Or a croak? Mr. Deering's frown deepened.

"What's going on?"

"Nothing!"

Max ducked his head in the door and peered up the stairs.

"Nothing! Please don't go up."

She seized his arm as he set his foot on the first step, but he shook her off and carefully — oh, so carefully — began to climb. Virginia listened to the swish of his sleeve against the bare plaster as he felt his way up the stairs and along the little landing and searched for the door handle. In her mind's eye she saw herself dashing after him and pulling him back by the hem of his trousers, but in actual fact she didn't move a muscle.

Mr. Deering went so quiet that Virginia thought by some miracle Lorna and Jozef had made themselves scarce, and that he was merely weighing up the evidence of their artistic enterprise: the wood blocks, the typewritten sheets, the ink-stained rollers. But it wasn't that — how could it be? It was just that he disliked himself when he lost his cool; he disliked seeming anything less than urbane. Virginia had seen him lose his temper on one occasion, and he'd been drunk then.

"Well, good afternoon," he said, after a very long pause. "I hope you'll forgive the interruption."

Virginia imagined their eyes locking on to his, and the three of them struggling for comprehension; searching for some way to break the unthinkable impasse they found themselves in.

Virginia heard a strangled yelp, which might have been Lorna saying *Max,* and then a lot of flapping, fumbling sounds as she and Jozef grappled with blankets and clothes.

"Please don't move on my account," Mr. Deering insisted politely, and they stopped at once. The coldness of his tone was like a sharp knife running from the nape of Virginia's neck all the way down her spine, and she felt as if she were being slit open like a fish and turned inside out. If she didn't ask herself *What have I done?* it was only because she didn't dare touch on such a question. It was bad enough that she'd just remembered — really remembered — who Jozef was: not a Nazi after all, and certainly not Clem's murderer, but the good man who'd written "Call of the Curlew" just for her, and made a gift of it for her twelfth birthday.

Virginia took a few steps down the landing, away from the attic door, because she had to get away from the possibility of Jozef's voice. She couldn't bear to hear him say her name — *Was that Virginia on the stairs? Was that Virginia who told you where we were?* She knew exactly how he'd say it, too. He'd sound sad, and a little bit surprised, but not the least bit cross — as if he blamed himself, more than anyone, for the whole fiasco. He'd have the same apologetic expression he'd been wearing that night when they first found him in the shed — she, Lorna, and the empty shotgun.

The shotgun. The idea of it went through her like an electric shock. She walked more quickly down the landing and broke into a run as she reached Clem's study.

The corner cupboard wasn't locked this time — Lorna couldn't have shut it again properly — but the bundle was there, exactly as it had been a year ago, and Virginia knelt down to peel away the cloth. Bracken must have heard the study door opening, or perhaps the scent of ammunition had tickled his nostrils, because he came padding up the stairs and nosed into the room with his stumpy tail wagging. Virginia tried to push him away but he refused to be discouraged, and when she pulled back the last fold he began panting and trotting around her in circles.

Even before she'd touched the gun, its dangerous smell and gleam gave Virginia heart. She pictured herself poking the muzzle into Deering's back — he'd be *Deering* then, not *Mr. Deering* — and forcing him to walk ahead of her, down the stairs, and out into the lane. He'd have to loosen the knot in his tie just to catch a proper breath. She thought about the things she could make him do and say. The groveling apologies. The promises. Lost for words, his shoulders sagging, he'd turn to look at her as she stood on the doorstep with the gun in her hands. He'd know what to expect, if he ever darkened the doorway of Salt Winds again.

She slid her fingers underneath Clem's gun and held it up, as if she were presenting a gift at an invisible altar. It was heavy enough to make her arms tremble, but not so heavy that she couldn't manage. She went back to the Deering fantasy, and watched his face turn white and sweaty, and his mouth drop open.

Virginia staggered to her feet, one hand gripping the wooden stock, the other supporting the barrel of the gun. Once she was up, she tried to swing it under her arm, but she was clumsy and the whole thing slid to the floor with a thud, narrowly missing her foot. Bracken barked excitedly just as Mr. Deering appeared in the open doorway. His expression was grave, but he didn't blanch or tremble or struggle for breath at the sight of her. If anything, his features lightened.

"Good girl," he said, swinging the gun into his arms as if it weighed nothing at all, and snapping it open. Virginia had forgotten that it wasn't loaded, but he seemed to know just by looking at it. "Great minds, eh? Now, where did Clem keep . . . the . . . ah, here we are."

Mr. Deering needed to look in only a couple of drawers to find what he wanted. He fitted the fresh cartridges in no time and clicked the mechanism shut with a practiced hand.

"Good old Clem." He raised the gun to his cheek and aimed it at Virginia's head before lowering it with a laugh and giving her shoulder a friendly prod. The feel of the metal through her dress made her catch her breath; it felt as tensed and alive as a tightened fist.

"Well?" he smiled. "Are you coming? Oh, hand me those binoculars, would you?"

Impossible to hesitate; impossible to ask why. Virginia unhooked the binoculars from the back of Clem's chair and passed them to Mr. Deering, and he hung the strap around his neck. She thought he'd leave the room first, but he bowed and made a little flourish with his hand, inviting her to lead the way.

The cardboard had been ripped away from the window and daylight seeped across the attic floor like dirty water. Jozef and Lorna sat side by side on the old settee, like two children waiting to see the dentist. At least they were semiclothed now: Jozef had managed to get his trousers on and Lorna was wearing his, or rather Clem's, jacket. She'd pulled it tight across her chest with one hand and over the tops of her thighs with the other, which kept her just about decent but wasn't effective at hiding her pregnant stomach. When the others came in, Jozef laid a hand on her bare knee.

Mr. Deering repositioned the rocking chair so that it faced the settee before relaxing into it with the shotgun under one arm. Virginia loitered at his shoulder with her eyes on the floor, but she felt like his stooge standing there.

"Where are you off to?" he inquired as she crept away, and she returned to stand beside him. Every time he spoke, he stroked the trigger of the gun with his forefinger, but other than that he sat completely still.

Virginia's gaze wandered toward the settee. There was a brown paper parcel on the floor beside Jozef's feet, addressed in big, bold letters to Corbett & Cole Publishing House, Bedford Square, London. Whenever Mr. Deering seemed briefly distracted — by dust on the wooden part of the gun, or the dog sniffing his legs — Jozef would feel about for the parcel with one foot and try to push it backward, out of view. He didn't try for long; Mr. Deering was too much on his guard.

Bracken pottered about the room, sniffing briefly at Lorna's toes. Nothing very interesting seemed to be happening, in spite of his hopes, so he yawned and flopped down on his belly. With his tongue hanging out and his mouth drawn up, he looked as if he were laughing quietly to himself.

"Now then, Herr Friedmann, where had we got to?" Mr. Deering settled back in his seat. "You were telling me how you bailed out of your burning plane, only to find yourself lost on the marsh, with the tide drawing in. And suddenly you saw a man coming toward you through the gloom, with a flashlight"

Jozef stared straight at his interrogator,

and his fingers tightened on Lorna's knee. Not just a man of words and kindnesses, thought Virginia, but a pilot. An ace. A dicer with death.

"That's correct," he said, haltingly. "It was Clem — he told me he was called Clem, and that he would help me. I was wet through and cold, and hurting all over, especially my arm. He gave me brandy from a little flask, and when I couldn't stop shivering he made me wear his coat. He kept pointing to the big house on the horizon and saying, 'Let's get you home, old chap.' I remember how he kept calling me 'old chap.' He wanted us to hurry because of the tides, but I wasn't very fast. I tried, but I kept falling down —"

"Enough!" Mr. Deering held up his left hand for silence. "It's a lovely tale, and you tell it awfully well, *old chap.* But it's not what really happened, is it? Would you like me to describe what really happened?"

Jozef looked at the gun and gestured helplessly. "As you please, but I think you will be wrong."

Mr. Deering jerked forward, his hands tightening on the gun, and Lorna recoiled. Her jacket slipped open as she tried to cover her stomach with her hands, and that made him laugh. He leaned back, pleasant and relaxed, and crossed his ankles.

"This is what really happened, Herr Friedmann. Along comes Clem, as you say, with his brandy and his nice, dry coat, and he says, *Let's make for that house over there, old fellow: that's Salt Winds, where I've lived all my life in peace and plenty. I'd be more than happy to let you sit in the kitchen for half an hour while you're waiting for the police to come and cart you off to a prisoner-of-war camp, because that's just the sort of generous fellow I am. My beautiful young wife might even make you a cup of tea, if you play your cards right.*"

Jozef opened his mouth to speak, but Mr. Deering shook his head.

"I haven't finished yet. So off you both plod, and Clem shows you how to dodge the tides, and the sinking sands, and before very long the ground starts feeling solid under your feet, and the sea is no longer so loud in your ears. *Well, well,* you think to yourself. *I believe I can manage on my own from here. I don't need this soft-headed Englishman to show me the way. What's the point of him? That comfortable house could be mine, and his pretty wife too, if I only —*"

"If I only *what?*" Jozef scoffed, standing up and sitting down again. "If I only put every instinct aside and murder this man —

my rescuer — in cold blood?"

Mr. Deering sighed gently and rocked the chair back and forth with his foot. An excitable opponent was a pleasure to him; Virginia had noticed that before. He seemed to find it calming.

"And please, how am I supposed to have done this murder, when I was injured and tired?" Jozef went on, his voice rising. "Did I strangle him with one hand? Mmm? Or . . . or stove his head in with a rock? I tell you, the tide snaked in and separated us. I saw him. I saw —"

"Please." Mr. Deering closed his eyes, as if he found the conversation wearisome. "I'm not interested in your version of events, Herr Friedmann. Really, I'm not."

Jozef lifted his hands impatiently and let them drop again.

"Clem said the conditions were not so bad," he insisted fiercely. "*Someone will come and help us,* he said. *My old boyhood pal, Max Deering, will come; he knows the marsh like the back of his hand; he won't let us down — not when it really matters.* That's what Clem said."

Mr. Deering got up and strolled to the window, and the lovers squeezed hands, quickly, while he wasn't looking. The sky was still stormy, but the marsh itself was starkly clear, as if it had just been washed and rinsed, and Virginia didn't need binoculars to see all the way to the ruler-straight horizon. Gulls blew about, their wings spread wide, like brilliant white motes on the black wind.

There were pink patches on Mr. Deering's cheeks as he lowered the binoculars and turned back to the room, but his tone was as reasonable as ever.

"All I'm asking," he said, "is that you go back where you came from. That's all."

Jozef frowned uncertainly. "You want me to return to Germany?"

"No, no. Not that far. Just . . ." Mr. Deering gestured toward the window with the gun. "Just back to the spot where Clem found you. And if you make it that far, which, knowing the tides as I do" — he clucked his tongue against the roof of his mouth and glanced at his watch — "is highly unlikely, then I want you to keep walking till you reach the sea." He dipped the binoculars, the way you might dip a glass if you were toasting someone at a party. "I shall watch your progress with interest, from here."

Silence lengthened like a shadow across the room.

"And if I get as far as the sea?"

"Well, then you'll have to start swimming, won't you?" Mr. Deering laughed. "Who knows? Maybe you will make it back to the Fatherland after all."

Jozef's fingers stirred on Lorna's knee.

"And if I fail to do as I'm told? What if I veer off, back to shore? What are you going to do about that, Mr. Deering? Take pot-shots at me from the window?"

Everyone's eyes followed Max as he stepped over the sleeping dog and settled in the rocking chair again.

"My dear old chap." The wicker seat creaked under his weight as he crossed his legs, resting the shotgun on his knee so that it pointed — casually, and with no apparent intent — at Lorna's belly. "You can, of course, do as you like. There's nothing to stop you from calling at the vicarage for tea."

Lorna stared at the pointing gun, and then at Mr. Deering's face, pulling the jacket as tight as it would go. Words hovered on the tip of her tongue, as if she was daring herself to speak out loud; her mouth formed the shapes, but no sound came out. She cleared her throat and tried again.

"You wouldn't, Max," she said huskily. It wasn't a plea so much as a shaky assertion of faith.

Mr. Deering watched her musingly, as if

wondering how best to reply, and then it came to him. In one long, fluid movement — as if it were as natural a gesture as shrugging his coat on, or smoothing his hair — he raised the shotgun to his shoulder and fired. The walls of the attic seemed to contract for a second before bouncing back into place, and Virginia felt — rather than heard — the explosion, like a pain inside her ears.

She uncovered her eyes and stood up straight, but it took her a while to work out what had happened. Lorna was hunching forward with her hands over her head, and Jozef was holding her body tight in his arms, and for a moment Virginia thought Mr. Deering had managed to kill them both with one shot. But then Lorna shouted, "What happened? What has he done?" and the two of them parted slowly and sat up, their lips and eyes drawn downward, like old people with a lifetime's suffering behind them.

"Bracken," said Jozef.

The dog was lying on his side with his legs stretched out, just as he had been before — only now there was an oozing crater in his head where there'd once been an eye, and there were strings of flesh and blood spattered across the floorboards and over

Lorna's naked toes.

"Poor thing," said Mr. Deering, lazily rocking the chair so that the runners made a rhythmic rumble. "It's not even as if he'd done anything to deserve it."

Lorna let go of Jozef's hand and shuffled forward, until she was sitting right on the edge of the settee. Perhaps it was just the dull light that made her face look gray, but Virginia couldn't shake the notion that the color was leaking, like ink, away from her skin and hair.

"Max," she began, in a low voice. "Please, stop this. Please. Listen to me. I will do anything. I will promise never to see Jozef again. We can turn him in to the police — today, now, if you like — and you and I will get married as soon as ever we can —"

That was the wrong thing to say; Virginia could have told her she was on the wrong tack. Mr. Deering stopped rocking and spat out a laugh.

"Get married?" he snorted. "You think I'd *touch* you, after this?"

Mr. Deering stroked the trigger again. It was the first time all afternoon that his voice had risen above a drowsy drawl, and it left him breathing heavily. When Virginia glanced sideways, she could see the whites of his staring eyes.

"It's me," she piped up. "It's me you want to do things to, isn't it? Not Lorna."

Her skin burned, not just because of what she'd said, but because she was speaking at all. A reedy little voice — a child's voice — had no place here, amid all this adult murk and gore. It sounded ridiculous. Irrelevant. Puny. No wonder Mr. Deering looked straight ahead, as if he'd gone deaf. No wonder Lorna turned and stared at her, as if she were speaking in tongues.

Virginia wished she'd kept quiet. Jozef was staring at her as well now, and shaking his head slowly from side to side. Lorna was putting her hands over her mouth. "I'm just saying . . ." Virginia bit her lip, remembering the feel of his spidery hand on her skin. "I just mean . . ."

"No." Jozef's voice had gone husky, but he cleared his throat and stood up. "No, Virginia, please. Don't say anything else. I won't let you bargain with this man."

Lorna tore her gaze away from Virginia. She seized Jozef's waist and tried to pull him back down, but there was no holding him. Once he was up, he turned and kissed her on the eyes, nose, and lips, lingering for a moment, pressing his forehead against hers.

"Don't go." The words dropped like stones

from Lorna's mouth — dull and emphatic — and Jozef closed his eyes. Then he gathered up her clingy hands and laid them on her lap, as if they were a gift he wanted her to have.

Jozef started pulling a navy sweater over his head, but Mr. Deering ordered him to stop.

"Why?"

"Just do as you're told."

Jozef took the sweater off again and dropped it on the floor. Mr. Deering ran the gun's snout over his prisoner's shoulders and down his spine, in the shape of a capital *T.*

"Your skin is as white as a girl's," he said. "I'll be able to see you better, like this, when I'm watching from the window."

On his way to the door, Jozef touched Virginia's arm, and she thought he was going to say something desperate, or reproachful: *Take care of Lorna,* perhaps, or *May God forgive you.*

Perhaps he thought about these things, because he hesitated for some time, but in the end, he kissed her on the cheek and whispered in her ear, so softly and swiftly that the others wouldn't suspect: "Remember the curlew."

Virginia opened her mouth. She wanted

to tell him that his story kept unfurling, word for word, across her mind, but her voice had deserted her and all she managed was a nod.

The three of them remained, still and silent, while Jozef's footsteps faded down the stairs: Lorna bunched up at one end of the settee, Deering at the window with his hands tight around the gun, Virginia like a pillar of salt in the middle of the room.

After the front door had shut, their silence deepened, and it was only when Mr. Deering said, "There he goes!" that Virginia managed to stir. She lowered herself onto the creaky settee, as cautious as if she risked waking someone, and slid the parcel out of sight with her foot. Five minutes went by, and the roof slates rattled like bones in a gust of wind.

"A golden light was dancing, like a fallen star, on the edge of the sea," Virginia murmured. *"She raised the telescope to her eye and spied a great galleon, painted in rich colors, starred all over with lanterns and straining against its anchors for the off."*

"What was that?" Mr. Deering looked round, but Virginia made no reply, and he turned to the window again. Lorna hadn't moved.

"Over the wall," he said after a while, "and across the bumpy grass. So far so easy. Now let's see how much your German's love is worth."

The daylight faded and Bracken's blood spread across the floor. When it was too dark to see, even with the aid of the binoculars, Mr. Deering came away from the window. He fell into the rocking chair with an exhausted moan and let the shotgun slide from his hands. It clattered to the floor and slid a few inches toward the settee, but nobody bothered to pick it up. It was as if nobody cared about it, or believed in its power, and so they let it lie between their feet like an old toy.

They sat on and on through the evening without speaking a word. They sat for so long that Virginia thought they'd never move again. She imagined the attic in a hundred years' time, and the three of them just the same, like figurines in a neglected doll's house.

Lorna was the first to move. She sat up straight and said, "Get out of my house."

Her tone was blank, but it must have carried some kind of authority because Mr. Deering got up immediately. He ran his palms over his jacket and moistened his lips as if to speak.

"Get out," Lorna repeated, in the same lifeless way, and he did. He slunk away without a word. The singing wind hid his footsteps and the slamming of the front door, but they knew when he'd gone.

Virginia reached for Lorna's hand. At first it felt cold and heavy, like a stone from the sea, but after a while it stirred, and then their fingers touched and linked and locked together.

New Year's Eve 2015

My dear Joe,
I know it looks odd, an old woman disappearing into the marsh on a night like this. I've just poked my head out of the front door, one last time, and I'll grant you it's cold: a proper "bed, socks, and cocoa" sort of a night, as Mrs. Hill would have said. But you never knew Mrs. Hill.

It's cold, but it's not so very dark; I shall be able to see where I'm putting my feet. The wind has blown those low clouds away at last, and the sky is awash with stars. I suppose that's why the snow streaks gleam so white along the wall and out on the marsh? They look like they're lit from within, but I don't know the science. There's also a light on the horizon, very low and yellow, which might be a ship.

So yes, I suppose you're bound to think it odd, but I do hope you won't be all tragic about it. I was feeling a bit that way myself when I woke up this morning, and I even filled my dressing-gown pockets with bits and pieces to make myself sink more quickly. For one reason or another, I feel quite differently tonight and I've emptied my pockets again, which is why the kitchen table is so untidy.

Do whatever you like with the house and its contents, Joe. Salt Winds has served its purpose, and if you want to let it go then do so with my blessing. There's one thing I should like you to keep, however, and you'll find it beside this letter. I used to keep it tied up in a scroll — that's how it was when your father gave it me — but the ribbon has frayed terribly over the years, and the last threads snapped just now as I was putting everything ready. No one other than me has ever read "Call of the Curlew" — not even your mother — so consider yourself privileged!

It was a good life the three of us had, wasn't it, Joe? I wish I'd said as much to your mother, before she died, but I wasn't conscious of it at the time.

Look after yourself, Jozef Leonard Friedmann, and enjoy what's left of the whisky.

Love, Vi

P.S. Take care of Silver, won't you? I know you're not overly fond of each other, but he can't have many years left, and I shouldn't like to leave him orphaned.

The cat knows that Salt Winds is his for the night, and there's nobody to shoo him off the kitchen table. He circles the clutter delicately, inspecting it all with trembling nostrils, but there's nothing of interest. It's just papers and photos, and a few pebbles.

Midnight, and fireworks flare over Tollbury Point. The cat's ears twitch uneasily and he turns his head, but it's only a distant rattle and a few dilute flashes that turn his eyes red and gold. He decides he doesn't care; he's seen it all before.

The wind has dropped, but every now and then a gust will shiver in from the sea, carrying some fragment — a feather, a straw, a grain of sand, the scent of snow, the dainty bone of a bird — by way of an offering to the house.

ACKNOWLEDGEMENTS

First and foremost I would like to thank my agent in the UK, Joanna Swainson, for her patience and wisdom, and for all her perseverance on my behalf. Huge thanks also to my US agent, Sarah Levitt, who has been so enthusiastic and supportive throughout.

Many thanks to the wonderful team at Tin House, in particular my very insightful editor Masie Cochran, but also Allison Dubinsky, Copyeditor; Erika Stevens, Proofreader; Diane Chonette, Art Director; Sabrina Wise and Priscilla Wu, Publicity; and Nanci McCloskey, Marketing.

Thank you to everyone at Transworld/Doubleday — especially my editor Suzanne Bridson — who was involved with the book in its UK incarnation as *Call of the Curlew.*

Thank you John Quirk, and all the Manx

Litfest crew, for your interest and support over the years. Manx Litfest is a fantastic institution, and it seems to go from strength to strength every September. Long may it continue!

I would also like to thank Mark Lloyd, of Pillar International Publishing, who put me in touch with Joanna in the first place, and gave me encouragement when I needed it most.

I am extremely grateful to my friends Katherine Reed and Linda Harding, for taking the time to read early drafts of the book and for giving such perceptive and encouraging feedback.

Thank you to my Mum, Marian Barrow, and my Dad, Paul Barrow — not just for reading and commenting on earlier drafts, but for giving me such a happy start in life and inspiring me with a love of books.

Last, but by no means least, thank you to my husband Christopher Brooks, without whose love and support I couldn't possibly have become a writer.

ABOUT THE AUTHOR

Elizabeth Brooks grew up in Chester and read Classics at Cambridge. She lives on the Isle of Man with her husband and two children.

The employees of Thorndike Press hope you have enjoyed this Large Print book. All our Thorndike, Wheeler, and Kennebec Large Print titles are designed for easy reading, and all our books are made to last. Other Thorndike Press Large Print books are available at your library, through selected bookstores, or directly from us.

For information about titles, please call:
(800) 223-1244

or visit our website at:
gale.com/thorndike

To share your comments, please write:
Publisher
Thorndike Press
10 Water St., Suite 310
Waterville, ME 04901